RAVE
FOR MORT CASTLE:

"Mort Castle is one of the best short story writers
in the horror field today. More than that, he's one
of the best short story writers around, period."
—Robert Weinberg

"The stories are by turns funny, moving, surprising,
and dark. Mort Castle is a writer who loves word play,
but like every writer worth his salt remembers that
even for kids, play is a serious business."
—Jack Ketchum, author of *The Lost*

"Mort Castle is a master wordcrafter. Fans know
the icy effect of the Castle chill, but not even a jaded horror
reader can pre-guess the garotte twist of the Castle kill.
He has taken the horror genre to new heights."
—The Star Newspapers

"Mort Castle's *Moon on the Water* is a dark, disturbing pleasure."
—Douglas Clegg, author of *The Infinite* and *Naomi*

"Mort Castle is one of the best horror writers we have with us."
—J. N. Williamson, author of *Affinity*

MOON
ON THE
WATER

MORT CASTLE

LEISURE BOOKS NEW YORK CITY

A LEISURE BOOK®

July 2002

Published by

Dorchester Publishing Co., Inc.
276 Fifth Avenue
New York, NY 10001

ISBN 0-8439-5032-3

My thanks to all the editors who thought these works should be in print: Jerry Williamson, John Maclay, Donald Davidson, Bill Wilkins, Paul Freeman, Gretta and Paul Dale Anderson, Robert Weinberg, Cynthia Sternau, Martin H. Greenberg, Joe Morey, Tina Jens, Maurice DeWalt, Nye Willden, Al Sarrantonio, Lin Stein, Merritt Clifton, Tom Suddick, T. E. D. Klein, William Raley.

TABLE OF CONTENTS

MOON
ON THE
WATER

Foreword

by

Robert Weinberg

Let me share a secret with you. It's something that most writers don't like to talk about. It's a topic they prefer not to discuss, not even at a bar where most writers will talk about just about anything under the sun—especially their own work. Raise the subject and they'll give you a blank stare. Persist and you'll suddenly find yourself all alone. But, the secret's true and since you're reading this book, it's one you need to know.

Writing short stories is a lot harder than writing novels. A lot harder.

Novels have space. They give you room to play. When you write a novel, there's plenty of time to set up the ending, put in the drama, fill in the characterization. Despite what readers and most beginning writers think, writing a novel isn't that hard. There's plenty of space to screw up, forget a name or two, leave some loose ends dangling (read Raymond Chandler's *The Big Sleep* if you doubt me), and in general, go totally berserk—and still produce a readable, often quite entertaining book.

You can't do that with a short story. A short story has to be concise. The plotting has to be tight, the characterization taut and convincing, and loose ends stand out like big red flags. Short stories are hard, hard work. You can get away with a multitude of crimes in a novel. In a short story you have to be perfect, or pretty damn close, if you want it to work.

Which, finally brings us to this book. (You thought I was just stalling, huh?) Mort Castle is a master of the short story. Not to say that he's not a fine novelist as well, but Mort's greatest talent is composing short stories with a punch. He's an expert, the real thing, the whole nine yards, and all those other clichés we read about famous people but that usually aren't true. Not the case with Mort. There's no exaggeration involved. The guy is just plain talented. He has a gift. He writes short stories that make a point, stick in your memory, remain with you long after you've put down the book in which they appear.

Mort knows the value of economy. He uses words like a master carpenter, constructing a story piece by piece, frame by frame, until when he's finished, the whole is much greater than the sum of the parts. He builds his houses out of words, not wood, but the result is the same. Each story is a work of passion, dedication, and most of all, craft.

If you've read Mort's work before, then I'm telling you nothing new. You know just how good he is. If you've not read his fiction before—stories like "Bird's Dead," "Buckeye Jim in Egypt," "Moon on the Water," and "Altenmoor, Where the Dogs Dance," then I envy you. You're holding a collection of stories that are as good as they get. A book of polished gems, of fiction that gives you hope that there's still a place for short stories in our constantly changing, media-dominated world. Mort Castle's a walking, talking, writing example of the power of the printed word. Read this book, then buy another copy for a friend. (Don't loan your copy because you'll never get it back!) Most of all, enjoy these stories because they just don't get any better than these. And believe me when I tell you that most professional writers can put together a novel. But few of them have the talent to write short stories like these.

Bob Weinberg—March 31, 2000

Foreword
by
Lucien Stryk

From the politically aware and bold, "Buckeye Jim in Egypt," to the sensitively atmospheric "Bird's Dead," a jazz elegy, Mort Castle's stories, piece after finely honed piece, give a full sense of what life can be like in our time. His world stretches from Crete, Illinois to anywhere in the U.S.A., painting a vivid sense of goings-on light and dark.

The jazz dramas in this collection are especially appealing to one who grew up on the south side of Chicago, immersed in White's Emporium and Dave's Place, enriched by great ones like Coleman Hawkins, Stan Kenton, Stan Getz. Indeed, I know that scene well enough to appreciate how Mort Castle, jazz musician in his own right, finds the right notes to deliver sound, mood, buzz, over and over.

The beautiful and tender "Altenmoor, Where the Dogs

Dance," which I first heard Mort read at a literacy conference, was a memorable happening, where the audience was as visibly moved as I was. Reading it now affects me just as it did then.

In this book, one can dip into spine-chilling love/hate moments in a beautiful junkyard, or a lyrical tale, like the jazz story which gives the collection its name, "Moon on the Water." Take one's pick of suspense, revelation, excitement, or quiet times, surprise or wonder, and above all, compassion and understanding for the lost and unfortunate. Mort Castle has crafted a more than worthy collection for all tastes.

(With over 20 books of poetry published since 1950, Lucien Stryk is one of the world's most distinguished poets. Emeritus professor at Northern Illinois University, Stryk is ranked alongside Alan Watts, Gary Snyder, and Allen Ginsberg for his introduction of Zen philosophy and art in the Western World.)

If You Take My Hand, My Son

—*Johnny . . .*

HE HEARD (THOUGHT HE HEARD?) the voice, thought he knew it (The Old Man . . . No, no way . . .) and he slipped away once more and he was floating (though he lay in a bed in intensive care). He could see (though his eyes were shut, though he had slipped beneath the level of consciousness) a serene circle of colorless light beckoning him.

He knew it was Death.

And he was afraid.

Even if you don't believe or don't know if you believe, you grow up, you hear all kinds of things, heaven with the benevolent Boss Man always smiling at you while you're on eternal coffee break and hell with the Devil shish–ka-bobbing your soul

1

at a constant one million degrees . . . Or maybe nothing, just nothing at all, not even blackness, dust to dust . . .

He feared death.

So his (silent) declaration was, *I am alive!* The spiking green EKG line proved he lived. He could watch it (see it in a way that was not exactly seeing but that was no less true than sight). The doctors (he'd heard them) said he had a chance, condition critical—but stable.

He drifted back toward life. Into the pain, the pain that was a ruined body with plastic tubes dripping fluids into him, sucking fluids from him, the (oh christ am I still screaming?) pain that told him straight flat–out for sure and for certain he was alive, pain that bloated him with a heavy hurting ballast.

The pain was an anchor to life.

But shit, not that much of a life, you stopped to think about it.

One fuck-up after another.

Guess you'd have to call this the Big One. The Ultimate Fuck–Up, rank it right alongside being born. A little self-pity there, Johnny? Sure. But if we can't feel sorry for ourselves, then . . .

Well, let's not forget it was funny. Three Stooges. (Nyuck-nyuck-nyuck.) Jerry Lewis. Pee Wee Herman. (Say, what are you trying to pull?!? Get it? Trying to . . .) Must have looked like two different kinds of asshole. There I am . . .

. . . telling the guy behind the counter at the 7–11, looked like a Pakistani, there's a gun in my pocket . . .

. . . all I got is my finger for Chrissake. Who's got money for a gun?

. . . and he'd better come up with everything, every god-damn dime in the register there . . .

. . . and Mr. Pissed–off Paki starts hollering, "I am a citizen! You are not stealing from the citizen. You get job, good for nothing shitheel!"

. . . Enter two cops, just going off-duty, and try this, one looks like Andy Griffith and the other like Don Knotts . . . Maybe they want a cup of coffee, maybe donuts, maybe a pack of cigarettes . . .

. . . so the Paki is hollering, "Here is now police protecting good honest citizen!"

. . . maybe Don Knotts' wife asked him to pick up a copy of the National Enquirer . . .

. . . with the Paki hollering, "He is making here the robbery!"

. . . but whatever the cops come in for . . .

. . . *what they get is me, Johnny Forrester, Mr. Fuck-It-Up* . . .

And they're telling me, just like on TV, "Freeze!"—and what happens is my hand freezes in my pocket, I mean, I cannot get my hand out of my pocket because my finger is stuck in the jacket lining, and they both have guns and they're shooting . . .

. . . and what he keeps yelling is "Ow!"—when a bullet punched into his thigh—"Ow!"—one in the gut, in the old labonza there—"Ow!"

They shot him four times.

And he actually said, at least he thought he did (remembered trying to say), "Now will you just cut it out?"

Hey, that's memory, something that happened—how long ago was it—and I must have slipped back to it. Can't. Have to stay right here, right now, where I know I'm alive.

Alive. Not more dead than alive but (a balance) just as much alive as dead.

3

He moaned.

"Johnny . . ."

Knew this time there was a voice, not what (who?) he'd heard before, different

Her voice . . .

"Johnny . . . Don't you die." A whisper. "Oh, no Johnny, you die and it's over, there won't be any more us." A whisper. "I need you."

He opened his eyes.

Nancy, dark hair parted down the middle showing clean pink of scalp, eyes green and big (big like those pictures of kids you see in K-Mart) and her mouth all soft (little girl's mouth), face tear-washed, Nancy, looking so young (they went into a tavern for a few beers, and sure enough, they always carded her, really studying the driver's license that said she was 23) Nancy, maybe not all that pretty, not to most, I guess, but they didn't know how to look at her in the right way, and she loved hearing him tell her she was pretty and he loved telling her that because when he said it, she smiled in a way that made her so just so goddamn pretty and she would be prettier still, you know, when they got the bucks together to have that one tooth of hers capped. Nancy, (he'd drawn pictures of her in pencil, gave her one on Valentine's Day, that was a nice day with Nancy), Nancy, standing at the side of the bed wearing a Disneyworld T-shirt (one of their dreams, a trip to Disneyworld) and those old blue jeans.

"Johnny . . . Be all right. You'll see . . ."

He wanted to tell her he loved her (only thing good and gentle and right in a fucked up life) and his lips tried

4

to say it, but what came out was a groan. "I hurt . . ."

"I know, baby, I know. Johnny . . ." She held a hand over him, as though afraid to touch him. "Johnny, I don't know what to do. I can't do anything . . ."

The light. Brighter now. Making him squint.

There, in the corner of the room, where the wall met the ceiling

Shimmering glow

The light was Death

And there in the center

eyes

couldn't be The Old Man's eyes because The Old Man's eyes were as hard and bright as beer bottle glass

he saw The Old Man's eyes, so gentle

he saw The Old Man's face long and horsey and good looking in a drawn Hank Williams country boy kind of way

> *He saw his father*
> *Who was dead*
> *in the light*
> *And his father said,*
> *—It will be*
> *all right, Johnny.*
> *I'm with you now.*

Johnny said, "You rotten old sonofabitch, when were you ever there for me?"

* * *

He eased away from pain and his father and dropped into remembering.

Mort Castle

A Memory:

His mother sat crying, night after night, and his father wasn't home, night after night, and now, his mother was drinking whiskey like his father drank whiskey. He kept asking (Yeah, even when we're little kids, we ask the questions we already know the answers to, there's something twisted in us that makes us grab onto the pain, like the way you keep poking your tongue at a bad tooth to get the hurt kicking up), "Where's Dad? When's he going to come home?" and after the answers his mother felt she had to give him, "He's got to be away for awhile, he's taking care of things, he's doing what he has to do," after all those sad lies, came the real answer:

"He's out drinking in every gin mill and tavern and low-life road house in Southern Illinois . . . He is gone whoring with every low-life tramp who'll spread her legs and give him diseases."

His father did come home. He was white-faced, shaky and sorrowful. "I'm sorry. I don't know what happens, like there's a nastiness in me, like there's a demon, just got to get out and do what it's got to do. But this time is the last time. You'll see. I'm going to change. Got it all out of me this time . . ."

They believed him. This time. And for many years, damned near all the other times.

Moon on the Water

It was one of his father's good spells. The Old Man was working regularly (heavy equipment operator, made damned good money when he worked, but you've got to be sober to work, always wanted The Old Man to put me up there alongside him on that big yellow Caterpillar), and in the evenings, nothing much, but they'd sit around and watch television, maybe some popcorn and cokes, and there was a feeling that they had a chance to ease into the familiar patterns of living that make everything all right.

So when The Old Man said, "Sure, I'll be there," for the Webelos ceremony, very big deal, advancing from Cub Scouts (just little kids) to that significant stage just beneath Boy Scouts, that time in your life when you thought you had a real chance to be something, well, he thought sure (this time) he could count on The Old Man.

But surprise, surprise! (Everything that happens is a surprise—if you're a damned fool.) Was The Old Man there at the Webelos ceremony? Oh, Charley Hawser's father was there, and Mike Pettyfield's father, and Clint Hayworth's father, Clint Hayworth's father who was in a goddamned wheelchair, for chrissake, paralyzed from the goddamned neck down!

And Johnny Forrester's father? Forrester? That was him up to the Double Eagle Lounge, watching the Budweiser clock, listening to Patsy Cline on the jukebox, getting royally shit-faced.

So the new Webelos went home and cried and stayed up waiting and waiting and waiting. The Old Man came in, all loose smiles and Camel cigarettes and booze stinking.

"You lied to me! You told me you would be there. You lied."

The Old Man laughed, phlegm bubbling and cracking.

"Guess I'm just a goddamn liar is what it is." Then he mussed up my hair. That's what he did, mussed my hair.

How could I ever forgive him for that?

"Good night, son," The Old Man said, and wobbled off to bed.

A Memory:

Maybe it really was a demon in The Old Man, one that grew bigger and stronger on liquor, because as the years went on, something turned The Old Man from a drunk to a mean drunk. The Old Man started hitting. (—*Huh, you like that? That's what you're looking for? I got plenty of it and I'll give you all you need.*)

Like that call (I was nine, maybe ten) from the dime store (I got caught stealing). Here's The Old Man (—A thief? I'll give it to you, give it to you so you remember!) pounding away, and Mother has her hands over her face (Stop it, you'll kill him, stop it!), she does what she usually does, that is, she can't do a goddamn thing, and The Old Man's got the rhythm going, a whack, and a gulp of air, and a whack.

"Come on, you old bastard, hit me again! Come on!"

—Want more? Why, sure! Here's more for you, Captain Snotnose! Oh, yeah, you little shit! I got plenty!

"Come on! You like it, don't you? It makes you feel good!"

—I like it fine, Johnny boy. See how you like it!

Memories:

(My) failures and fuck-ups. Kept back in seventh grade. "It was Johnny Forrester took my lunch money." Asked Darlene Woodman if she'd go to the eight grade graduation dance with me. Said she couldn't. Went over to her house and threw eggs and Mike and Dallas, her two older brothers, grab me and pound the living shit out of me. Next week I slashed the tires on Dallas's Ford.

Get to high school and right off I'm flunking classes. Like biology. Cut up a frog so you can see its guts. Me, I cut it up so all you get is this mushy mess. Like English, half the words in the things we're supposed to read, I have no idea what they mean. Like auto shop, and I mean even the shit-for-brains kids do all right in auto shop, but me, only reason I can tell an air filter from my ass is my ass has two parts. Maybe it's because there's nobody to be proud of me if I ever manage to do something right or maybe it's because I was born to fuck up and that's it.

Except once I thought maybe, just maybe . . .

I was sixteen and I sent off for this learn-art-by-mail course (working as a bag boy at the Certified so I would have had the money to pay for it). Always did like to draw, couldn't take art class in high school, not for "lower track vocational ed students." But there I am at the kitchen table, working on lesson one, horizon lines and perspective, and then The Old Man comes up behind me.

—*What is that shit?*

So you ignore The Old Man

—*I said what is that shit?*

And then you can't ignore The Old Man anymore, so you tell him.

And he's laughing his ass off.

—*You're going to be an artist like I'm going to be Emperor of fucking Ethiopia.*

And that's when you tell him you hate him, you hate his fucking guts, and he's smiling, fists ready.

—*Not any more than I hate you*

so you slug him

but The Old Man is still tough, or maybe the booze has fixed him so he doesn't feel a thing, but he's got you by the throat, pressing you back onto the table, and filling up your face with his fist again and again and then you're on the floor on your knees and The Old Man is ripping up your drawing and your learn-art-at-home lesson book and laughing like crazy

—*Emperor of Ethiopia . . .*

10

Moon on the Water

A Memory:

    His mother died. Something went blooey in her brain and that was it. That left him and The Old Man.

A Memory:

    until he was seventeen, old enough to join the Army. The Old Man told him
    —*Yeah, the soldier boy who'll be keeping the country safe, now that's a thought you can sleep good on . . .*
    He fucked up again, smoking dope one night and a fight with a black guy who said he talked like a goddamned redneck country-ass cracker. He punched the black guy in the nose and the black guy broke his jaw so it had to be wired shut for ten weeks.
    He got a general discharge, which meant the army didn't have to give him any benefits and proclaimed to the world, "Here is one certified asshole to be hired for any position in which fucking up is required." He moved to Chicago. He worked shit jobs when he could find shit jobs, got welfare and food stamps sometimes, and he was always close to broke or broke.

A Memory:

    The Old Man died. Myocardial infarction. His heart shut down.

And of course the questions came, the "if only" and "I wish" and "what made" and "how did it happen" questions—which were all one question: Why?

A Memory:

He met Nancy. She worked in a storm door factory. He had no job at the time. He liked to go to the Art Institute on Thursdays, when there was no admission cost, and, Nancy, once a week, on her lunch hour, went to the Art Institute, because, as she explained later (when she knew he would not laugh), she wanted to be in a building that held all those pretty things.

A good Memory:
A Realization:
The Truth:
I love Nancy.

*   *   *

"Johnny, you can't die . . . Oh, please, baby, oh baby . . ."
He thought if she knew just how terrible the pain was, she wouldn't ask him to go on living. It would be so easy, an end to pain, to die, to die now but he was afraid
                                                —No, son
The Old Man's voice came to him from the light
                                                —Do not be afraid

*   *   *

Moon on the Water

Old bastard, old sonofabitch, you're dead

                                                    —Yes
dead and in hell, right where you belong

                                                    —No
in hell

                    Son, it's not hell, not heaven. I don't
                    know what you'd call it, Beyond or Eternity
                        or maybe just someplace else. It's a
                    better place, Johnny. There's no time here
                        so there's all the time in the world.
                                        That's how it is.
                        There's time to think about things, to
                                    realize all you did
                            wrong and how to set things right.
                    Listen to me, Johnny. I want to help you.

Help? Your idea of help was always to give me shit and shove
me in it.

                                    I said I did a lot of
                                        things wrong.
                                I know that now. I wasn't
                                        a good father . . .

You weren't a good father? Christ! You were a drunken, rotten, rat-fucking sonofabitch.

                                Johnny, get it all out of you
                                    now, all the poison
                                    so you can leave it

behind
forever.

I hated you. I hate you.

*I know, Johnny, I
know.*

*But that isn't what you
wanted, is it, Johnny? . . .*

* * *

—Johnny?

No

Say it, Johnny.

. . . I wanted to love you . . .

I know

I wanted your love

*There's something I want to tell
you, Johnny, something I can say and
mean—now . . .*
*—Johnny, I'm sorry,
I am sorry*

* * *

He floated up and away from the pain, from his body,
nearing the light and the promise of a timeless time and
peace and reconciliation

* * *

"Johnny!" Nancy cried

Moon on the Water

*   *   *

                              —*I love you,*
                                    Johnny

The Old Man stretched out his arm.

                              —*Take my hand,*
                                      son

*   *   *

"Johnny!"

*   *   *

He wasn't afraid
Not anymore
He took The Old Man's Hand

*   *   *

He died

*   *   *

and he was screaming in agony as the marrow of his bones boiled (though he had no bones, though he had no body) and a thousand whips lashed his back and razors slit his eyeballs (though he had no eyes, though he had no body) and corkscrews twisted into his skull into his brain and all about was the cacophonous shrieking chorus.

15

Mort Castle

souls in hell

and flames, tinged with black

                              we are souls in
hell

and the stink of suppurating wounds and shit
And The Old Man laughing like crazy

            —It's a pisser, huh, Johnny?

laughing his ass off

You lied to me!

laughing

YOU LIED!

laughing
            —Guess I'm just a goddamn liar

                              is
                                 what it
                                    is.

Fear in Children,
in general
and in Mulbray, in Chenoa, Illinois
in Particular

RETURN WITH US
  Now . . .
  to when:

In the United States it is illegal to hit anyone wearing glasses. The FBI has a special, secret division devoted to the pursuit and capture of anyone who does hit anyone wearing glasses. Anyone wearing glasses walks in corrected myopia safety, free to be an absolutely rotten bastard, safeguarded by the Constitution of the United States.

to when:

Lonny-down-the-block is a geek. Lonny-down-the-block will eat anything. Pluck a potato chip from the blue and white

17

Jay's cellophane bag, rub it in dirt, garnish with green-bodied brown spotted caterpillar, and voila! Hors d'oeuvre for—Lonny-down-the-block.

These are, God help us, typical fragments of everybody's American childhood. They are illustrative of the force and emotion that tyrannically ruled our days when you and I—and Mulbray—were young:

FEAR

Fear, yes, that is it, simple and foul.

To explain:

1. Anyone wearing glasses. Fear of the LAW, Someone big and powerful always watching, always waiting. The Law that strapped Cagney into the chair while Pat O'Brien prayed to Our Lady of the Electric Instant; The Law that slapped away Al Capone, Scarred Face of Chicago; The Law that unerringly guided the bullets of Wyatt Earp, Bat Masterson, Hopalong Cassidy, Roy Rogers; The Law that does forever speak in the omnipotent voice of Mr. District Attorney; The Law that's going to pickle your ass the minute you mess up.

2. Lonny-down-the-block. Fear of Ourselves, the inner yearnings we dare not acknowledge. Lonny-down-the-block goes to school, as we do, and there he answers some questions and cannot answer others, as we do, and he has a wagon and a cold sore, and blue jeans, as we do, and he eats horrible fucking things. So, we sing songs of greasy, gooey gopher guts and laugh after each verse and pretend that there is not a Lonny (who does not live all that far down the block) inside us.

Yes, and all the others. Step on a crack and that's it

for Mama's spine. Cut yourself in the web of thumb and forefinger and you die. The trips to the doctor's or dentist's where wait the implements of a Twentieth Century Inquisition; at the doctor's they usually go right up your personal behind and you yell like crazy. At the dentist's, down your throat, and you can't even yell because the old bastard is strangling you! And hey, God—or Santa Claus—or The Boogeyman—will get you for saying or doing or thinking or being that. The journey to the antiseptic death nursing homes to see cancer-shriveled Aunt Shirley looking just like a turkey carcass. All these myths, totems, and taboos come with our passport into the world of childhood. We have the certain knowledge that the Cosmos exists to get us. This is the Universal Fear.

Now wouldn't you think it enough? It is not.

Unsatisfied with our portion of the Universal Fear, we explore our small realm and create new objects of fear and make them singularly our own.

These belonged to the child, Mulbray:

1. His father. A cool, white Arrow shirt man, who believed in a time and a place for everything. He was the principal of a junior high school in Chenoa. He always looked as though he were posing for an oil painting, the kind that hangs on the wall behind the secretary's desk in the front office of a junior high school in Chenoa, Illinois.

2. The kidnappers. Late at night, just as he as about to fall into dreams and nothingness, they came for him. One at the foot of the bed, the other at the head, they carted him bed and all down the stairs. He kept his eyes shut. Had he opened them, the kidnappers would have killed him.

3. The Russian bomb. At age four or so, Mulbray watched the twelve-inch television from a distance of under two feet, so he became part of the endless Civil Defense warnings about the precautions to take when the Commies hit us. At school, the first grade took monthly shelter under their desks, awaiting further instructions from the teacher on how to stay alive.

He seldom went far from the house so that when the night winged bombers blotted out the sun and the sirens shrieked and the Great! Flash! came, he would have a wall to shield him, and he would not be caught in the fire wind, and would not become dust.

4. *The Godfield. A vacant lot next to the white frame Presbyterian Church on Arthur Street. A buggy, ragweed sanctuary for children, where they could hide from parents, other children, where they could sink down and disappear. Now, Mulbray never heard anyone else refer to it as the Godfield, so that must have been a name known only to him. That is a strange name, in a way, because, even before he became an adult and stopped believing in God at all, he only believed a little bit.*

But the Godfield was his right and secret name for the half-acre of weeds, just as a butterfly is exactly a butterfly and the sky is the sky.

What did Mulbray fear in or about the Godfield?

Some Thing.

Or rather . . .

Some Thing that would Happen.

In the same way he knew The Godfield's name, he knew that if he ventured too far into the Godfield, Some Thing would—indeed—Happen. Were he to go to the exact center of The Godfield, Some Thing would Happen and he would be changed in so strange and miraculous a away that he would never be the same again!

All right, you can say this is strange and ridiculous and incredible. But pause, reflect, and above all, remember yourself as a child. Remember yourself as a deeply religious pagan, afraid of everything and nothing and able to leap tall buildings at a single bound or burst into tears at the memory of some nebulous nothing that had frightened you.

This is Mulbray, the child, like all children with emotions the same as any adult and thoughts those of a race apart.

And so, Mulbray feared the Godfield, and feared the Some Thing that would Happen, and so he was forever lured to the edge of the field to stand, only stand. Fearing, he did not seek the exact center of the Godfield. He was an always-lurker on the edge of The Godfield.

Fearing the Godfield, and his Father, and The Kidnappers, and The Bomb and damned near everything else, he grew up, as we did.

Somewhat.

And now, we're all grown up.

And nobody's afraid anymore.

Henderson's Place/The Girl with the Summer Eyes

HE CARRIES THE PLACE WITH him *always*, but it is at night, in dreams, that Henderson sees it most vividly:

A secret place, a hidden-away place, a place far from this universe that has gone to concrete and neon and plastic.

A time-out place, a time-slowed and time-melted place.

Dew-gleaming grass. Sky a layered blue. Tall trees. The easy slope to the brook where water flows snake-softly over flat stones.

This is Henderson's Place.

It is his, his alone.

Except for the one with whom he is meant to share it.

Who is:

The Girl with the Summer Eyes.

Who is—

22

—in dreams (and Henderson knows that dreams are dreams and that dreams can tell you so much if you know how to be in the dream in just the right way)—

With Henderson, in Henderson's Place

Who is:

of The Place . . .

So Henderson sees The Place in his dreams.

But dreams end with, "For Chrissake, I've called you three times. Will you puh-leeze get up?"

Will he get up? He asks himself that question (and that has been the question of the morning for how many days now?) and he opens his eyes.

Another beckoning from down the hall, the summons of the kitchen: "Come on!"

Henderson rises. In his pajamas, he goes to the window, raises the shade, almost expecting to see summer, but though the sun shines, there is a flatness to the day that tells him this is autumn.

And that is a surprise, in a way, a mild amusement.

In the bathroom, he lets the shower run, very hot, while he stands naked at the vanity, razor in hand, face lathered by an aerosol shave cream that smells like burnt plastic.

The mirror fogs. He erases an oval of mist, erases another patch, sees stubbly cheek, shaves it. Another clear spot; the razor again, and so on until his face is smooth. He sees a cut on his chin, a line of blood. It does not hurt at all.

A few minutes later, he is dressed and in the kitchen. His wife, in housecoat and slippers that snap against her heel when she walks, gives him a paper plate with two breakfast tarts on it and places a cup of coffee on the table. She says it is harder to wake him than it is to raise the dead.

Henderson's teeth crack the tasteless toaster-tart shell. He looks at his wife's eyes. They are hard and lifeless.

"Going to the office or do you have calls to make?"

He is a salesman for Educational Enterprises, Incorporated. Henderson goes to the office on some days. On other days he visits schools. He doesn't recall where he is to go today.

"Well?" At the counter, his wife pours herself coffee. She yawns.

"I swear, I don't know what's gotten into you. You act like you're missing half of what's going on."

Henderson smiles, enjoys his so secret, so special knowledge of The Place.

Soon he is on the tollway, going to, going to . . . The office.

That's right.

In the rush hour traffic, he pulls into line at a toll booth behind a new, blue Chevrolet. The sun's reflection on the Chevrolet's bumper is a blazing fireball that pulses in a steady, insistent rhythm.

Suddenly a horn blares. Now there are three lengths between him and the Chevrolet. Henderson pulls up. The Geo is at the toll booth in the shade.

The flashing, compelling fire-eye is gone.

* * *

When third period ends, Linda and Karen, her best friend, go to the "safe" restroom where teachers seldom bother to check for smokers. "God!" Linda says, "Wagner's class is a total bore!"

She stands at the mirror combing her long blond hair.

"For sure," Karen agrees. She lights a Kool, rests her blue-jeaned backside on the edge of a sink. "School is one big bummer. Totally."

"Yeah," Linda says. "How come if school's supposed to be for kids, we all hate it?"

" 'Cause it sucks. That's the American way," Karen says. "If it's big time dumb ass and boring and all, it's supposed to be good for you." She waves her hand. Her cigarette is a baton and she is conducting an orchestra, singing, "My country misery, you keep on shafting me . . ."

Linda giggles. She looks at the mirror. She decides she is pretty. Well, not pretty exactly, but she has nice, even features. Clear skin, thank God. And—no brag, just fact—she does have pretty eyes—big and green.

And so if she is young and pretty—almost pretty—and she is—if she is exactly the way an American teen of her American time ought to be—and she is, she thinks, all things considered: Upper-middle class family. Way upper. Ten years older brother faraway and gone in San Francisco doing something with spreadsheets and probably wearing ties and (how the hell would she know? Ten years after all. Maybe he's a queer for all she knows). Her college education guaranteed by parents' careful financial planning—

(What college? I don't know. I should start thinking about it except I don't want to think about it.)

So everything is *Boring!* Better than the Brady Bunch, right?

Then just why does she feel so damned shitty so damned often?

What is it, she gets up, you know, goes to school, comes home, breezes through homework. She doesn't have to work some dumbass job at Greasy Arches or Fashion Fart or anything, not with the Parental Units agreeing that Teen Time is the Time to focus on studies and self identity and shit like that.

She dates on weekends—guys she likes "okay" and her parents don't much dislike—and all in all, she has what is supposed to be a "pretty fun time."

And usually she feels like a shuffling-along zombie in a grade-Z horror movie, just shuffling through it, shuffling on through all of it.

Feeling nothing.

Nothing.

"Hey, Kar?"

"Hey what?"

"Want to ditch next hour? I don't feel like my daily dose of American history."

"Yeah. Okay."

"We can stay here and smoke a little. You got herb, don't you?"

Karen laughs. "For sure."

They light a joint as the bell rattles the washroom windows.

*   *   *

At the desk in the office he shares with four others, Henderson takes invoices from a wire basket on his left and transfers them to a basket on the right. Henderson is a "paper man." The computer thing, sure, he learned what he had to learn when computers came along, but, thank you, pencils and paper.

More and more pencils these days. Not pen. There's a sound made by a pencil point that is subtle and real that you cannot get from a pen.

Henderson glances at a brochure for Educational Enterprises's new United States history text and discovers that not one word in the first sentence of the copy is related to any other word.

He looks around. It's as though everyone and everything in the office were pressed between two sheets of glass, flat—two-dimensional, like television cartoons.

"Henderson, what are you doing here?"

Tom Beamer, sales manager, has suddenly appeared.

"Nothing," Henderson says.

"You were supposed to . . . Say, Henderson, something bothering you?"

"Oh, no," Henderson says, "everything is fine."

Yes, yes indeed. Everything is fine. He has The Place. And it comes to him that, why, whenever he wishes, he can go to The Place, flee this drab, silly, and—oh so strangely flat— world.

Yes. The Place.

". . . appointment, Henderson. It's big. They want to toss out all the texts they're using and kick in a whole new line across the grades, one through twelve. And Henderson, there's the multimedia . . ."

"Yes," Henderson says. Multimedia. He might remember what that is. It's possible.

". . . That is one school district with serious money. No tax caps for those suburbs. Mom and Pop want the fruit of their loins to go to Harvard and Brown and Yale so they can be just like Mom and Pop who went to . . ."

Henderson folds his hands on the desk. Beamer glances at his wristwatch.

". . . get moving, right? Don't want to be late."

Beamer is still talking. Henderson can see the mouth open and close in the flat face. Beamer's voice fades away and then . . .

is gone—

And Henderson hears:

the bubbling of water skipping across stones.

Henderson pushes back his chair. He stands and smiles at Beamer.

Beamer's open mouth stays that way. "Now," Henderson says, "I forget. Where is it I am supposed to go?" Henderson forces himself to hear the sales manager.

Tom Beamer says, "Christ doing cartwheels, Henderson . . ."

water over stones

"Look we can send Martelli out on this. I can go myself. It's okay."

"Oh no," Henderson says. "That's all right. That's all right. I'm already on the way."

He has The Place. Its serenity fills him, and he pities poor Beamer, Multimedia Beamer, who does not know, cannot know, has nothing.

Blue sky,

tall trees

water over stones.

A minute later (time) Henderson is on his way—

"Pine Forest High School."

Yes, he is on his way.

But before he leaves, he gazes back where everyone has become trapped in a gigantic ant farm, sandwiched between the transparent glass walls.

Henderson laughs pleasantly.

*   *   *

They are sitting on the window ledge, passing the third joint. A serious joint. Reggae-ska-ganja express *el bomber grande*.

From time to time, others have come in, some to sneak a cigarette, most to use the facilities, a couple to share a hit with them. No teachers have spot-checked, though, and while some of the "goody pies" have given them nasty looks, there is no need to worry about anyone ratting them out. Pull that shit at Pine Forest High and poof! Ostracism—instant exile.

"I don't know," Karen says. "Guess it's sixth period."

"Huh?"

"See, you asked me what time it was—well, what time it is—really was, I guess, 'cause time takes a while, you know how it is with time. If you think about it, it's funny. Really."

"Oh," Linda says. "I am totally destroyed. This is good shit."

She takes the joint from Karen and decides she doesn't like or dislike being destroyed. It's just another way to be, that's all.

But to be . . . what?

That is the question. Nothing.

That is the answer.

That is the answer most of the time and it makes her sad

as hell when it gets to her at all and sometimes she wishes she could really sob about it, big gulping nose-running sloppy sobs . . .

"Let's play," Karen says.

"Play what?" Linda shifts her weight. The window ledge is hard.

"What do we play when we're stoned?"

"Nah, I don't want to."

"Sure you do."

"Sure I don't."

Linda has a chill.

"Come on," Karen says. "The only time you can really talk is when you get stoned, right? It's no bullshit time. Let's play the Truth Game."

"Uh-uh," Linda says. She is colder now, and she has a sudden moment of absolute clarity, of shining frozen vision. They *must* play the Truth Game.

This is what is meant to be.

"Please," Karen says. "I want to talk and we are best friends and everything."

"Okay," Linda says, "but you have to start."

"True-true-true," Karen says. She whispers, "You know that party last Saturday? You didn't go."

"Yeah." Her period. Cramps making her pull her knees up to her chin.

"Well, everyone got real crazy. Drinking and smoking. There was this guy, Marty. He goes to Ridge. He's a senior. He's pretty nice, I guess. I don't know. I was kinda stoned."

A pause for air. "So anyway, it was him. Definitely. Marty."

30

Then the words rushing together, true-true-true "So I guess I'm not a virgin, anymore."

"Oh, Karen," Linda says. "Oh." She knows she should ask the right stuff: "Did you take precautions?" and the stuff she should want to know, like, "Did it hurt?" and there should be all sorts of things to say and ask. Instead, she says it once more: "Oh."

Karen sighs. "Now it's your turn."

* * *

As Henderson drives, all color is fading. At last, he sees only black and white and gray. A world of dim, shimmering outlines.

Henderson amuses himself by blinking. In the fraction of a second that his eyes are closed, The Place springs magnificently into view, into life.

The grass is a throbbing green. The brook is a billion diamond encrusted hearts, beating, beating, beating. The life force of the trees roars through the veins in their leaves.

A horn screams behind Henderson as he drifts into the left lane.

He swings back. A Toyota passes in a blur, the faceless driver—no more depth to him than to a sheet of paper—gives Henderson the finger.

Henderson's hand moves to the radio—
then the song of the breeze through treetops
water over stones
and now—so complete the vision—
The Place.
And The Girl with the Summer Eyes
who waits for him

31

Now

who sings—her song, his song—the Song of The Place

   Henderson, Henderson, Henderson

Come now Henderson . . .

Soon, then, soon Henderson will make the certain journey to The Place.

Where she awaits

The Girl with the Summer Eyes

   Henderson, Henderson, Henderson

But there is yet something he must do, something to be taken care of in the flat world, this world without color, this dead world.

Lines wriggle and take on a rectangular shape. For an instant, there are letters: PINE FOREST EXIT.

Henderson slows and pulls onto the exit ramp.

*   *   *

"True-true-true," Karen says. "Okay," Linda says. The memory comes welling up from so deep within.

It has been with her a long time, buried, and re-buried, and it is only now, the Truth Game, that she can dredge it up, vomit it out.

Yes, the dope has opened the door to understanding. All is clear. She can perceive the wispy connections between things that were and things that are and things that will be—and won't be.

Now she understands. She sees herself not as she appears to be but as she is. The real Linda. Someone so different. Someone so bad.

"You know how down from our house it's so woodsy and everything?"

She is talking. No, the fake Linda, the go-to-school, big-eyed, nearly pretty Linda is talking. That is not who she really is . . .

"I was six years old, I guess."

She is stalling. She is not playing the Game. She is keeping the Truth inside.

"I was playing down there. By myself. Dad said I couldn't go there alone, but I did. The ground was all rough, and I could have gotten hurt, I guess. I found this nest that fell out of a tree. There were three baby birds."

Linda closes her eyes.

She tries not to see it, tries to see her father's face as he warns her about where she is never to go alone, that place that is going to get her something she won't like if he ever catches her down there—

She tries to imagine Karen and the guy screwing, Karen eye-rolling stoned with her legs up and that guy ramming it into her while the worst retro-disco trasho is playing somewhere in the background—

But she sees it all again as she knows she has to:

Because it rushes at her and happens again. It happens as it happened.

It happens.

The bird nest. The baby birds are ugly, scraggly heads tipped back, beaks open impossibly wide in constant, noisy demand. She stoops, takes a bird in her hand. Its heart beats like a frantic moth at a lighted window.

"Stop that," she says. It continues its cry. She is so much bigger than the bird but it will not be quieted.

She tightens her hand, squeezing. The baby bird's body makes the small noise of potato chips being crunched or of autumn's dead leaves underfoot. Something oozes from the bird's beak and the bird is silent.

Linda is crying.

"Hey, come on, kid," Karen says. "It's the grass, Lin. It's got you paranoid or something. It's no big deal, okay? Really!"

The bell rings.

* * *

Henderson pulls into the parking lot as other cars—like faint pencil strokes—pull out. He parks in a space for "Visitors" and has a feeling of anticipation and irony. There is a rushing all about him as he walks to the two-dimensional building.

He goes in and finds the office.

"May I help you?"

Squinting, Henderson is able to discern an outline, empty, like a hurried cartoon. A woman.

"I'm Henderson. Educational Enterprises."

The woman consults an appointment book on the desk. "Mr. Henderson, Dr. Thompson, that's the curriculum director for the district, you know, thought you weren't coming. You are two hours late, after all. Mr. Thompson is gone for the day. School's out. Everyone is going home now."

"Oh," Henderson says.

It is time for Henderson to go, too.

To The Place.

* * *

"Hey, that was the last bell, Lin. We've got to move it to catch the bus."

Linda has finished crying. She is free and weightless. Now she wants to be alone, just for a little while. "You know, Karen, to get my head together. Go ahead. I'll catch up with you."

"You okay?"

"Sure. You go ahead." Karen turns to leave, then looks back. "Linda . . ."

"Don't worry," Linda says. "It's all right."

Then Linda is alone. Shit, that grass did a number on her, she thinks. Crazy thinking; paranoia-plus! Baby birds and a six year old kid and it was just something that happened, that's all.

That's all.

* * *

Henderson wonders why he has wasted so much time in this vanishing nowhere when he has—has always had—The Place. He will not delay another moment. He steps out of the office. He is on his way.

Color explodes before him. Green. Golden. Warm pinks. In this world of flat and gray, Henderson sees life.

Sees:

The Girl with the Summer Eyes.

Eyes of wonder and excitement. Eyes meant to gaze upon the forever beauty of The Place. The Place.

And that is why—She is here—He is here—Now. It is here that she has been awaiting him, It is here they are meant to find each other

Now

Mort Castle

Henderson
and The Girl with the Summer Eyes.

*   *   *

Well, shit, she could wait for the activities bus, another hour and a half, but God! All she wants to do is get home, lock herself in her room, and sleep until there's not one single scrambled-up thought left rolling through her mind. She'll ask him for a ride. He's got to be a new teacher. He's got a suit and tie. There are more than 190 teachers on the staff so you can't know them all. This guy might be one of the poor dudes who gets stuck teaching the nerds in the remedial classes. He looks like it. Like he holds out his hand and the shitty end of the stick goes there automatically. Check out that half-ass smile, will you?

"Say, I missed the bus. I live close. Could you give me a ride?"

The way he's looking at her makes Linda wonder if the guy can tell she's still pretty stoned. "My name is . . ."

"I know you," he says.

It is so weird with teachers. They always seem to know everyone whether or not they've had them in class.

"You come with me," he says.

*   *   *

Henderson is surprised that she has to give directions. He thought he'd be able to find the route to The Place simply by listening and following the sound of water over stones.

36

But she says, "Left," and "You go right here," and he drives.

When the car turns onto a narrow gravel road, he knows—he knows—that they are close.

Ahead, colors glow, there, where the branches hang heavy. He gives it more gas.

Then

*   *   *

"Why are we stopping here?" Linda asks. She doesn't want to be here.

Here is where a baby bird dies.

*   *   *

"This is The Place."

*   *   *

She understands that he knows, knows everything. This is where it has all been leading, has always been leading, the end of the path found in dark woods when she was six years old.

They get out of the car. He takes her hand, leads her into the trees.

*   *   *

Something is wrong. Henderson does not see the brook, does not hear the water over stones. Something is wrong.

Yet he is here.

He is here with The Girl with the Summer Eyes.
He touches her.
She screams.

*   *   *

She knows it is all crazy. It is something that should not be happening. Goddamned marijuana has made her think crazy.

She has to get away from him.

He touches her.

She screams.

*   *   *

She has to stop. She must stop screaming, the Girl with the Summer Eyes.

It is all going wrong.

He touches her.

She screams.

He feels the grass wither beneath his feet. The trees are disappearing, growing dim. The color, the color drips away.

He touches her.

She screams.

"Please," he says, "please stop." His hand covers her mouth. He holds her and pushes her and tips back her head.

*   *   *

Something breaks inside her. She knows the sound: autumn's dead leaves underfoot.

He is touching her.

She is trying to scream.
There is more breaking.
She cannot scream.

*   *   *

*She lies on colorless grass. Her eyes are closed. Henderson
is confused. Something has gone wrong.*

Henderson has—somehow—made a mistake.

This is not The Place.

It is only

Her Place.

The W.W. II Pistol

THE TAVERN SMELLED OF COAL and of the drying sweat of men who worked in the mines. The jukebox's neon glow and the illuminated face of the Budweiser clock over the plastic Imperial sign behind the bar provided the only light. It was the end of the work week and the men seated at the six Formica-topped tables and at the bar were drinking beers and boilermakers and highballs. It was quiet, with just an occasional nickel for a Hank Williams or Red Foley song. There had been no accidents in the mines for seven weeks and no one had bought a new car; there was little to talk about.

Even Lori, the barmaid, fat, a bleached blonde, wasn't kidding around with anyone. She greeted new arrivals with "Hey," or "How you doin'?" and then brought beer or whiskey.

Joe Heane threw the door wide when he entered. It took a long time to close; the sunlight that followed Joe in made everyone blink. Joe's head swiveled on his tight neck as he looked around.

Curley Raymond, at the end of the bar, bottle of Stag beer in hand, moved his stool a quarter-turn and said, "Guess who?"

Ron Adkins sipped beer. He sighed. "I'm getting tired of him. I'm getting real sick and real tired of him."

"Yeah," said Curley. "Me too."

Joe Heane's eyes again made a circuit of the tavern. He put his hand in the pocket of his blue vinyl jacket. He walked to the bar and stood behind Curley and Ron. They said nothing.

"How're you, Joe?" Lori said.

"I just want a beer," he said. "I want a Stag."

"Look, Joe," Lori said.

Joe Heane interrupted her. "I just want a beer. All I want." His mouth was tight. "Know why I only want the one beer?" The light of the Budweiser clock shone on his face. His teeth were widely spaced. A spot of dried blood where he'd bitten his lower lip glittered like hard coal.

Curley circled his fingers on the neck of his nearly empty bottle. Ron took another drink.

"I drink too much," Joe Heane said, "screws up my eyes. Makes everything all soft, fuzzy-like and I can't see so good. I want to see real good, though"—the tip of his tongue touched the scab on his lower lip—"so I can see every goddamn sonofabitch in this place for the goddamn sonofabitch they are."

Ron shrugged and turned on his stool to face Joe

41

Heane. So did Curley. "No need for trouble, Joe," Ron said.

Joe Heane stepped back. He looked at Ron, then Curley, then back to Ron. "No," he said, "no need for trouble. Just 'cause you're all goddamn sonofabitches. That don't mean there's a need for trouble." He smiled and his mouth got tighter. "Not scared of you, Ron Adkins. Not scared of you, Curley. You're sonofabitches the both of you."

Curley laughed. "Okay," he said, "you called us what you come to call us, I guess, so now you can get on out of here. Or you can sit down and have a beer with us."

"No," Joe Heane said, "I don't drink with sonofabitches. Got something better for you. Got it right here in my pocket."

"Yeah," Ron said. "We know."

"Yeah, yeah," Joe said. Then the words came quickly. "Got my World War Two pistol. Ought to take it and put a round in every goddamn sonofabitch in here. Blow you all to hell. Carried this gun in the big war. You don't think I know what killing's all about?"

"Right, Joe. We know."

"That's what I should do. Make you sorry for the first day you and all the other goddamn sonofabitches thought to make a goddamn fool out of Joe Heane."

There was silence and then Ron said, "Oh, for chrissake, then you do. Just you do it, Joe. You take out your pistol and then we see what happens."

"No," Joe Heane said. "I won't do it now. Get my World War Two pistol half out my pocket and you and all the other sonofabitches jump all over me."

Joe looked like he'd said something clever. "So, I won't

do a thing. Not now. But I killed men in the war and I know what killing is. Every Mr. Sonofabitch can stand some good advice ought to remember that."

"Well, good enough then, Joe," Curley said, "so what you do is take yourself and your pistol home now. Your pretty little wife is probably missing you, missing you real bad. So you go home."

"Curley, you are a sonofabitch for certain and I will settle all with you someday."

"Maybe so and maybe no, but for right now, you go on home," Curley said.

Joe Heane said nothing. The hand in his jacket pocket moved so that his knuckles took on a layer of blue vinyl skin. Then he turned and left.

Ron and Curley swivelled their stools back toward the bar.

"A couple more beers here," Curley said to Lori. Then he said to Ron, "We're going to have to do something."

"Yes," Ron said, "I think so."

* * *

Duane Sellers sat behind his polished desk. A stray lick of black hair had fallen onto his lined forehead. He brushed it back, then folded his hands on the green desk blotter. "All right," he said, "what do you want me to do?"

Curley rubbed his chin. "I don't know. Getting to be some kind of problem."

"That's right," Ron said. He slid forward on the upholstered armchair. "That's why we came to you, Duane.

You're a big man now. Assistant State's Attorney. But you never forgot who you were."

"That's right," Curley said. "You know folks around here. You know how they think."

"I guess so," Duane Sellers said softly. "I guess I do, that's right."

"Look, Duane," Curley said, "Joe Heane's getting crazier and crazier. He's carrying that goddamn pistol . . ."

"Yeah," Duane Sellers said. He smiled. "The World War Two pistol. Lots of kids in town used to want to see that pistol. Getting out of high school, thinking about joining the marines or the army, they'd go talk to Joe Heane. Want to see the pistol he carried in World War Two. Wanted to hear what all he did over there. Sometimes he'd let 'em look at the medals and everything, but then, after a time, he stopped doing that. Still tell the stories, though. Sometimes."

"Joe's not telling war stories anymore, Duane," Curley said. "All he talks about is how everyone's a goddamn sonofabitch and he's going to take the pistol and put a round in every one of us. Tell you, Duane, he is getting crazier and crazier every day goes by."

Duane Sellers nodded. "Guess that's so. Guess it is. I know he is a problem. Started acting crazy right after he got that pretty little wife from up in Decatur. Pretty little thing like that in a town like this.

"He goes off to work and all the time he's chopping coal he's thinking about that pretty little wife. That would be fine if his thinking stopped right there. But next you know, he's thinking how maybe everyone else, all the men he works with, the men in town, are maybe thinking about that pretty little wife of his, too. Then he's dead certain that's just what they are thinking. So he goes a little crazy, thinking about what everyone's thinking about.

"Then he gets real crazy and figures maybe some men are doing more than thinking about that pretty little wife of his." Duane Sellers nodded again and said, "So, that's it all right. He starts in thinking crazy and now he's acting crazy, carrying that World War Two pistol all the time and making threats and the like."

"Wants to be crazy, he's welcome," Curley said. "I don't want him come up behind me some night and blowing my head off. And I'm not the only one that feels that way, Duane."

Duane smiled. "I see your point. I don't want anything like that either. That would be bad trouble, a real mess."

Curley laughed. "Yeah," he said, "especially for me."

Duane Sellers laughed with him. "Especially for you. And not all that good for me or the town or anyone else, either."

"Can't he go to jail for a while, Duane?" Ron said. "Give him time to cool down and maybe get thinking right again."

Duane Sellers shook his head. The stray lick of hair flopped down and he did not push it back. "No, no," he said. "Around here you don't put a man in jail for talking crazy. Lots of people talk crazy. Lots of people carry guns. Can't have them all in jail. Can't sign Joe into Clarewood, either. Be a lot of folderol to get him in there and he's nowhere near crazy enough for them to keep him more than ten days or so. And then he gets out, he won't be all that amiable, if you see what I mean."

Duane Sellers frowned. "Of course, Joe does sometimes beat that pretty little wife of his."

"I know," Ron said.

"No good," Duane said, shaking his head. "She won't press charges. I asked her a time back. Hell, my daddy used to hit Mom when he was feisty and she said that was nobody's damn business and certainly not the law's damn business even if the whole town knew all about it.

"Shit fire and save the matches, boys, but Joe doesn't make enough racket beating and she doesn't make enough noise hollering so that we could jug him for public disturbance. Even so, throwing Joe in jail wouldn't help. The man has gone crazy in the mines. Let him out of jail and he'd be twice as crazy. Then he'd sure come after all us 'goddamn sonofabitches.' "

"Well, then," Curley said. "So what do we do?"

Duane Sellers thought a moment. "Kill him, I guess."

"Are you sure?" Curley said.

"Yes, I think so," Duane Sellers said. "Just do it right so there won't be much trouble about it. Maybe use his World War Two pistol and stick it in his own hand. Or knock him goofy and put him in the river.

"Don't want a lot of trouble about this. None of us do. Thing is, we just can't have a man running around town with a pistol ready to shoot everybody he thinks has been thinking about, or seeing, or messing with his pretty little wife. This is the only way I can figure."

"All right, Duane," Curley said. "Thanks a lot."

"That's all right," Duane Sellers said. "People expect me to take care of problems. That's my job."

"Thanks, Duane," Ron said.

*   *   *

It was Sunday afternoon and Joe Heane was seated on a wooden bench in the town square. Curley sat down on his right, Ron on the left. Joe Heane's old Chevrolet was parked in one of the marked spaces at the curb.

"I talked with Duane Sellers," Joe Heane said. "Called me in to his office. Said he had to talk to me."

Joe Heane licked his lips. His right hand was in the pocket of his blue vinyl jacket. He did not look at Curley or Ron. He kept his eyes on the old Chevrolet.

"You are all of you sonofabitches, you know."

"Yeah, Joe," Curley said. "We know. You told us all about it."

"Joe," Ron said, "that record has been spinning around too many times on the phonograph. That's just about enough of it, okay?"

"I don't know."

"What did Duane Sellers tell you, Joe?" Ron said.

"Said it was open season on Joe Heane. Said that's what he told you. Said it was going to get known around here that there wouldn't be a whole lot of trouble if I got killed. No trouble's, what he said." Joe Heane's voice was flat. "What he said was that it's all right to kill me for carrying my World War Two pistol, and marrying a pretty little wife, and calling you all the sonofabitches that you are. That's what I heard from Duane."

"Guess you heard right, Joe," Ron said.

"What I ought to do, goddamn it," Joe Heane said, "is take my pistol right now and kill you both. Kill you dead right in the middle of the Town Square here. Then I ought to just keep on killing until they kill me and it would mean something that way. Maybe I could get to kill that sonofabitch, Duane Sellers, and, goddamn it, that makes just as much sense as anything, I would say. Hell, I killed men in the war with my pistol."

"You won't do that, Joe," Curley said quietly. "We know you won't. Whole thing is just about done. You know that."

"Yeah," said Joe Heane, "I guess I do." He sounded tired.

Curley said, "See, you talked about it too much, so you can't do it. You talked about it the way you talked about all those men you killed in the war. And so now it's just like a story and it doesn't mean anything. It's all over, Joe, and you know it."

"That's right," Joe Heane said, "so I guess what happens now is you kill me. Is that it?"

Curley laughed. "No," he said. "No need to kill you now. Sitting here and chatting like this, you're making good sense. I talked this over with Ron. We decided if you got in your car, just you by your own self, and drove on out of here—say maybe a couple hundred miles south—there's big mines there and you could get work— just you going off by yourself and never coming back, then we don't have to kill you. Killing you is nothing we want to do, you see."

"You'd like that, wouldn't you?" Joe Heane said. "That's the way you sonofabitches are."

Ron laughed. He said, "Best thing for you to do, Joe."

"Is it?" Joe Heane said.

Neither Ron nor Curley answered him. Joe Heane

looked at his old Chevrolet. "All right, that is what I'll do then. I won't ever come back."

"That's right," Ron said.

"One more thing, Joe," Curley said. "Before you go, you'd better give me your pistol. It's made a lot of trouble for all of us."

"No, it didn't," Joe Heane said. But he took the .38 caliber pistol from his pocket and handed it to Curley. Then he rose, walked to his car, got in, started the engine, and slowly pulled away.

When the Chevrolet was out of sight, Curley hefted the pistol and said, "Gun like this has been through a lot."

"Guess that's so," Ron said.

"Genuine World War Two pistol like this," Curley said, "might be of value. Could even be worth a lot of money."

"Might be."

"We don't have a right to this gun," Curley said. "Joe Heane's wife ought to have it. Might bring her some money. She'll be needing money now with old Joe gone off to who knows where."

"That's right," Ron said. "We ought to drive on out there and see that she gets Joe's World War Two pistol, pretty little girl like that."

"Yeah," Curley said, "I think so, too."

Pop is Real Smart

LONNY GAZED AT JASON. HE loathed him with all the egoistic hatred of which only a five-year-old is capable. He was supposed to be happy he had a new brother. He was supposed to love him. Oh sure. Right. Damn.

Lonny's eyes measured the baby's length and studied the pink fingers curled in tight fists at the top of the blue blanket. He watched the fluttery beating of the soft spot on Jason's head as, under skimpy down, it palpitated with the tiny heart.

"Damn," Lonny said. Pop said "damn" a lot, like when he was driving and everybody else was driving like a jerk, or when he was trying to fix a leaky faucet or something.

And "damn" is just what Lonny felt like saying whenever he looked at Jason. The only thing the baby could do—his ookey-pukey brother!—was smell bad. Jason al-

ways smelled no matter how often Mom bathed him or
dumped a load of powder on him.

Jason wasn't good for anything!

Now Scott, down the block, Scott was lucky. Scott had
a *real* brother, Fred, good old Fred. Yessir, Fred was a fun
kid. You could punch Fred real hard, he wouldn't even
cry. And Fred didn't go running to tell, either. Uh-uh.
But Fred had these clumpy cowboy boots and if you
punched him, then he would just start kicking you and
kicking and maybe you would be the one who wound up
crying!

Fred, that was the kind of dude you wanted for a little
brother.

Not Jason. This damn baby, hey, he couldn't do anything.

And this was the kid Lonny had helped Mom and Pop
choose a name for? Jason. That was a good name for a
good guy.

Damn!

Jason—this stupid thing with that stupid up and down
blob on its head going thump-a-thump, thump-a-thump.
No way, José!

Somebody must have fooled Mom. When she'd gone
to the hospital, Mom had somehow got stuck with this
little snot instead of a good brother for him.

Lonny wondered how Mom could be so damn dumb.
Well, she was a girl, even if she was a grownup, and girls
could be pretty dumb sometimes. But damn, how did they
put one over on Pop? Pop was real smart.

Lonny reached through the crib slats. He lightly
touched Jason's soft spot. At the pulse beneath his fingers,
he yanked back his hand.

Damn, this baby was just no good. No. Good.

He left the room. There had to be some way to get rid of Jason. He would ask Mom to take the baby back to the hospital, tell her she'd made a mistake. Oh, he'd have to say it just the right way so she didn't get pee-owed, but he'd figure it out. Then she could go get him a really good brother, like Fred.

Yeah! He knew just how to say it. He'd talk to Mom right now.

"Mom!" he hollered, running down the stairs. He hoped he would wake the baby.

Mom did not answer. Jason did not cry. "Mom!" Lonny went to the kitchen. The linoleum buzzed beneath his Nikes and he heard the muffled thud of the washing machine in the downstairs utility room.

Mom was doing the wash. Damn, it was never a good idea to talk to her about anything when she was into laundry.

Lonny decided he might as well make himself a sandwich or something. He dragged a chair from the table over to the cabinets. He climbed up and took down the big jar of peanut butter. He got the Wonder Bread from the breadbox.

He set the bread and peanut butter on the table. He hoped he could open the new jar by himself. No way did he want to ask Mom for help when she was doing the laundry.

Okay! The lid came right off. "Yeah," Lonny said. "She's gonna have to take it back. It's no damn good, and if it's no good, you just take it back."

Hey, sometimes he wondered how a smart guy like Pop

got stuck with Mom, anyway. For real, it was Pop had the brains.

Like once Lonny had goofed it. He had spent his birthday money on a rifle at Toys R' Us and damn! It was wrong. It wasn't a Rambo assault rifle. It was a stupid Ranger Rock rifle. No way did you want a Ranger Rock rifle. Who ever heard of Ranger Rock?

So he and Pop took it back to get the Rambo rifle. "No refunds on sale items, sorry." That's what this real dipstick at the store had to say.

Then Pop showed him how you couldn't even pull the trigger and the way the plastic barrel was all cracked and everything. No problem, man! They got back his birthday money, went to another store, and bought the Rambo rifle.

And you know what? That nerd at Toys R' Us never even had an idea that Pop had busted up the stupid Ranger Rock rifle himself! That's how smart Pop was.

With his first finger, Lonny swirled out a glob of peanut butter. He popped it into his mouth. Yeah, peanut butter was great. He could live on peanut butter all the time. He'd make a nice, open-faced sandwich, and then maybe Mom would be done with the laundry and he could talk to her about getting rid of smelly Jason.

He went to the drawers by the sink. He opened the top one.

Mom always spread peanut butter with a dull knife.

It was the sharp knife that caught Lonny's eye.

Healers

1. *What Is*

HE PEERED DOWN AT THE child who lay in jockey shorts on the twisted sheets of the day-bed. The living room of the housing project apartment was close with the smell of sickness and grease and poverty.

"Mister, he dyin'," the boy's mother said. "Maybe gone by mornin' tomorrow, maybe next day, and then my baby boy ain't no more."

It was not yet eleven o'clock at night and it seemed the mother's "mornin' tomorrow" might well be optimistic. The boy's skin was the color of putty, stretched taut on a body bloated with its own poisons. His eyes floated in poached egg yellow and each time he breathed, a tiny bubble of spit burst between his lips.

"Not yet seven years old," the mother said, "and it's not right. You tell me, Mister. Is it right a boy like him should get no more time than that to walk this Earth?"

He shook his head. "I can't tell you. I long ago gave up thinking about what is right and what is wrong."

"What is it you do think about, Mister?"

He said, "Only what is."

The boy's mother said, "Mister, I tell you what is. My boy dyin', that's what is. Dyin' cuz he's black and dyin' cuz we're poor. They says 'Money can't buy health,' now that's a damned lie and a double-damned lie. You a rich white boy needin' a kidney transplant and you get a kidney and you live. Don't work that way for poor black folk, Mister. We ain't like them 'cuz they got and we don't, and we ain't like them 'cuz we're black and they white. And they hate us 'cuz we different, and what you hate you afraid of, and what you hate you try to pretend ain't there, an' more than anythin', what you hate you don't never give no help to—and if it goes away, goes away like my boy goin' away, forever, well you damn glad of it."

She paused. "I guess I talks a lot, but Mister, I guess maybe you know all about bein' different. So you tell me . . . Am I saying what is?"

"Yes," he said. Then he asked, "What do you want of me?"

She pointed at her son. "Don't let him die, Mister. Please."

He bent and his fangs found the boy's jugular.

When he straightened, the child's mother said, "Thank you, Mister. My boy's gonna live."

He said, "He will not die," and he left.

55

Mort Castle

*   *   *

2. A Billion Monstrosities

It was so late that it was early when Rafael Martinez returned to his home, but when one visits the city, as Martinez did more nights than not, a Mexican turista city built to cater to the needs and desires and whims of wealthy gringos, there is much to do, much pleasure to be found and taken in places that are devoted exclusively to pleasure finding and taking. Martinez felt greatly welcome in the city, and why not? He was wealthy, BMW, Mercedes, Jaguar wealthy, Rolex watch, IBM computers, and Pierre Cardin suits wealthy.

When he turned on the light in his bedroom, Rafael Martinez felt a flash of surprise—but half a moment's appraisal convinced him that he had nothing to fear from the stranger who somehow had invaded his home and now sat in the arm chair by the balcony window. Rather than fright, Martinez felt anger that his privacy could be impinged upon—but no less did he feel a reassuring familiarity.

Had he not seen many who looked like this—and had they not brought him a fortune? The stranger looked old, but it was not the natural aging that mankind is heir and prey to; rather it seemed the result of grievous wasting sickness that had stripped away layers of flesh to leave only a parchment skinned skeleton, with a bald head the color of old ivory and too bright, fever-glittering eyes.

"Who are you?" Rafael Martinez asked sharply. "What are you doing here?"

"You don't know me?" The stranger's voice sounded the way his eyes looked, a fever-glitter sound. "You should. I know you, Rafael Martinez."

"Dr. Martinez . . ."

"Rafael Martinez, you are no doctor."

Rafael Martinez sighed. Whatever this was, he was tiring of it. It was time to summon the police, he decided, and because he saw no threat from the stranger, Rafael Martinez, as he reached for the bedstand telephone, announced such intention.

But the stranger was out of the chair, and he gripped Martinez's wrist, and his fingers were remarkably strong and no less remarkably hot, and Martinez could not pick up the telephone.

"I've come because of the clinic," the stranger said.

"I see," Rafael Martinez said. "But this is quite irregular. We can make the proper arrangements if you will come tomorrow directly to the clinic . . ."

"To Rafael Martinez's famed clinic," the stranger interrupted.

"Where I treat the afflicted . . ."

"With purges that twist their guts and foul-tasting elixirs that make their heads spin, with hot baths that draw their tiniest bits of remaining strength streaming from their pores in rivers of sweat, and cold baths that freeze their pain within them, with brutal massage and spinal realignment that bends their already bent bodies into bizarre postures of screaming misery . . . I know the work of your clinic, Rafael Martinez, and I know you do all this—and you do that which is far worse. You sell false hope to the hopeless."

With the stranger's strong hot grip on his wrist, and

the stranger's eyes unblinking and piercing, Rafael Martinez began to feel fear.

"Who are you?" he demanded.

"You know me," the stranger said, and he let go of Martinez's wrist.

And it was now that Rafael Martinez felt within his blood, within his bowels, within his lungs, within his bones and the marrow of his bones, the peculiar movement of a billion and a billion times a billion multiplying monstrosities.

The pain swelled inside him, waves of pain without diminution, as his body inexorably began to consume itself.

Rafael Martinez fell to his knees.

"You know me," the stranger said once more.

Rafael Martinez looked up through curtains of thick red and screamed the stranger's name.

"Cancer!"

*   *   *

3. Miss Hazeltine's Miracle

Lord Jesus, blessed Jesus, merciful Jesus, my own sweet Jesus, help me . . . Heal me—this time! That was the silent prayer Lois Anne Hazeltine prayed as she hobbled into the tent on her two canes, her bent body vibrating with the always pain, the pain that filled her so that she thought on the worst days (there were no good days: only bad days, worse days, and worst days) that she would burst with it.

The diagnosis, made five years previously, when she

was 32: rheumatoid arthritis. The prognosis: pain for the rest of her natural life, pain that would cripple and twist her body, that might be (sometimes) alleviated (slightly) by aspirin, by anti-inflammatories (indomethacin, cortisone), but pain about which medical science, "Well, quite frankly, Miss Hazeltine, there's not a great deal we can do for you."

No question then that she needed a miracle. And she'd prayed for one ("Ask and it shall be given"), and sought one ("Look ye to the Lord"), but though she avidly watched and prayed along with TV preachers, putting her clawed hands on top of the Sylvania console and opening a humble heart to the Holy Spirit, and though she'd gone to faith healers in 33 counties in Kentucky, and Missouri, and Illinois, and though she'd sent in coupons from supermarket-sold tabloids, receiving for a dollar, two dollars, or ten dollars, miracle beads, miracle statues, miracle crosses, miracle pictures, miracle water, she had not yet received a miracle.

But she would. (I believe) Lois Anne Hazeltine did not doubt. (I believe) Her faith was real and unwavering and it would be her salvation. (I believe I believe Ibelieve-IbelieveIbelieveIbelieve!!!)

This time!

Because Jimmy Smalley had a reputation.

He was the man who could work miracles.

There was no organ playing as the miracle seekers found seats on the wooden benches. No choir sang hymns to God.

There was just Jimmy Smalley striding to the platform, moving like a tall man and not a pudgy five-footer, Jimmy Smalley raising his arms, the jacket sleeves of his polyester leisure suit riding up to reveal a good three inches of none too clean cuff, Jimmy Smalley greeting everyone in the piercing voice of an amphetamine-fueled munchkin:

"Well y'all, hello, hello, hello! We're gonna get movin, right here and right now and right away, 'cause you come here for miracles, and miracles you're gonna have. Get some lines here, and bring your sick and wasted and twisted selves right on up here, why doncha? Got some cancer in your colon? We'll clobber it! Take care of epilepsy in an instant and scoliosis in a second. Gonna mash your miseries, heal your hurts, and pull the pain plumb out of you and throw it on over the moon. Maybe you was born deaf, but tomorrow night you're gonna be singin' along with the theme from Love Boat. Maybe you was born blind, but tomorrow morning when that pesky bluejay wakes you up with its squawk, you can pitch a bit of chat and knock it right square in the head. Come on, come on, come on! Get a move on! Got us some miracalizing to do—and I do mean NOW!"

Lois Anne Hazeltine wanted to hurry, to claim a place at the head of the line, but she was barely capable of movement, let alone rapid movement, and so, far back in the line, she had plenty of time to pray (Oh Lord, let it be, this time, my sweet Jesus, grant my prayers!) and to watch:

As Jimmy Smalley put his hands on the shoulders of a man in a wheelchair, a man who had muscular dystrophy, and commanded: "Now you just get on up out of that contraption." And the man did. Jimmy Smalley, his hands still on the man's shoulders, walked backward and the man, who had not walked in four years, walked,

walked forward, walked without a lurch or stumble or hesitation. "Now on your knees, friend," said Jimmy Smalley, and the man knelt easily, Jimmy along with him, and Jimmy Smalley whispered in his ear and the man threw up his arms and screamed: "I believe! I do believe!"

Jimmy Smalley said, "You are healed."

And the man was.

And in more or less the same way . . .

—so was a woman who had a short leg (and the leg grew, right there, with everyone watching) . . .

—so was a man who could not speak, whose first words—ever—were "I believe! I do believe . . ."

(And getting closer now, closer to the miracle that was waiting for her, Lois Anne Hazeltine prayed to God and told Him she believed, had never stopped believing during her trials and travails and torments.)

—so were all those who came to Jimmy Smalley for a miracle.

—until at last it was Lois Anne Hazeltine's turn, her moment for her miracle.

With Jimmy Smalley's hands on her shoulders, she felt the power, a buzzing glow, spreading through her, (Yes! Oh, yes dear God, at last!) and when Jimmy Smalley said, "Drop those canes, you're not needin' those silly things no more!" she did—and she felt herself straighten, felt an incredible life-rightness within her, as though she were a springtime plant bursting from the dark and cold of the ground.

"Now claim your cure, woman!" Jimmy Smalley commanded. "On your knees now!"

She fell to her pain-free knees (hurt gone—the hurt is gone—Jesus, this is my miracle!).

Jimmy Smalley was kneeling with her.

(Thank you, Jesus, Oh, thank you, dear Lord . . .)

Softly, so softly, Jimmy Smalley whispered in her ear, whispered a promise of radiant health and a promise that brought her the most profound pain she had ever experienced: "Woman, now you know what he can do. This is the Devil's work, woman; believe in Him and be healed."

And Jimmy Smalley asked, "Do you believe?"

With Father, at the Zoo, then Home

"WELL, WHAT SHALL WE DO first?" he says. It is a Saturday, sun-washed, and they are at the zoo. Mulbray is her father. She is Debra, five years old, a little thin.

"I don't care, Father," she says. They walk in no particular direction, which takes them to the reptile house, where he says, "Want to go in here?" and she replies, "Yes, Father."

The snakes are hardly moving. Occasionally, a split tongue touches the one-way-glass barrier and lazily retreats. The rattlers are not rattling. The coral snakes are too small to be easily seen, no more deadly than dried twigs. The boa constrictor is only a sprawling, blown-out inner tube.

"Would you like to see the lions now?" Mulbray asks, when they emerge from the cool, dark snake house into the sun, into the heat. "The big cats are just over there."

"Yes, Father," she says.

Like the reptile house, the inside of the feline house is dark. It smells. The great cats are all indoors. Their outside cages are too hot for them; they lie on their bellies, forepaws stretched before them. Giant eyelids, sandpaper colored saucers, cover dreamy eyes that will become alert only at four o'clock feeding time.

He leads Debra over to where a group of children, accompanied by two vigilant nuns, stand at the railing in front of the cage of a mammoth lion, who lies on his back, lazier than the others. The children have questions for their nuns.

"Sister! Why ain't he doin' nothin'?"

"He dead, Sister? He dead?"

"Look! He's a man lion!"

"They feed 'em live horses, don't they, Sister?"

"That's a man-eating lion. Where do they get the man for him?"

He has a question for Debra. "He really is big, isn't he, honey?"

"Yes, Father," she says.

And so he says, "Let's visit the children's zoo."

Adults are not permitted entry to the children's zoo. He directs Debra through the gate and sits down under a sign, "Adult Waiting Station." A dripping fat lady with a dripping smile joins him on the bench.

"Oh," she says, "they're so cute." He looks at her. She quickly adds, "Oh, not just the animals, although God knows they're just the sweetest things. Those tiny deer, and the lambs and the big turtle. But the little ones are so cute with those darling little baby animals."

He nods to the fat lady, who is pointing a sausage finger. "That one's mine, my little Nancy," she says, indicating a fat girl who is holding a black and white rabbit.

"Which one is yours?" the fat lady asks.

"There," he says. Debra is passing a fence that imprisons half a dozen kids. They climb the center rung of the fence rail, miniature hooves sliding off the wood.

"I wonder if we should buy her a bunny of her own," the fat lady says. "She just loves the precious little dears."

Debra walks by the giant tortoise, who lifts his leathery head, then lowers it slowly.

Nancy, the fat girl, still has the black and white rabbit. The rabbit struggles, twitching ears, kicking its hind legs.

"Oh, I do think she would just love a little bunny pet," the fat lady says. "Don't you?"

He nods.

When Debra emerges through the "Exit" gate, he says, "Nice to meet you," to the fat lady, stands up, and rapidly walks to his daughter. He takes Debra's hand.

Later in the day, they see the polar bears, playing in the green, slimy-looking water of their pool. They stop at the elephants' cage. The ponderous gray beasts, skin flaking off in dead white patches, sway from side to side and spray each other with pulsing gushes sucked from their trough into their trunks.

Kama, the last cage they stop at, is the world's third largest gorilla in captivity. The ape blinks constantly, stupidly, and bats at a tire swinging on a frayed rope.

"That is really a giant of an ape, isn't it, Debra?" he says.

"Yes, Father," she answers.

And then it is time to take Debra home. It is a silent

ride. He pulls into the driveway. Debra's mother is waiting at the open front door. Debra runs from the auto, slamming the car door behind her, and even though Debra runs and he walks, they reach Debra's mother at the same time.

"Did you have a nice time?" she says, one arm around Debra's thin shoulders.

"Oh Mommy!" Debra says. "The lions have tails like paint brushes! And I saw a big, big monkey! And elephants with hose-noses . . ."

"I'll pick her up about the same time next Saturday," Mulbray says, and turns, and walks to the car.

Buckeye Jim in Egypt

Prologue

IN THE BEGINNING, THERE WAS darkness.

Then came light.

That is the beginning of everything.

I

The more mundane among us contend Southern Illinois is called "Egypt" or "Little Egypt" because of its southernmost town, Cairo, on the Mississippi River.

More probable is that the term came into usage because we are still waiting for a Moses to lead us out of here right to the Promised Land, although every time one appears on the scene, we kick him flush in the backside and tell him to let us tend to our own affairs.

> Brian Robert Moore, weekly columnist,
> 1920–1973, "I'll Tell You What!" for the
> *Sesser Sentinel, Eads St. Publications,*
> *Sesser, Illinois*

> Way up yonder, above the sky,
> white bird nests in a green bird's eye.

> *"Buckeye Jim"*
> *An American folk song,*
> *usually performed on the banjo*

Monday, July 12, 1925

Sometimes he forgot who he was.

Sometimes he forgot what he was doing here.

It was just past 7:30 in the morning, and already the thermometer had hit a swampy 80, but it was not the temperature or fatigue that caused the man in the light weight suit coat to set down his straw valise and banjo case and lean on the rail of the half-mile long bridge. He needed to think. Gazing down at the rippling, sun-reflecting waters of the Washauconda River helped to bring about a mind-calming focus.

He reached into his pocket. He found it: a lucky buck-eye. Every time he reached into his pocket, there would be one—and one only. The seed of the horse chestnut was brown and brittle; it felt as though there were something magical and off-center within it. It was exactly like the world.

His smile came slow and easy. Nobody would ever mistake him for handsome, but when he smiled, it made most folks like him.

He knew who he was.

He was Buckeye Jim.

This time. He knew what he had to do.

Buckeye back in his pocket, he hoisted his grip and banjo. Just then a new, deep green, Oakland All American Six pulled up, the powerful Phaeton model. Of course, in this weather, the windows were down. The driver, in a straw fedora, tie knotted in a half-Windsor, a prominent American flag pin on his collar, leaned toward Buckeye Jim. "How do."

"How do," Buckeye Jim answered, bending down, face framed by the window. "Your automobile is a beaut."

"I do thank you. Might I offer you a ride into Ft. Lorraine? I assume that is your intended destination."

"Yes, sir," Buckeye Jim said.

"The Devil is always hiring fiddlers and banjo pickers in hell, but if you're after employment in the mines, Mr. June Legrand's got a one hole privy operation in Ft. Lorraine that is likely to oblige. If you don't mind working next to niggers. And if you don't mind being forced to join the union."

Buckeye Jim said nothing as he stowed his gear in the back.

The driver added, "Not saying Legrand's a Bolshevik. Not saying he's a nigger lover. I do wonder if he's a true-blue American."

The auto felt massive. Buckeye Jim wondered if he

would ever get used to cars. He did enjoy the smell of new cars. He liked the smell of gently flowing rivers and hot sun on steel bridges . . .

He suddenly remembered the strong and surprising odor of light, a smell that was itself pure radiance, shattering and banishing the darkness.

The driver's name, said the man who wore his nation's flag on his collar, was Mark E. Dupont. ("Thank you for the ride, Mr. Dupont, and people call me Buckeye Jim.") He seemed a friendly fellow, not too jolly or too serious.

Not too much one or the other . . . He could be a dangerous man, Buckeye Jim reckoned. On several occasions, Buckeye Jim had been killed by this sort of man.

Mark E. Dupont casually mentioned he was assistant superintendent up to the new strip mine owned by Illinois Coal and Power north of Herrin. A new process, strip mining would be the wave of the future, and it was swell. It meant more profit for everyone. Also, Mark E. Dupont mentioned (casually), he'd been elected to Herrin's town council. There had been talk—casual, but who could tell—about his running for mayor.

He started to say something else casual when Buckeye Jim said, "Sure a fine automobile. A real ace."

Dupont chuckled. "Well, I would have been most happy and satisfied with just your standard model, but my boys would not have it."

"You have sons?" Buckeye Jim asked.

Dupont said, "Why, yes, yes, I do have a family, and I am blessed with boys. Two boys and a girl, and a fine, Christian wife who dotes on me.

"But I was not referring to my offspring. I meant the boys in the Klan."

70

"Clan," Buckeye Jim said quietly. There were times when his mind became a tedious and troublesome thing.

So many memories . . .

He did remember clans. The MacEldoes? The Mc-Cutcheons? In Scotland. He recalled Scotland as a land of thistles and foggy mornings more gray and ominous than anywhere else on earth. And cutting through the grayness, he could remember the swirling—squeal of the pipes, eerie and mysterious, a summons to war and death . . .

He remembered . . .

". . . I'm the leader. What it is is what you call the Cyclops. That's sort of like a code," Dupont said. " 'Course they have to inflate it some, call me the 'Grand Exalted Cyclops.' "

Mark E. Dupont sounded like he didn't mind that "his boys" wanted him to be "grand" and "exalted" and to drive a Phaeton.

"Well, I don't know," Buckeye Jim said.

"A lot of people don't know," Dupont said, "and among 'em is one Mr. C. Cooper Legrand, Jr. I'll be jawing some with him today. Rich man like him, what he can't realize is this was hard-scrabble, bare bone, poor country 'fore the mines come. And if all the really big companies from out east choose to leave because Legrand has a head full of foreign thinkin' and a heart that beats pure nigger time like a shufflin' pickaninny . . ."

Buckeye Jim said nothing. He was confused. Not infrequently, people thought him dull-witted.

But if you live many lives, and you don't know what you should know and you do know what you shouldn't know . . . My, oh, my, and wasn't it a perplexing business?

Mr. Dupont was talking about—

71

". . . the Klan is four-square for the Bible. I'd imagine a right-looking American fellow such as yourself, why, you wouldn't be having any moral or spiritual argumentations with that, would you, Mr. Buckeye Jim?"

With all his poor head had to tote, sometimes Buckeye Jim felt he had no room left over for a sense of humor, but doggone! That did make him laugh!

"Mr. Dupont," he said. "I would testify in any court of the land or on Judgment Day that I have no dispute with the Bible."

"Well, good, good," Mr. Dupont said. He went on to tell how the Ku Klux Klan defended Americans from foreigners and Communists and Catholics (especially those "Eye-talian Catholics but also those Bohunk and Polack" Catholics), and he went on to tell how it brought true Christianity to those as needed the Gospel Truth, and he went on to tell how it put the fear of God in the bootleggers, like those East St. Louis Shelton Brothers, or that Jew Charlie Birger with his road house, the Shady Rest, and he went on and he went on and on and on . . .

Buckeye Jim said, "Looks like we're here."

Like virtually all southern Illinois town squares, Ft. Lorraine's was a circle. In the center, an imposing island of civic sanctity, stood the municipal building, new red brick, with broad, white concrete steps. Merchants on the town's center hub included Walker and Sons clothing, the Vick-Cline Pharmacy (where the forty cent size Fletcher's Castoria was on sale for twenty-nine cents), and Ulricht's Shoe Store.

Buckeye Jim got out and pulled his gear after him.

"Good luck," Dupont said, shaking his hand through the passenger window portal. "You find Ft. Lorraine isn't exactly to your liking, that maybe it smells more niggery than you care for, you come on up north of Herrin way and perhaps I can do you some good."

"Why, thank you," Buckeye Jim said. You know, Buckeye Jim felt altogether humorous today. "Mr. Dupont, you are the very first Grand Exalted Cyclops I have met in my entire life and I am likely some older than you take me for."

Mark E. Dupont waved a "Pshaw" hand in pleased self-deprecation.

"And by the way," Buckeye Jim said, "I'm a Jew."

II

With Britain's defeat of France in 1763, the dreams of a French empire in Illinois ended. In the south of the state, such lasting place names as Vincennes, Prairie du Rocher, and Bellefontaine are usually so mispronounced in southern Illinois twang as to be unrecognizable to any Frenchman.

But today, in Ft. Lorraine, Illinois, in Union Grove County, "an experiment in planned living" is being conducted that makes many of the local citizenry proclaim their community "a heaven on earth." The "social scientist" responsible is C. Cooper Legrand, Jr., who owns the Old Legrand and Washauconda River Mining Corporation, one of the smaller operations in the region—"but one of the safest," Legrand stresses. A childless widower, C. Cooper Legrand is usually addressed good-naturedly by his employees as "June," or "Juney." With enthusiastic forthrightness, he states, "Yes, we are working together to create a utopia, an earthly paradise if you will. After all, my father created hell."

In addition to owning the mines, the Legrand family built and owns much of the town of Ft. Lorraine itself, renting living quarters to its laborers. But these houses are a far cry today from what they were in "the not so good old days." According to the Illinois Coal Report for 1898, these dwellings "lacked central heating and running water. One outhouse privy served six homes. Workers led 'joyless, brutal, dangerous lives,' and had little opportunity to 'even dare to dream of bettering themselves.' "

"My father died in 1910, and I bear him no grudge, and I hope others do not. He was not cruel, merely unenlightened," states Legrand. "I was 22 at his passing, and I felt myself ready. I had studied in Europe, in France, England, and Germany. I had visited Russia. I knew that if capitalism did not change, it would be brought down, that there would be a revolution in blood and fire. History would condemn those who reaped inhumane profits from the sufferings of the masses. I envisioned a decent, compassionate capitalism, one that has at its root the understanding that the human experience is one we all share."

Upon assuming the mantle of leadership, Legrand immediately instituted new safety features in the mining operations, and transformed the workers' "squalid huts" into real homes. He opened negotiations with the United Mine Workers of America and his operations today are 100% union.

Not infrequently, C. Cooper Legrand, Jr. is asked if he is a "leftist," or even a Socialist or Communist, and in this part of the country, these are damning labels.

But Legrand laughs at such allegations of "Un-

Americanism." "What I am is a progressive," he maintains. "I believe in people. I'm working for a better world for all of us, without the invisible walls that have kept people apart for too long.

> *"From "Utopia in Illinois?," a feature article by Roy L. Potts, in The St. Louis Tribune—Leader, May 10, 1924.*

"Horseshit."

> *Mark E. Dupont, Grand Exalted Cyclops of the Knights of the Ku Klux Klan; a private response to the above article.*

The Knights of the Ku Klux Klan stand for the purest ideals of native-born, white, Gentile four-square Americanism:

The tenets of the Christian religion.

The protection and nurturing of white womanhood.

The freedom, under law, of the individual.

The "right to work" of the American workingman; his individual liberty to enter into such business negotiations and private and personal contracts as he chooses.

> *From a two color handbill entitled "The Fiery Cross: America's Guiding Light," written by Mark E. Dupont and the Rev. James E. Scurlock, January, 1924*

"Horseshit."

C. Cooper Legrand, Jr., in a private response to the above quoted handbill, prior to his ripping it to pieces as he laughed.

III

He liked it.

By that afternoon, he'd walked here and he'd walked there, and after a time, he knew Ft. Lorraine was the right place.

A little girl on the east side sold him a one-penny lemonade, ferociously cold and snapping with lemon.

He saw a bluejay.

A negro woman on the front porch of a neat little house in a neighborhood of neat little houses called to him.

"Sir?" She held her little boy by the hand, a child of perhaps five or six.

Buckeye Jim went up the walk. He liked the way she sounded, not the "hiding away" voice black folks often use for white people.

"You lost?"

No.

No one is lost; no one is forsaken; those were the words that came to his mind.

There were flowers in the yard. Impatiens. Pink and yellow roses. And tulips. July, and so hot, and yet the tulips were still here and lovely.

A happy perplexity filled his head, and he felt a small grin growing that he knew to be silly. Maybe at last, at last, it was coming around! Coming around here, in Ft. Lorraine, and maybe this town would be a light unto the nations . . . He was, he said, just sort of scouting the territory, and he told her his name.

She was Mrs. Willoughby. Her little boy was Paulie Jason. The child drew closer to her. "My Paulie can't talk. He can hear, but he can't talk. Doctors don't know as to why it is."

Buckeye Jim put his small straw suitcase down on the walk. He reached into his pocket. "Yes! I thought I had me one. And it's an extra special lucky one!"

A snap of thumb launched the buckeye. At the top of its arc, it hung there and there it hung . . .

Then Paulie Jason let loose his momma and slowly, slowly, his hand swam out as the buckeye dropped through weighted depths of air to land on his palm and his fingers closed over it.

Buckeye Jim turned and walked away.

Paulie Jason said, "Goodbye, Mr. Buckeye Jim."

IV

Socialism, communism, and other doctrines have played no part in the violence and murder which have brought such ill fame to the "queen of Egypt."

William L. Chenery in The Century

. . . respect to Mr. Chenery, this self-proclaimed Sage of Sesser holds that we are just as willing to kill for doctrines as your most radical, bearded, bomb-toting, Eastern European anarchist. Many of our law enforcement officials and politicians are willing to kill for the doctrine, "Under the Table and in My Palm," while our bootleggers resort to violence to enforce the "Right of Americans to Get Drunk." Our Kluxers, of course, will take up arms in defense of every town's prerogative to conduct festive lynching bees, while I personally know at least two Methodist churches whose congregations load the cannons if you try to take away their covered dish pot luck dinner, which they hold as a sacrament.

Of course we Egyptians, when we lack doctrines to kill for, will quite happily kill because A) we've nothing more interesting to do and B) our nation expects us to act like savages.

Brian Robert Moore, "I'll Tell You What!"

* * *

Son of a bitch! Mark E. Dupont, THE Grand Exalted Cyclops, did not hold with unnecessary violence, but at this particular instant, he could violently put a new Montgomery Ward steel-toe work boot all the way up that man's . . .

Mr. C. Cooper Legrand, Jr., "Call me June," trying to be "plain folks," but oh, the man was just so full of himself!

Talk reason to him. That's what the Illinois Coal and Power Company wanted its designee (and rising member of the management team!), Mark E. Dupont to do.

Illinois Coal and Power would like Legrand to sell them his enterprise. Not that Legrand was real competition, not with I C and P's far cheaper strip mining process and non-union operation . . . *But I like having a coal mine, Mark! It's a challenge! It's exciting! It's entertaining!*

Negotiations could begin immediately. Accommodations could be reached with the union. Mr. Legrand could play a role on a board of directors . . .

Mr. Legrand, whether you know it or not, there was trouble stirring, many of Egypt's citizens did not hold with white people and the colored living and working together like that—

—Mark, when the men come off their shift, all you see is eyes. You can't tell a colored coal miner from a white one!

—this union thing, well, in the long run, it might DEstroy individual incentive . . .

—meant no one was cheated and everyone got what was coming to him. Do unto others and all that, Mark . . .

Like to give you what's coming to you! Like to do unto you until you're done for certain, chucking Bible at me when nobody ever sees you at church!

Hmm, could be some of the fancy learning you got overseas included how to spurn the Lord your God? You an atheist, Juney-Bug? By the way, how long your wife's gone and you still single and no lady around but that giant mammy housekeeper? Could be you more of a Jane than a June, Mr. Legrand?

At sunset of a frustrating day, Dupont pulled up in front of his home in Herrin. If Dupont had been able to get things moving right, he'd been virtually promised the super's position at the Illinois Coal and Power's Ft. Lorraine mines!

But . . . say, what the hell?

He picked it off the seat of his new Oakland All American Six Phaeton.

A buckeye.

That guy this morning, that sort of a mush brain . . .

The buckeye felt damn bad, he thought.

That's when lightning hit.

Lightning did not blast down from the heavens.

It burst from deep within him, and he felt the searing anguish in his eyes, felt his blood boil, felt his heart blaze and burn and turn to hard, black coal. And he felt a hellish hand wrap around his soul and squeeze!

The power of it threw him against the car door with enough force to spring it. He did a back somersault, losing his hat in the process. He pushed himself up to his hands and knees.

"Aaaaah! Aaaaah!" he shrieked, but it was a thin shriek, all breath and tightness. Jesus! Jesus!

Save me!

In spiritual and physical agony, his American flag collar-pin falling into the disgusting Niagara as he vomited and vomited . . .

. . . in the fetid black and green foaming spew from his guts, he could see incredibly tiny frogs, obscenely clean and shining eyed . . .

The Devil had him! He could not doubt! The Devil . . .

In his anguish, he comprehended it. The Devil could don many guises . . .

Buckeye Jim! Oh Lord, deliver me, Dupont begged, *for The Devil has laid his fiery hands upon thy servant!*

Somehow, somehow, Legrand *atheist nigger lover* DEVIL WORSHIPER! had arranged it all. He understood that without any evidence but the revelation of his tormented spirit.

Dupont staggered to his feet, slumped against the car. A sudden cramp, and drool and frogs—he could feel them on his tongue and palette!—leaked out of his mouth down his clothes.

Up at his house, he heard the commotion. "What is it? What!"

What it was was he was DAMNED!

He lurched into the car.

He needed God's help.

"Please, God, please . . ." he whispered. The automobile jerked away, as he squinted to see through his tears.

He had to get to Granny Gunger!

* * *

> Give me that old time religion!
> It's good enough for me!

Granny Gunger had a regal and hideous demeanor as she presided at the rickety table in her hovel out near the tracks at Whittington Curve, a prime location because, when a train slowed for the turn, coal would tumble from the tender and she'd reap the bounty of Luck and the Illinois Central Railroad.

Granny Gunger came from the hills. She knew dowsing and how to draw fire out of wounds. She could stop bleeding or set bones. She could not regrow an eye, however, and so there was the mucus and muscle rippling empty socket where her drunken father had accidentally thumbed her when all he'd meant to do was punch her.

"You stink, Mister Dupont. You stink like you crawled up an old OH-possum's ass," Granny Gunger said. Granny Gunger was known for her plain speaking.

Dupont told her why he'd come.

81

"Frogs," she said. "Frogs is bad. You got strong enemies doin' Satan's bidding. Mister Dupont, the Old Deceiver wants you. You're in sorry shape now, and I don't think you'll like eternity in Hell much better."

"Help me, Granny!"

"You got faith, Mister Dupont? You got true faith and the courage of it?"

"Yes."

"You got a RE-solve for God A'mighty to put you to the test?"

Dupont shivered. "Yes," he whispered.

"You got five dollars?"

He nodded.

Granny Gunger slouched over to the black box, unfastened the chain, opened the padlock and reached in. Mark E. Dupont prayed as he had never prayed before.

At just under three feet, Sweet Mercy was not the biggest diamond back rattlesnake in the universe, but he was a lovely one, with radiant coloring and perhaps the snakiest eyes ever to grace the mean triangle of a rattler's head.

Granny Gunger kissed Sweet Mercy right at the bony ridge of his nose.

Sweet Mercy rattled happily.

"They shall take up serpents," Granny Gunger quoted scripture. Then she improvised, as she hobbled to Dupont. "For if they be a generation of vipers, what profiteth a man to dwell far from the tabernacle as he goes up to the Land of Goshen?"

Mark E. Dupont thought, prayed, and entreated the Lord.

"Pucker up now," Granny Gunger said. "Let the kiss of salvation come to you."

Dupont closed his eyes. He puckered. He heard Sweet Mercy's rattle. He felt the snake's subtle breath—sugary, like the breath of a baby.

Then Sweet Mercy's forked tongue flicked against the dry, chubby, pursed lips.

Dupont flew to the floor, landing on his heels and the back of his head.

And when he could rise, he did not doubt.

He knew it—because he FELT it! HALLELUJAH!

Free! Saved! Praise God!

Delivered! he thought, as Sweet Mercy got delivered back to his box.

"Now, Mister Dupont," Granny Gunger said, "we got to do us some plannin'! We got to take some precautionary actions. We got to make sure. We must confound your enemies."

"Yes."

"I got somethin' special," Granny Gunger said. "It's got nightshade and a bloody thorn and the lips and eggs of a stone blind fish in it."

"What does it do?"

"You'd best believe it does just fine."

After Dupont's departure—preceded by her reminding him of the five dollars he owed her—Granny Gunger sat with Sweet Mercy in her lap, petting the diamond back like a tabby. "Well," she said, "told him the Old Deceiver wanted him, and now the Old Deceiver's got him."

She laughed.

"Don't you?"

Sweet Mercy rattled in a way that sounded almost exactly like Granny Gunger's laugh.

V

Prior to beginning another insightful commentary on our ever-interesting Egypt, I wish to thank those who have been kind enough to write the Sentinel comparing me with Mr. H. L. Mencken, and offering to tar and feather us both as soon as we can find the time for this singular honor. While I greatly admire Mr. Mencken's writings, I find him far too optimistic about the future of the allegedly human race.

Now, let's talk about the pride of Egypt: A true crime lord.

With the passing of the years, it becomes more and more difficult to distinguish Charlie Birger from the "legend of Charlie Birger."

I knew and liked Charlie. On occasion, I bought him an illegal beer at his illegal road house, and he bought me one. We told one another jokes, few of which could be printed in this newspaper.

As his acquaintance, then, I will tell you I do not believe that the shady owner of Shady Rest rode the rodeo circuit with Tom Mix, but I have seen him on horseback and cannot doubt his formidable skills.

I do not believe that, following an argument in a St. Louis speakeasy, Charlie fought to an impromptu bloody draw with Jack Dempsey, but I believe he would go to the line against anyone of any size because I have seen him do just that.

More folks liked Charlie than not, and they had reason. The poor of Harrisburg knew his charity. A good number of men found employment, if not necessarily of the legal variety, because of Birger. He had wit, grace, and courage. He was a man's man, and on occasion displayed a streak of sentimentality that would have been derided in a less masculine fellow.

Above all, Charlie Birger was the steadfast friend.

If Charlie liked you, he'd kill anybody for you.

Brian Robert Moore, "I'll Tell You What!"

* * *

Tuesday, July 13, 1925

A slow afternoon at Shady Rest, so, nothing much else to do, the boys wanted to see him shoot. Charlie felt frisky and in the mood. They went out back, behind the pole barn.

Though a Tommy was his weapon of choice these days—you had to stay modern and keep up with competition, to say nothing of your enemies!—he took his old Winchester. The boys tossed beer bottles and he snapped off shots from the hip: eight shots, eight hits.

"That's the way it is done by a shootist, ole hoss," Charlie said. Born in New York City, Charlie Birger spent his youth in the west as a cavalry soldier, a wild horse breaker, a gambler and a gunfighter, and he still often spoke the palaver of the range. It had been a good life out there; folks played you straight. You were what you were, what you said, and what you did, and that was all that counted.

Here in Egypt, well, let's just say it was considerably different. You couldn't count on all the cards being on the table. But Charlie had done well; they called him the "King of Egypt."

Now the King needed a suitable chariot.

So after a beer, Charlie and some of the boys drove off to West City, where Joe Adams, mayor, gin mill owner, and proprietor of a Stutz dealership, was working on a new conveyance for His Royal Majesty!

* * *

Buckeye Jim got hired by the Old Legrand and Washauconda River Mining Corporation.

In the weeks following this uncelestial event, there were other happenings that might be viewed as more interesting or even "curious."

One of them involved K. J. Pritchard. One afternoon, when, as usual, he was standing on the square, dark glasses and a tin cup, a cardboard sign around his neck saying—

A VETERAN
I WAS BLINDED
FOR LIBERTY'S SAKE

—he sensed someone standing in front of him. He said, "The big war. I was in the big one."

"I was in that one, too."

"It was gas. They didn't have to gas us! It was NOT FAIR!"

"Nothing ever is, not in war."

"Help me?"

K. J. Pritchard heard something drop into the tin cup. It didn't sound like a coin. Cheap bastard.

With his left hand, he took it out. It felt like . . . it felt like a buckeye!

He held it up. Yes, that was just what he was looking at, a . . .

He ripped his dark glasses off, shattered them on the pavement.

The bright sunlight burning his eyes, he wept.

*   *   *

There was a car wreck late one night out past Crenshaw Crossing. A rattle-trap Ford full of young boys and younger girls who were full of shine. In the moonlight, you could see the silvery white of bone punching through flesh, and a head squashed the way you'd swear a head couldn't be squashed, and a bloody mess in which you could not tell twisted metal from human meat.

One of the victims, 15 year old Anna Beulle Diggs, would later say, "I had this strange dream. I heard a voice, kind of like Daddy when he's disappointed and angry both. It said, 'This is foolish, but children ought not to die for being foolish. So all of you, you live. And sometimes you think about just how precious life is.'

"Well, we all did live. Maybe it was plain luck, but such a great big lot of luck like that might be a miracle. I think, anyway . . .

"I don't know why I've kept it, but when they found us, I had this buckeye in my hand, and I have had it as a lucky piece ever since."

*   *   *

It was heavy dark, the frogs and crickets and night sounds, loud, so loud in his throbbing head. Out in front of The Jolly Sports roadhouse, Sam Washington had a gun and no options. With just the one arm, the other blown into sausage in the explosion at the fireworks factory where he had worked, he couldn't find a job, not anymore. He was colored and he couldn't read and he was as tapped out as a man could get.

Once he'd been a pretty good gut-bucket piano player. Not a real professor like Jelly Roll or Willie The Lion, or even the white boy, Art Hodes, but he might have had the makings of a tickler. He used to dream, one arm ago, of going to New York and making records and playing for the swells, just like Mr. Jelly Lord.

Once he had a dream and now he had a gun.

Then there was a white man standing in front of him. He seemed to pop up just like a haunt, but his smile was a man's.

"Mr. Washington, let's make a trade. Let's swap death for life. You give me the pistol. I give you . . ."

. . . *the buckeye was in his hand. Suddenly, Sam Washington knew: It was all right It was all all right.*

The man said, "Now . . . what you do is take your dream and go on and live it. Play the piano, Mr. Washington."

"I don't know, sir. You need ten fingers to play piano."

"How many you got?"

"Five."

"So you move the five twice as fast."

88

*   *   *

... strange reports that none other than a renowned citizen, formerly of Nazareth, is paying a visit. Call me a doubting Thomas, but I fear our Egypt an unlikely locale for the Second Coming. Our civic minded Kluxers (and mindless clucks!), enforcing the Volstead Act, will not tolerate His turning water into wine, the unions will move if He attempts to practice His carpentry without getting a card, and few of our churches will listen for five seconds to this "foreigner's" ludicrous doctrines of compassion, charity, and tolerance.

   Brian Robert Moore, *"I'll Tell You What!"*

*   *   *

Tuesday, August 17, 1925
First Shift at Old Coop #3

No matter how many years they'd been in the mines, the other fellows knew that moment's hesitation, that instant of fear when you understand it is possible for the blackness to engulf you forever.

Buckeye Jim knew darkness. *I was summoned forth from the darkness.*

Don't fear, don't fear. That is what he wanted to tell them, what he wanted to tell everyone. Love one another and do not be afraid.

But they were not ready to hear it yet.

So he smiled the smile that made the others think him

a "nice fella," though "no winner in the Mental Olympics, if y'know what I mean." Not that you had to be a chess champion to heft a shovel in a coal mine, and he certainly was one for that!

Buckeye Jim liked the work. He liked the feeling of using his muscles, his back, arms, and legs. He liked the idea that darkness, the coal, became heat and flame.

There was much for Buckeye Jim to like these days. He lived in Spartacus House, one of two company-owned residences for single men. It was a lot like an Army barracks, clean, fresh sheets every week, showers with limitless hot water, and detective and science magazines, and a Victrola and a player piano, and pretty pictures on the walls; he paid two dollars a month room and board. He liked the men he lived and worked with. Tonight, he'd go on out with them and have him a beer or two.

And of course he liked to play the banjo—

*   *   *

. . . one hell of a picker! Carrying his Thompson submachine gun, Charlie Birger walked over to the table of Ft. Lorraine miners at his roadhouse, The Shady Rest. After 11, but the joint still had a good crowd, even though tomorrow was a work day. White and colored drank at the Shady Rest—and if somebody purple showed and had a nickel for a beer, he'd be welcome, too—and here was even a gigantic Ojibway Indian, Big Tommy Tabeshaw, and so at the place, you might hear Italian, Polish, Lithuanian, Rumanian or Ojibway. (When he was really lost in the firewater, Tommy talked to himself and to the "Ojibway ghosts" in his head.)

Charlie told the banjo player that he plainly admired the way he could fram away on that five string.

The banjo player said he appreciated the compliment, but hoped Shady Rest's owner wouldn't get to framming away on his instrument.

Charlie Birger laughed like hell. No, no, no, his Tommy meant protection for himself and his guests. There were some shit heels, Kluxer bastards mostly, didn't like his catering to a "mixed clientele." And, for that matter, they weren't too delighted with Mr. C. Birger, Esquire's, being a co-religionist of Moses.

"My name is Buckeye Jim." The banjo player offered his hand.

He said, "Shalom Aleichem," the traditional Hebrew greeting, "Peace be unto you."

Charlie Birger blanched. "Aleichem Shalom," he said softly. "And unto you, peace." The gleam in his eyes might have been tears. "You're . . ."

Buckeye Jim shrugged. *"Vuden?"* Loosely translated, the Yiddish term meant, "What did you expect?"

"I'll be damned," Charlie Birger said. "A hillbilly Yid! A Yid-billy! Well, me, too, I reckon!"

Birger bellowed to the bar, "This gentleman and his friends drink free! Tonight and every night."

He turned back to Buckeye Jim. "You have yourself a friend in Charlie Birger."

"Thank you," Buckeye Jim said. "A man needs all the friends he can get."

VI

Sunday, September 12, 1925

God forgive me, Opal Rae Brown thought. If He did, it would be long before she forgave herself.

Opal Rae puttered about, a huge woman who seemed to fill up all the space in the vast kitchen that had so long been her domain. Oh, Lord, he was a good man and she had to . . . He was a white man, she tried to tell herself, and if every white man in the country America decided to swallow a Mason jar full of iodine, lye, and turpentine, now wasn't that just too bad? Besides . . .

Besides, she was scared, she was scared in every one of her 280 pounds. That man, that Mr. Dupont, had never raised his voice as he told her this, and told her that, as he asked her this and then asked her, "You ever smell black skin burning? You are sort of heavyset, so I imagine it would take a long time for the fire to bubble and blister and cook all the meat right off your bones."

He gave her orders and the "secret potion" she was to add to the food (*Now don't you worry, just some fish eggs and stuff*) and 100 dollars. The money would take her north, she vowed. Nobody burned colored people in New York, not as she had heard, anyway.

She took a deep breath, then another.

Then she took Mr. C. Cooper Legrand, Jr. his evening meal.

The next day, he was in Ft. Lorraine's hospital.

Condition: critical.

* * *

Buckeye Jim couldn't sleep. He went for a walk, moonlight his guide. At midnight, that empty moment that is neither one day or another, he was far from Ft. Lorraine, deep into the rolling woods. He relished the coolness and earth smells, the myriad night sounds, the eternal celebration and affirmation of life.

Oh, he did not want to die. Not again.

Ahead, on the path that wasn't a path but simply the way he chose, he saw the gleaming eyes. The rattler's precise, gorgeous diamond patterns shone hypnotically. It rose up like a cobra, shifting left and right, the forked tongue a flicker-blur.

Surprised?

"Not hardly," Buckeye Jim said, "Sure you're here. You're everywhere." He took out the lucky buckeye and flipped it, caught it, flipped it. "But you're not going to win, you know. Each time, we get closer."

Fool!

"Fool? Maybe. But God needs His fools."

Do you not see? Each time and every time Man is given a chance to damn himself, he says, "Yes, thanks, and might you have a few extra opportunities for my friends?" The victory will be mine!

"No," Buckeye Jim said, "Man is not born to lose." The buckeye flew up high and then higher and came down in his palm. Buckeye Jim grinned.

"Man is born to win."

*   *   *

On Wednesday, condition now "serious/guarded," Legrand had visitors, representatives of the Illinois Coal and

Power Company—Mark E. Dupont among them. They did not want to tire him out, to do anything that might slow his recovery.

Inside of 15 minutes, C. Cooper Legrand sold them everything.

VII

Buckeye Jim, weave and spin,
     Time to go, Buckeye Jim.
        "Buckeye Jim"
        American folk song

There will always be questions, but I knew C. Cooper Legrand, Jr. I drank coffee with him, went to New York with him to hear Emma Goldman, and spent a long, memorable, mentally exhilarating night, arguing with him over the nihilistic philosophy of Bakunin; both of us agreed that the man had to be an idiot if all he would allow to go undestroyed would be Beethoven's Sixth, the closest the composer ever came to failure.

Juney Legrand was all right.

So to my dying day, I will not accept that he willfully betrayed the people of Ft. Lorraine or his dream of a world of brotherhood and harmony.

They did something to him. They destroyed Legrand's will or twisted his mind or threatened him with consequences so dire that I cannot imagine—nor do I wish to. As incredible as all this may sound, coming from a man who is reputed to be sane, if surly, I have come to believe there are conspiracies meant to stifle and suppress Mankind as we struggle to attain the next step on the moral and ethical evolutionary ladder.

A conspiracy of . . . ???

The Left will tell you it is a wicked collusion of Capital and Government. Too-imaginative pulp magazine fans will offer you theories based on a wicked cabal inside our hollow Earth. Then there are preachers who will tell you it is all the work of the Devil . . .

Brian Robert Moore, "I'll Tell You What!"

* * *

Monday, September 27, 1925

In the basement of Ft. Lorraine's Masonic Temple, they argued and argued, called each other names, threw about the words, "scab," "fink," and, a phrase frequently used in the American labor movement: "Dumb son of a bitch!" They would march on the state capitol! The nation's capitol! A splinter group said there was a case for assassination—if they could figure out who to assassinate.

They waited to hear from the president of United Mine Workers of America, John L. Lewis. Last time, he said the wrong thing. He gave his UMWers carte blanche in "taking care" of scab laborers. Carte blanche: the scabs were herded together to provide sport for miners wielding shotguns, rifles, pistols, baseball bats and jack handles. The resultant deaths by brutality of unarmed citizens became known as the 1922 Herrin Massacre, Williamson County earned the sobriquet "Bloody Williamson," not likely to attract either tourism or venture capital, and the United Mine Workers suffered serious public relations damage.

This time the usually eloquent John L. said nothing.

The Illinois Coal and Power Company meant to take possession of the mines—the town. But damn all and double-damn, it was not the property of IC and P; Ft. Lorraine was their town! The mines were their mines. It was their labor that gave them ownership, their muscle and sweat and not a capitalist's dollars!

It was theirs, damn all!

They meant to keep it!

If it took guns to . . .

It went on and on, until, at last—

Now they are ready to listen, Buckeye Jim said to himself. He was sad. He liked these men. He did not want to leave them. He thought about bitter cups. He thought about the Lord's will. He thought about what he had to do.

Then Buckeye Jim said he wanted to talk. He talked easy and slow, flipping a buckeye.

He talked and they heard him.

Funny, how a guy you don't figure all that equipped with smartness can talk to you in a way that makes you say, "Why, yes indeed! That is what we have to do."

That is what they did.

They barricaded the northern approach to Ft. Lorraine. They left their guns at home, but they turned over worn-out tin can cars, piled up bales of hay, and strung barbed wire the way some had learned in the War to End All Wars.

Behind their barricade, they linked arms, the black men and the white men.

They were a living chain across the Washauconda Bridge.

They were ready.

Moon on the Water

*   *   *

To assist in the IC and P's taking possession of its properties were men in smart-looking uniforms, all duly deputized, bayonets on their rifles.

From Sesser and Marion and Ina and dozens of other towns came non-union miners, needing work, armed with baseball bats, shotguns, pistols, and pitchforks, determined to get these sorry niggers and Bolsheviks out of their way.

Mark E. Dupont led the largest delegation, the stalwarts of the Klan. The Grand Exalted Cyclops, in his robes of flowing white, a regulation Army Springfield under his arm. Now he'd claim . . . his!

His, damn all! Mr. Mark E. Dupont, the new General Superintendent of ICP's Ft. Lorraine holdings, had the might and purity and right of the Klan stepping smartly behind him, armed with everything from a Quackenbush boy's model single shot to a log chain!

The forces of the Illinois Coal and Power Company tramped onward.

The men of Ft. Lorraine waited.

The army of the Illinois Coal and Power Company came closer, ranks tightening as they trod upon the vast length of the Washauconda Bridge.

Waiting them, someone called out, "Stand firm! Union men, comrades in the war!"

Men with bayonets, men in miner's hats, men in KKK garb, moved forward.

The men at the barricades sang:
Hold the fort,

Brave union miners!
Show no fear,
Be strong!

At the other end of the bridge, taunting voices called, "Let's kill us some niggers!"

"Turkey shoot! They ain't got a gobbler's chance!"

The IC and P troops drew closer. The bridge shook with their out-of-step march. The collage of sounds was sinister and portentous: muttering and shouts, the hiss and whisper and bubblings of the Washauconda below, the click-ready sound of firearms.

You could smell oil and gunpowder.

"You are an unlawful assembly, blocking a public thoroughfare!" Dupont called out. "Give way immediately or perish!" He liked the formality of his proclamation.

He did not like the roared response it drew from a defender of Ft. Lorraine: "You get up on your momma's shoulders and kiss my ass."

When less than a hundred yards separated the men of Ft. Lorraine from the IC and P forces, Buckeye Jim suddenly appeared between them.

Quizzical in a way, because nobody really saw him walk there, but there he was.

It stopped them all. Buckeye Jim wasn't flipping a lucky buckeye. Not this time. He had his arms up and out, as though he were Moses helping God, pushing back the walls of water to part the Red Sea. There are some still living who, even to this very day, will tell you the man was transfigured.

Buckeye Jim had something to say.

*　　*　　*

Nothing happened he didn't know about. Not in his kingdom.

Because—you'd better know it and you're mighty well told!—Charlie Birger was the King of Egypt!

Ft. Lorraine? Good boys, there, and his Yid friend, Buckeye Jim, so . . .

Time for damned sure to hitch the horses to the king's chariot.

Except he didn't need horses.

*　　*　　*

Everyone stayed quiet. Everyone heard him.

He said, "Some of you don't know me, and some of you know me as Buckeye Jim. But years back, years and years and years ago, I was the one they talk about in the Bible. They call me 'The Widow's Son.' I was dead, just as dead as Mr. Lazarus, but then Jesus called to me and said, 'Come forth from your tomb.'

"Well, I was grateful and such, and I politely thanked Him, but I asked him why He had summoned me from the ever-dark of death into the light of life.

"Didn't I like being alive? Didn't I want to do the work of the living God, the God of the living?

"I thought about that and thought about that—

"Until I said, 'Why, yes, I guess I do.'

"Now this is what Jesus told me. This is what He wants me to tell you.

"Jesus came to bring hope. He said it was my job to be hope, because I'd been dead and now I was alive.

"We are all the children of God. The Devil and the darkness will never defeat us!

"Jesus told me something more.

"He said He would come again.

"He said He would return—on the day after He no longer was needed!

"That means it's up to us to set it all right.

"And we can start to do that. We can start now."

There was silence.

And almost everyone stood frozen.

But not Mark E. Dupont, who thought, *The Devil can quote scripture for his own purpose.* Dupont slammed the stock of his Springfield into his shoulder and fired.

The bullet caught Buckeye Jim just to the left of the heart. He flew backward, slammed into the bridge railing a slice of an instant after his blood and fragments of bone did, and, loose limbed, flipped over. If his body splashed as it plunged into the river, no one heard it.

The IC and P forces let out a collective yell that drowned out a sudden roar of thunder in the clear sky above. They charged.

*   *   *

"Give it all you've got," Charlie Birger commanded. The driver of the brand new armored car obliged. The powerful Stutz engine thrummed. The heavy sheet metal riveted and welded to the auto slowed it and guaranteed nothing could stand in its way. Instead of a windshield or windows, the car had gun slits. Except for treads, it was a tank—and its solid rubber tires weren't about to be knocked out by any varmint hunter's firepower.

It was the lead vehicle of three. Two cars loaded with Birger men followed.

Charlie might have been confused, once they hit the bridge, but the KKK bastards, decked out like Monday wash on the line, why he knew who to shoot! So Charlie popped the heavy hatch, and rose up to let loose with a quick spray from Mr. Tommy. One blast felt so fine, the gun a roaring quiver in his hands, that he fired off another. He heard the guns of his army behind him. He saw the befuddled ICP men turn, trying to figure what the hell. There was sporadic return fire, slugs pinging off the metal around him.

"Welcome to Egypt's O.K. Corral," Charlie yelled. He laughed and fired off another burst.

Then another.

With the next one, he totally hem-stitched Mark E. Dupont. Inside of three minutes, 43 men lay dead on the Washauconda bridge, most of them Kluxers; another 75 or 81 or 58 (depending on which account of the conflict you believe) were wounded and conveyed to area hospitals.

Most historians cite the "Battle of Washauconda Bridge" as the end of the Klan's power in southern Illinois.

Charlie Birger and his warriors retreated to Shady Rest and drank beer. The King could not figure where Buckeye Jim might have disappeared to. He hoped he would turn up. He wished him luck.

Fellow played one fine banjo.

EPILOGUE

Mark E. Dupont received one of the most elaborate Klan funerals in the history of the organization. A vice-president of IC and P gave the eulogy, saying Dupont was one of the company's finest assistant superintendents; after the funeral, he presented Mrs. Dupont with a check for 50 dollars.

Virtually everyone employed by the Old Legrand and Washauconda River Mining Corporation was fired and had to leave Ft. Lorraine. The union did not regain any foothold in the region until FDR.

Charlie Birger had a falling out with Joe Adams, who'd built "The King of Egypt's" armored car, and was convicted of arranging the man's murder.

Charlie was hanged on April 18, 1929, the last man legally executed in this way in the state. Legend has it that the night before his execution, Charlie had a lanky visitor, who talked and joked a while with him, then handed him a buckeye.

Perhaps that is the reason that, on the scaffold, Charlie's last words were, "It is a beautiful world.

"Goodbye."

Bird's Dead

THERE'S A SIGN WITH A tipped top hat out in front. It's as tawdry as Sammy Davis Jr. wearing love beads.

But don't worry. It's got nothing to do with nothing because this is The Commodore's Blue Note.

You walk in. The smoke encircles you and drags you in. Drags you into the music. And there's always music, even when there is no one on the stand. There's a jukebox. There's a phonograph. There's a battered-to-hell upright in the corner—it's Mr. Jelly Lord mainly tickles that one. There's a violin on the wall, supposedly carrying with it a Gypsy curse, but when Stuff Smith comes in and he's feeling all right, he takes down that fiddle, says, "Curse of the Romany, I defy you!" and he sets to hard swinging, and though the notes don't always come in tune, the man is pure virtuoso.

103

Here. That is right where you are.

The Commodore's Blue Note can be like staying high all the time.

The Commodore's Blue Note can be like when you are under the lowest.

This is it, the place, the joint, the saloon, the pad, the locale of . . . hipsters and shysters and mooches and backsliding preachers. And tailgatin' muffaletta-chompin' juke-jointers and swingers and malingerers and zoot-suiters and add in a shouter and a professor and a half dozen unclassifiable unreconstructed originals.

In The Commodore's Blue Note you sometimes find Ben Webster. Ben Webster at the bar, floating on reefer and slugging down Scotch and there is something pinning the eyes that isn't Scotch or reefer and Ben Webster looks for all the world like an obsidian statue of a gorilla. An ugly gorilla. An acrome-galic, brow bone bulging, lantern jawed, lowland gorilla. But did anyone ever play a sweeter horn? Could anyone do that sweep up the register into nothing but breath and heartbreak like Ben Webster?

Ben Webster is the Ugly who plays so beautiful.

However, unless you want your next suit of clothes to be made out of pine, you do not want to insult Ben Webster. You do not want to hurt Ben Webster's feelings in any way, because Ben Webster is sensitive. He is a soulful man. He is a man who can all too easily take umbrage.

I saw this once. We were at a rent party. Ben Webster came in, sax around his neck, scotch fumes trailing him like Mighty Clouds of Glory. And some damn fool, this little bit of a country boy, with his hair all country parted down the center, this hayseed, rube, chicken plucker, happened to give offense to Ben Webster.

Moon on the Water

What country boy said to Ben Webster was, "Sir, even with that saxophone hanging on the neck, you look like a statue of a gorilla. Obsidian." Ben Webster's feelings were hurt. Ben Webster sort of whispered sometimes when his feelings were hurt and he wanted to sound like Dexter Gordon. Ben Webster whispered to the country boy, "I take umbrage."

The he took Country Boy to the window. What he said was, "I am so full of umbrage that I feel like throwing you out the goddamned window."

Well, if you know anything about Ben Webster, then you know for Ben Webster to fool was no different than to do. He threw Country Boy out the window.

Did I mention that we were about fourteen or fifteen stories up?

As I said, Ben Webster was a sensitive man.

You know who else you might find at The Commodore's Blue Note? Damn near everybody, that is who. One night in walks Miles Davis with Billy Eckstine. Billy was trying to get back into Miles' good graces because Miles had tried to punch him out over five dollars he had tried to cheat Billy out of and Billy had raised up several major lumps beneath Miles' eyes. (He never hit Miles in the mouth. Billy Eckstine was a good friend to Miles and he also understood commerce.) Now Miles was sulking.

Miles' father was a dentist. This shaped Miles. The offspring of dentists are likely to become architects or abstract painters or Existential Christian theologians. Anything but a goddamn dentist.

On any given night at The Commodore's Blue Note, this could be your—

Roll Call!

Behind the bar. It is The Commodore. They call him that because some years ago somebody who claimed to be Wallace Beery gave him a pirate hat. "This here, matey, be the very chapeau I was a'wearin' in the movie Treasure Island. Now, if you could give me a drink on the house."

Nobody drinks on the house at The Commodore's Blue Note. Forget it. But the Commodore liked the hat. He gave the man who claimed to be Wallace Beery a drink for it. He perched it on his head. "Avast, lubbers," the Commodore would say. "Keelhaul the bilges. Mizzen the poop deck." Even bartenders dream of the sea.

Roll Call:

Sound off!

Who's here? Who's here now?

Billie Holiday, she is right here. Right now. That gardenia in her hair. Oh, doesn't she think she is the stuff?

That is because she is the stuff. Ethel Waters did not like her. Ethel Waters said, "She just thinks she's the stuff, don't she? And when she sings, she sounds like her shoes are too tight."

Ethel Waters. This is the real Ethel Waters. This is not the Ethel Waters who got to being the Godly Negro Lady for the Billy Graham rallies in Madison Square Garden and The Cow Palace and Comiskey Park and Ecuador and the South Sea Islands. This is the Ethel Waters who starred in *Blackbirds of 1928* and quite possibly coined the legendary bit of advice, "Walk softly and carry a big razor."

Roll Call! Roll Call!

Roll Call at The Commodore's Blue Note.

Buddy Bolden?

Present.

Jelly Roll Morton?

Here. Where the hell else has he got to go, now that his career is in the toilet and the hoo-doo is on him?

Eddie Condon?

Present and drunk as Cooder Brown.

Bix? Bix? Biederbecke, you here, boy?

Yeah, I'm here . . . That smile. Jesus, that smile. That smile was so shy and easy, you knew he came from Indiana.

Yeah, Bix is here. He's lost in a mist.

You know who smiles like Bix?

Chet Baker. A man utterly lacking in guile. Mr. Innocence. Right. My ass in two parts. Baker the Faker swiped the smile and about three-quarters of Bix's chops.

Not that Chet Baker smiles like that anymore. Drug thing, you know. He burned some people, you know. People who were called names like The Bear, and Perpetual Scar Tissue, and Emergency Warning Buxton, and Guido and Fat Tony, and Big Tony, and Large Tony, and Tony Kick Your Ass Esposito. What happened was the people he burned in this drug thing—and this is just something I heard, okay?—they got together and knocked every tooth out of Chet Baker's mouth.

It did nothing for his looks.

Of course, with what he had picked up from his father, Miles Davis could have fixed Baker right up, but Miles hated Chet. Miles hated everybody.

And of course, there at the bar, tonight and every night, it is The Detached Cop. He is Webster's size. He wears suits that make you think of Bulgaria. Some nights, he sits and drinks and listens to the music and he weeps. Sometimes someone tries to talk to him. Usually, the Detached Cop says, "Get away. I am undercover." You want him to say more. You want him to confess all, become maudlin and confidential. You hope he will reveal, "I am investigating the Lindbergh baby snatch. I am investigating crop circles and Judge Crater and those mysterious strangers and the celebrated rain of frogs that would have been the clincher for anyone except that dumbass Pharaoh. I want to know if Ambrose Bierce and Pancho Villa changed their names and became a tag team on Wrestling from the Marigold. I'll sure as hell find out who threw the overalls in Mrs. Murphy's chowder. And who was it played poker with Pocahontas when John Smith went away?"

The Detached Cop never says anything like that, though. I think he's afraid it would make people like him.

Every night, every night, you will find the Two Metaphysical Wineheads at their table.

They are good luck for the joint.

They somehow always have money for Dago Red.

They have discussions which are so laden with insight and all that the Dali Lama would instantly give them his Rolex and autographed picture of Marilyn Monroe and one of those funky Sherpa hats if he heard them talking. Consider this conversation:

Man, what time is it?

Now.

Yeah, now. What time is it?

Now.

Yeah, I say now. What the hell you think I say? What time is it now!

Now.

Oh, hell with you. Just drink some wine, that's right.

I will, says a profoundly philosophical Metaphysical Winehead. *I will drink some wine . . .*

Now.

Thing is, everyone is alive. Everyone who ever was in jazz, everyone. Alive! They're alive, I tell you. 100% guaranteed and bona fide and assured by an electrocardiogram on record.

They are alive.

Right.

Now.

Except for Bird.

Charlie Yardbird Parker.

Yardbird is dead.

That's is why The Commodore's Blue Note is down tonight.

Nobody wants to believe it. Nobody believes it. Paul Whiteman is alive, for Chrissake, and he's so lame nobody even thinks he should be, and Fats Navarro is alive and Bill Evans is alive and Benny Goodman is alive and Robert Johnson is alive.

Robert Johnson. Poisoned and shot and stabbed and chopped up in a cotton baler and with his head caught in a punch press! Acid thrown on him by one old girl, ice pick stuck in his nose, ear, and ass by another, Robert Johnson is alive.

But the word has spread throughout the community.

Bird is dead.

Naw, says one Metaphysical Winehead.

Naw, says the other Metaphysical Winehead.

Bird joking. Bird always one for the jokes.

Bird, naw, he ain't dead.

I hope he is, says the other Metaphysical Winehead,

'cause they done gone and buried him. Oh, my, ain't I a stitch? Ain't I a caution?

Naw, says the other winehead.

It is precisely then . . .

That a touch of the mystic and unexplainable, of the awesome and of the pure enters The Commodore's Blue Note.

The door swings open. No one sees a human hand upon it.

And if there is no human hand, then there is no human being attached to that no hand and so no human being enters The Commodore's Blue Note.

What flies in is a white dove.

Get it?

A bird comes flying in.

Say what you want about the brilliance of Yardbird, the creative genius, the inspired lunacy, but the man was not always subtle.

Everyone is silent. Even Jelly Roll Morton stops noodling on the battered old upright in the corner of the joint. That's about all he can do these days, about all that gives him comfort. He is convinced that there is a serious hoodoo on him and that is why nobody wants to hear his music anymore. Mr. Jelly Lord's music is called moldy fig music. Moldy oldie. Moldy Mush and Moldy Gramma. Aw, that is stale, that is square, that is . . . Moldy. The A and R man at RCA told him, "Well, you and your Hot Peppers, you ain't so hot now. So toot sweet, and write if you get work, but I bet you won't."

Whoo! And how's that for a hurt? Whoo! And who was it that just plain invented jazz? Why none other than

110

Jelly Roll Morton, and if you don't believe it, just ask him.

But now we are back to smoky silences and a white dove winging its way to the bar. For a moment, it hangs suspended in the air. Some that were there that night swore the dove glowed brilliantly, as though it were becoming a halo, needing only an angel beneath it to complete the religious experience. The Commodore, trying to remember lines his mother and her faith used to inflict on him, thinks The Kingdom of Heaven has come, and he says, in a reverential whisper, "Blow me down."

Then the dove alights on the bar. He is strutting as though he is the literal cock of the walk.

Everyone is saying it, not quite simultaneously, but saying it. "It's Bird. Bird's here. Bird lives."

"Horse manure," is what Jelly Roll Morton says.

Now what some folks don't know, because Jelly told a lie or two in his time, is that Mr. Morton's claim to have been a sharpshooter with the carnival was 100% veritas.

These days, not knowing if the hoodoo would come at him like a Swamp Dog or a Dhambala bat, Jelly Roll has taken to carrying around an 1873 Colt Peacemaker.

Which is what he yanked out.

He let fly.

And anyone who saw that shot does not dispute the Jelly's claim to have been a carnival sharpshooter. Because in one bang and one burst there is nothing but some splatter on the bar and a feather in the air.

Then Jelly Roll Morton says, "Bird's dead."

He sets the Colt on the piano and, grinning his diamond tooth grin like he has not since being given the RCA heave-ho, he starts in playing "Graveyard Blues."

And there ain't one moldy thing about it.

The Running Horse, the High, White Sound

SOME STRANGE THINGS HAVE HAPPENED to me lately. That's why I'm writing this. It seems things make more sense if I put them on paper, then, later, read over what I wrote.

I think writing's okay, even if a lot of jerks at John Dewey High think it's for the creeps and the faggots. I get "A's" on all my themes, and Miss Bertello says I could maybe be a writer. We're not doing themes now, though. Miss Bertello is trying to teach the morons not to say, "I have went."

English is probably my best class, a lot better than Civics with old Neederkorn the Nosepicker who's always yapping about how we have to be involved young adults, knowing current affairs like if Ike shot a three under par or had another coronary. Frankly, school would be a real douchebag if it weren't for English.

The problem with getting all this on paper, though, is I'm not sure where to start. Okay, "Begin at the beginning and end at the end" is what you get in English class, but I just don't know for sure where the beginning begins.

I guess I should probably just write about the rumble we had with the nigger gang, the Del-Sonics, when my brother Vince got killed. It was at the baseball diamond in Douglas Park. Rangers and Dels were spread out all over, beating on each other. It was tough, but it was clean, no bats or blades or aerials like a lot of the gangs. That was the way Vince, he was the chief man in the Stilton Street Rangers, always set it up and you could count on the Del-Sonics because when Beau Dooley—he was their warlord—laid it down, he laid it down.

Vince and I were back to back on the pitcher's mound. That was the best way. Nobody could Jap us from behind. The truth is, I think Vince was looking out for me; he made sure that was how we always fought.

But I wasn't candy ass, okay? I took care of things. And it worked. Soon as a Del got in close, I had him or Vince had him.

The Rangers were doing all right. Monster, who looks like he was born in Dr. Frank N. Stein's lab, had a head-lock on Beau Dooley and was clouting him in the middle of that niggery curly wool with a bowling ball-sized fist. Colored guys are supposed to be hard-headed, but you could tell the way Beau was starting to sag that Monster's message was getting through. In center field, Lonny and Ron were doing a number on a tall skinny Del. Lonny'd clip him, spin him, Ron would nail him, and turn him right back to Lonny for more.

Of course Mumbles, who's just as smart as your average head of lettuce, was getting his ass stomped. He was flat on his back with three Del-Sonics kicking away. That kind of thing never got to Mumbles. He'd show up the next day, bragging and mumbling, "Man, did they kick my ass, man."

Seven or eight Dels got smart and made a circle around Vince and me. "Get set," Vince said, so I picked my target, a dude about my size. I'd let him have the knee, slam him one in the mouth, then grab him and use him for a shield. As soon as Monster finished creaming Beau Dooley, he'd see what was going down with Vince and me and come charging like the Seventh Cavalry to the rescue.

Vince and I just had to stay cool, keep on our feet, and pound away. No Del or anyone else was going to stop the Monster unless they used a cannon.

It didn't work that way. A sawed-off guy broke out of the Dels' circle and came running right at me. He swerved at the last second and I missed with a left.

"I got him," Vince said.

Then Vince grunted. He fell back against me and nearly took me down. I swivelled my head to see what was happening and got tagged under the left ear.

Then Vince screamed.

Once I saw this scabby-looking dog get scrunched by a beer truck. It pulled itself to the curb, dragging its hind legs, letting out a pinched *yip, yip, yip*, until it died. That's kind of the way Vince's scream sounded, only it didn't last so long.

The Del-Sonics ran for it. They piled into their cars in the parking lot and took off, tossing gravel.

Most of the Rangers beat it, too, except Monster, at second base, his jaw hanging.

When I lowered my hands and turned around, Vince was on his knees, hands inside his Ranger jacket. Blood poured down his white chinos.

"Man," I said. I was going to touch him, I think I was going to touch his face, when he looked at me. "Ah, shit, Jimmy," he said. Then he pitched onto his face and died.

So, that is the beginning, I guess. I could write about the cops, coming on with questions like they watched too many *Dragnets*, but who the hell tells cops anything?

Like usual, the old man was soused at Vince's funeral. My little sister, T, and I stood there wearing new clothes. Father Zeranti did his number about dust to dust. Aunt Carmella, Anthony, her slob husband, and Suzie and Liz, her pain in the lower neck kids, were there. Aunt Carmella filled up a couple handkerchiefs with her bawling, same as she did when my old lady died. Come to think of it, she cried like that when Pope Pius XII kicked off.

And sure, the Rangers were there. That night, I got loaded with them on Tango and Budweiser.

It's weird, but it wasn't until four weeks later that it hit me that Vince was really dead. It was a Saturday morning and I was in bed, halfway between awake and nowhere. The furnace in the basement is about ten years past tired out, but I had a couple blankets so I was warm and kind of drifting.

I kept thinking that I ought to be feeling good. There was no school today. Maybe tonight I'd take my some-time-steady, Cookie Bamonti, to The Grand. Last time they had a horror movie, I got her bra off just when the giant lizard was eating some scientist's Oldsmobile.

But I wasn't feeling good. I wasn't feeling anything. Keeping my eyes shut, watching the red and purple blobs fly around in my skull, I finally got it.

Vince wasn't singing.

Vince was always the first one up. He left our room quietly, but when he got in the shower, he let loose. The first thing I was supposed to hear on Saturday was the water rushing in the tub, the pipes clanging and knocking, and, right in the middle of all that, my brother Vince.

Vince had this great voice, a lot like Dion or Neal Sedaka, only bigger. He could hit notes that were way, way up there. It was a pure, high, white, sound. He knew all the hits, note for note, "Runaround Sue," "Valerie," "Duke of Earl," "The Wanderer," you name it, and he made even the drippiest words sound like absolute truth.

Vince always used to say he was going to be a big recording star. "You know, man, they're always grabbing Italian guys off the front porch and wham! Next thing you know, you're a Frankie Avalon with three gold records and a Cadillac."

Vince used to joke about it, but I think he believed it.

It came to me slowly, but I got it. Vince wasn't going to make any records or own any Cadillacs. I'd never again hear him singing in the shower.

He was dead.

I didn't want to get up, but staying in bed when you're wide awake is a drag. I tossed off the blanket. When I sat up, the cold grabbed me. In my underwear, I stood in front of the dresser mirror. My hair stuck out all over. I'd have to shampoo before I gobbed on the Brylcream and combed it into a solid DA.

I turned to snatch my robe from the hook on the back of the door, but I stopped to take a look at the picture Vince had taped over the mirror. You could make out a dark horse's head and a wild mane in the center, but all the rest was swirling black lines. T drew it last year in her sixth grade art class. It looked kind of like a horse, but it was more supposed to be the way a horse felt when he was running across the plains or something like that; that's what T said, anyway. Vince used to kid T, tell her she was going to be the famous artist in the family just like he was going to be the famous singer.

After a hot shower, heavy on the shampoo, I went back to my bedroom and put on my regular Saturday clothes, jeans and a black t shirt, and fixed my hair right. Then I went downstairs.

The old man's bedroom is just off the living room and his door was closed the way I figured it would be. The old man was snoring like a choir of chain saws. He always brags he's never missed a day's work, but every other hour of the day is his boozing time.

He was sleeping off another Friday night so that when he got moving at three or four in the afternoon he'd have plenty of energy to suck down the whiskey.

T was at the kitchen table with the cornflakes and a package of Hostess crap-filled cupcakes. T eats about a zillion Hostess cupcakes but she stays a toothpick. She still looks like a little kid, with big brown eyes and pale skin, and nothing at all round to her body. She even has a little kid's mouth, bright pink, with no real shape to her lips. I boiled water and put together a cup of instant.

117

T was halfway through the white squiggle on cupcake number two when I sat down.

"Aunt Carm's picking me up," she said. "She's taking me and Suzie and Liz to the show."

"Okay," I said. "That's nice."

Suzie and Liz are little creeps, but it was probably better for T to be with them than to sit home and watch the old man pickle himself. I sipped my coffee. T dabbed at chocolate frosting on the tabletop. Without looking at me, she said, "Whatcha gonna do today?"

"You know," I said. "Mess around."

"With the Rangers?"

"Yeah, I guess."

T mashed more chocolate dabs.

"Jimmy?"

"Yeah? What?"

"Oh, nothing."

T was real quiet. She even looked quiet. That bothered me somehow, so I said, "Hey, you haven't brought home any pictures for a while."

"I know," T said.

That was the end of our breakfast talk. When I took off, wearing my Ranger jacket, T didn't say anything; she gets like that sometimes. She just went on squishing chocolate.

It was cold enough outside to freeze both cheeks off your ass. I walked slowly down Stilton Street, watching the tips of my roach kickers. The scenery wasn't worth looking at, nothing but two-story frame houses, every one of them the same. Twenty years ago, this was supposed to be a "class" neighborhood. Now it's a worn out island of white, surrounded by all the blackies in the high-rises the city built. My old man, when he isn't too bombed to talk—which isn't that often—says it's a very big deal how we're keeping the "goddamn jungle bunnies" out.

Ron and Lonny were at the schoolyard, sitting on the steps. I sat down and Ron handed me his pack of Luckies and a book of matches. I lit up. "Wanna do something?" I said.

"Yeah," Ron said. "I want to milk a coconut."

"Not me, man," Lonny said. "I think we ought to wash a reindeer."

"You guys are incredibly funny," I said. "Shit."

We sat there shivering and smoking. I had three Luckies, one right after the other. After a while, Monster showed up.

"Hey, man," Lonny said. "What's shaking?"

Monster nodded at me. He jerked his thumb over his shoulder. "Lonny and Ron," he said, "you guys take a hike."

"Yeah, man."

They disappeared like they'd had lessons from a magician. Hey, Monster is a frightening guy. It doesn't matter if he's on your side, he can still make you mess your pants because he's the kind of guy that busts heads just because it is what he does.

Monster sat down. I took the cigarette he gave me. My throat felt blow-torched already, but I didn't want to get Monster hacked.

"Look, man," he said, "I been doing some talking with Beau Dooley. That nigger, he knows, Jimmy. The Dels, they know. It was supposed to be straight."

"Piss on Beau Dooley," I said.

"No," Monster said. "Listen. See, Beau Dooley's been

119

laying it on his guys. It was a bad scene and 'cause it was Vince it's even worse. Beau Dooley knows that."

"So?"

Monster sunk a meathook in my shoulder and made me look right at him. "Man," he said, "what I got to know is could you break the guy's ass that got Vince?"

"How do you mean bust his ass?"

Monster told me.

I didn't even have to think about it. "Yeah," I said.

Monster said, "Sure, you're his brother. You got balls."

"What're you saying?"

Monster said, "The Dels will hand us the asshole, man. He's not one of theirs. Just a punk. Some guy's shitbird cousin who was with them, that's all he was. He had a knife. He was showing how he was a hot shit and all."

"Okay," I said.

Monster told me the rest. Monster's half-sister—who was pretty cute, actually—was going with a guy who'd done time for liquor store and gas station stickups. The guy could get ahold of a clean piece. Monster would take care of the rest, pretty much. That was it.

"You got it, man?" Monster said.

I did.

He told me a couple more things—where to meet him and when and all—and then he took off. I sat there wishing I'd bummed a few smokes. See, I never buy my own; I don't want to get into a heavy habit. I just hit on the guys when I want a butt and I make it up with money for gas when we go cruising or buy the guys cokes or something.

If I'd had a weed right then, I could have concentrated on lighting it, taking the first drag, feeling how the second drag tasted a bit different, feeling the heat get closer to my fingers, studying the black mark it made when I ground it out on the concrete. I wanted to think about something like that, something simple.

My ass was starting to freeze to the concrete, so I got up and went over to Cookie's. Her old man and old lady were both home, a double treat. Cookie's mother made me a salami sandwich (She always had the Jew salami, the Sinai, and not Genoa) and gave me a Pepsi. Cookie, smelling of hairspray and Juicy Fruit, sat across from me in the kitchen while I ate. Her mother rattled on about Vince and what a shame it was and how sad and all.

I kind of wanted to tell her it was okay, not to sweat it, because I was going to kill the guy that did it. That would have shut her up.

Mr. Bamonti was sprawled in a stuffed chair in his guinea T-shirt, sucking on a Pabst as I followed Cookie upstairs. "You kids keep that door open. Ha, ha, I know what it's all about. I was young once myself, you know."

Ha, ha, I thought, as Cookie gave her cute little behind an extra wiggle, maybe for me or maybe to say that she knew her old man was a real jerk.

When we got to her room, Cookie kissed me. She tried to get some tongue action going, but I really wasn't in the mood.

"What's wrong?" she said. She backed off. Her eyes were like marbles circled by Bozo the Clown blobs of mascara. She looked pretty and cool and somehow frightening all at once.

"Nothing," I said. "Maybe I'm on the rag. You ever think of that?"

"Jimmy!" Cookie dropped her chin. You could tell she

was trying to be shocked—just like a movie actress or something. "That is so vulgar. You shouldn't talk to me that way."

"Hey, man," I said. "Shut up, okay?"

"You shouldn't tell me to shut up, Jimmy. If something's wrong with you, you know you can always talk to me."

"I know," I said. "You're a regular Dear Abby, except she never lets me feel her tits."

"Jimmy!"

I sat down on her blue bedspread under this picture of Vince Edwards tacked to the wall. Cookie turned around. She was very hacked off or pretending to be very hacked off, but I was also sure she wanted to remind me what a sweet little ass she had and how if I wasn't vulgar and started acting nice, maybe I could pretty soon have a little piece of it. Even standing still, Cookie kept her little tail wiggling as she fooled with a stuffed toy on her dresser. Then she picked up a bottle of cologne and set it down. She was reaching for a tube of lipstick when I said, "All right. Shit. I'm sorry, okay? Forget it. Just forget it."

Cookie turned back to me, all smiles and true love ways. "Okay," she said. "You know, you got moods and so do I and everything. It's okay as long as we understand each other. We've always got to do that, Jimmy. When something is wrong with you, baby, you know you can count on me. That's what true love is all about, Jimmy."

"Okay," I said. I wished I had my notebook so I could mark that down. Words of wisdom and all.

"Hey," Cookie said, "I bought a new record. Want to hear it?"

"Sure," I said. Really, I didn't give a damn. Cookie's

"new record" was usually something everybody else already had for a couple of months. Cookie didn't really dig music the way some people did. I think she tried to dig it because you were supposed to dig rock and roll if you were a teenager and that was it with her.

She slapped a black and red label 45 on the spindle of her Webcor phono on the shelf by the window. The record player clicked and the tonearm lifted and the disc dropped. The needle hissed in the opening grooves.

Then the music started and it screwed into my head like a dentist's drill. It was Frankie Valli and the Four Seasons: Walk Like A Man. Frankie's voice took off like a wailing police siren on a summer night when the rain is pounding the pavement and that nutcase voice just kept going up there and up there and up there.

"Turn that goddamned noise down!" Old man Bamonti was hollering downstairs.

I stood up. "Stop it," I said.

Cookie was snapping her fingers and shimmying her hips. "Huh?"

"Turn the fucker off."

Cookie slashed the needle across the record, nearly slicing it in half. She turned on the waterworks. "You are crazy, Jimmy! You are crazy and you're mean! Talking so nasty and dirty like that to me. You're just nuts."

"Yeah," I said.

"You don't know how to act with a lady. You don't even know what true love is."

I got out of there.

Frankie Valli screamed in my mind all the way home.

I was later than I thought because, when I stepped into the kitchen, the old man was already drinking supper. He had his big hand wrapped around a water glass and he was staring at the half-full bottle of Ten High on the table.

I picked the bottle up by the neck.

"Hey Jimbo? What's this? What you doin'?" The old man sounded like he was chewing a sweat sock.

"I'm taking your booze, man," I said. "I want to practice so I can be just like you when I grow up. Dig it, Daddy-o?"

"Hey, Jimbo? Don't be like that, huh?"

I just stood there with the bottle in my hand. "Are you going to stop me, man?" I said. I waited until I knew for damned sure he wasn't, and then I went up to my room and slammed the door.

Sitting on the end of my bed, I unscrewed the top of the Ten High. Then I had a drink, the lip of the bottle clicking against my teeth. The first swallows burned like I was gulping down hell, but they went to work right away. Frankie Valli was getting fainter by the second.

I knew Ten High could do the trick, so I slowed it down, but I drank a hell of a lot.

It was some time before I passed out that something weird happened, something like on the TV show *The Twilight Zone*. I was looking at T's picture. I was trying to follow one black curving line from where it started to where it ended but I kept getting lost.

Suddenly, it was like the picture was getting closer and closer, dragging me into it. Did you ever stand on a tall building and look down? You get this feeling that there's something below, something with a power working on you to yank you down. It is scary as hell.

That's pretty much what it was like, except nobody I

know ever went off the building but I got pulled right into the picture.

Now this gets wilder, crazy even, like something a guy in the booby hatch dreams up. For about a second there, I was a horse. I was running wild and free and all alone, running so fast I was a part of the wind.

Then it was just T's picture again and I was so plastered I was seeing two of it. I flopped back on the bed. I slept and I didn't dream.

It didn't take an alarm to wake me. I left the house without checking on the old man.

The moon was bright. You could see gobs of pigeon crap on the statue of the Douglas guy the park is named after. Monster leaned back with his elbows on the pedestal.

"You okay, man?" he asked.

"Yeah," I said. "I'm cool. Give me a weed."

I watched my hands as I struck the match. I wasn't shaking. The cigarette tasted good. Monster put a hand on my shoulder.

"Don't do that, man," I said. "Don't touch me, okay?"

Monster took his hand away. "Jimmy, man," he said, "you sure you're okay?"

"No sweat, man, I'm fine," I said and I felt fine. I smoked, taking deep and easy drags. Then I said, "Got something for me?"

Monster took the gun from his jacket pocket. It was small, a .22 or .25. I took it. It felt right in my hand. I slipped it into my pocket. It felt right, knowing it was there.

"Walk like a man," I said.

"Huh?" Monster said.

"Nothing."

We went to the diamond. Where else? It all made sense right there, right? We waited by the backstop. I watched the parking lot. Monster checked his wristwatch.

"They'll be here," I said, and I knew they would. "It's cool. It's all cool. Don't sweat it."

I bummed another smoke. Just as I was grinding it out in the cold dust, a beat up Ford pulled in. Beau Dooley got out on the driver's side. The passenger door in the front opened and another Del stepped out. He reached back into the car and pulled a guy out. The dude came tumbling out and fell onto the gravel.

He was the one.

Fine.

Walk like a man.

Beau Dooley, walking cool-tough, circled the car and he and the other Del-Sonic stood the guy up. They even had him tied, like this was some old gangster movie or something, with his arms behind him, and there was this white gag in his mouth. The dude's eyes were as big as the moon. Beau Dooley clipped him, open hand, on the back of the head.

"Here we go, man," Monster said. They marched him over, the guy who killed Vince, and Monster and I walked to home plate.

They were three shadows. I could smell the guy in the middle.

"Hey, man," Beau Dooley said, "this ends it, right?"

"Yeah," Monster said.

I didn't say anything.

Beau Dooley and the other Del-Sonic leaned on the guy, made him drop to his knees.

"Man," Monster said, "do it!"

I was cool. I stuck the gun in the guy's face. His eyes went crossed. It was pretty funny.

There was no reason to hurry. There'd be all the time I needed. I could feel myself smiling, this was so easy.

Then I blinked.

For that little bit of a moment when my eyes were shut, it was just like I was back in T's picture again. There was nothing to me. I was only air.

Then I heard this choking noise slide through the colored guy's gag. It was a strange sound. It reminded me of something I'd heard before. It might have been on a record. It might have had something to do with a ratty dog hit by a beer truck.

It might even have made me think of a pure, high, white sound.

Now this is where everything gets weird, real weird. Sometimes, when I think about this, I figure I'm ready for a trip to the funny farm. What happened was, I stopped being me.

I was Vince and I was Monster and I was Lonny and I was Ron.

I was Beau Dooley.

I was a nigger on my knees on a cold night.

It was just a flash like that, but it stayed with me. I blinked my eyes a couple of times, real quick, but nothing changed.

I was . . . Everyone.

"Kill the fucker!" Monster said that. I think he yelled, actually.

I gave Monster the gun. He took it with both hands. It was small. He looked at the pistol like he couldn't figure out what to do with it, and then he put it in his pocket.

His face told me he didn't understand what had happened.

"All right," he said to Beau Dooley, "get this asshole out of here."

"No more, dig?" Beau Dooley said. "We call it done and settled and over."

"It's done," Monster said. "Just get him out of here."

I went over by the backstop. Beau and the other Del didn't even take the gag out of the guy's mouth or untie him. They just dragged him back to the car, tossed him in, and took off.

Monster came towards me, shaking his head. "He was your brother," he said.

"Yeah," I said.

Then Monster said, "You goddamn pussy!" and he punched me in the gut. All the air exploded out of me. Bent double, I wrapped my arms over my stomach. "You fucking faggot!" Monster said.

I squeezed my eyes shut, saw red and black pools seeping into one another. My head was filled with bad radio static. I didn't try to breathe, not yet. I hugged the hurt into me, pressed it in deep and held it there.

A little later, all shaky but pretty much okay, I straightened up and Monster was gone and I was alone.

I guess that's the end of it. I don't understand that nutty scene in the park when shit got in my blood. I don't know why the hell I went chicken. I don't know what the hell happened to me. It just doesn't make sense.

So maybe I ought to quit writing right here and go off

to get measured for one of the white coats that ties in the back.

But there's another thing that happened, too. I don't understand it either, even though it's not as goofy as the other stuff, but I have a feeling it goes along with everything else so I'll put it down.

The next few days, all I did was hang around the house. I didn't go out. I didn't go to school. The old man and I had nothing to say to each other. Maybe I gave a "Hello" to T a couple of times but that's all.

I had no energy. I stayed in my room, sleeping, getting up to eat a little something once in a while, and then going back to my room to look at the ceiling.

Then it was Wednesday, late afternoon, and there was this knock on the door. I didn't answer.

"Jimmy?"

I started to say, "Go away," but what the hell. When I sat up in bed, it made me dizzy. "Come in," I said. The door opened. T had on her school clothes. She was carrying an envelope. "What is it?"

T licked her lips. "Jimmy, I got a note. Dad's supposed to see it."

"So show it to him," I said. "Don't bug me, okay?"

"You know Dad," T said.

Yeah, I knew Dad. Old Ten High Dad. I told T to give me the note.

It was from T's art teacher. T hadn't turned in four drawings. She was going to flunk. Her teacher wrote, "I am worried about this drastic change in attitude for a student who has always done so well."

I said, "You know what this is?"

"I guess," T said. "Yes."

129

"Then what the hell's wrong with you? You want to flunk?"

T looked down at the floor. "I don't care," she said. "It doesn't matter."

That's when I stopped being tired. I got mad. I think I was madder than I'd ever been in my whole life.

I slapped T.

Her head jerked. Instantly, the lines of my fingers were bright red on her cheek.

Then I grabbed her and I held her. "Goddamn it," I said. "Shit."

T was so awfully skinny and she was crying. Not loud, but this deep, awful shaking crying. I put my face close to hers. "I'm sorry, I'm sorry, I'm sorry," I said. "Oh, man, don't cry, don't cry, okay? Don't."

I was crying, too.

That's it, I guess.

Yeah, I don't always know where to begin, but I know that has to be the end.

A Someday Movie

SOMEDAY I'M GOING TO HIT it, hit it so big. The policy, maybe. Put my buck on 9-7-2 or 4-6-8, or maybe shooting craps some night and fall into a run of real good luck, nothing but sweet 7s, and 11s, and all those easy 8s! Yes! These big old black fingers around all that green, all those dream dollars, and won't that be something, now, won't it just.

You know what a lot of the brothers would do if they scored that way, don't you? Go after that Cadillac with the tiger skin upholstery and the closets full of 800-dollar suits and a different pair of shoes for each and every one of them. Sure, they'd blow the whole roll in a week and there wouldn't be one real god-damned thing to show for it.

That's not for me. I'm a serious man and I've got a serious plan.

I guess this plan of mine first came into my mind when Mama and I came north. I was about nine years old, so that would be 1942.

Now Mama was a church woman, a strict one, so damned near anything that was any fun at all was something she'd whip my behind for doing. Mama had this terror that I'd be in trouble with the police. She feared policemen like they were devils right from Hell, so she kept one eye on me always—and usually had the other eye keeping it company.

We were getting some money from the county welfare, so Mama didn't have to work full days, and when she went off to clean white peoples' houses, she left the same time I was off to school and she always seemed to make it back before I did, so she was able to watch me real close—nine months of the year.

But in summer! Summer was trouble time for a child and Mama knew that. All the kids playing in the open hydrants in the streets and pinching stuff from stores and sometimes sneaking on the streetcars and going off to the Loop where there was more to see and a whole lot more to steal.

So in summer, Mama used to drop me off on her way to work at my Aunt Lorinda's. Aunt Lorinda lived a couple blocks away. She didn't have a job and she never went to church.

Years later, I learned Aunt Lorinda had enough boyfriends giving her "gifts" so she didn't have to work. I'll bet it bothered my Mama's soul plenty to leave me with a woman like Aunt Lorinda—but she must have thought it was better than my running with all those "trashy nig-gers"—that's what Mama called them—who were always getting into it with the Law.

Aunt Lorinda had a Victrola in the living room, not like Mama's wind-up one she was always playing church songs on, but a real electric phonograph that never got slow and shaky when the spring ran down. She must have had three or four hundred records, too, the kind Mama wouldn't allow in our house because they were "sinful"— Louis Armstrong, Big Bill Broonzy, Petie Wheatstraw, Victoria Spivey, Bessie Smith, people like that. Some-times now when I'm working in the warehouse shoving this crate over here and lugging that one there, I start singing something like "Whiskeyhead Buddies" or "Dig-gin' My Potatoes" and it comes back to me that I learned it sitting on the floor by Aunt Lorinda's Victrola with my ear up close so that the sound went boom-boom inside my brain and stayed there ever since.

I used to play a lot of cards with Aunt Lorinda, gin rummy and casino mostly. Once she was going to teach me poker but she changed her mind. " 'Cause your Mama kill us both, sugar," is what she said and she was probably right about that.

Anyway, one day I was over at Aunt Lorinda's, drink-ing a bottle of Nehi orange and listening to a new Jazz Gillum record. Aunt Lorinda was at the table, reading the newspaper. After a while, she said, "Sugar, you want Aunty take you to a movie?"

"Yes'm," I said. I jumped right up. I was so excited I dumped the Nehi all across the floor. If I made a mess like that at home, you can bet Mama would go on. But Aunt Lorinda didn't. She just took a wet rag, cleaned up the spill, and then we were off to the show.

The Paradise Theater on Madison Street was the most beautiful moviehouse there ever was. There was deep red carpet in the lobby, and pictures like in the museums on the walls, and this big fountain squirting water under different colored lights. They didn't have any kids for ushers, either. There were all these fine looking older gentlemen in uniforms that made them look like generals or admirals. Oh yes, the Paradise was really *someplace!*

This usher that could have been a five star general took Aunt Lorinda and me down the middle aisle. Aunt Lorinda told him, "Don't want no stiff neck from sittin' too close," so he pointed out two seats in a center row with his flashlight.

It was just early afternoon so there weren't many people in the show. The movie wasn't on yet and in that cool darkness I sat there trying to think of an extra-special way to say, "Thank you" to my aunt. I didn't see too many movies, not real ones. Oh, once in a while Mama would drag me off to something at church, movies that showed you what fine work our missionaries were doing for the savages. And there was that time I tried to sneak in with some other kids to see The Wolfman, but a man grabbed us and threw us out and said if we ever tried anything like that again we'd be off to jail for a thousand years. So, you know, going to a movie show was a real big deal for me.

The picture Aunty and I saw was Gentleman Jim. Errol Flynn was in it and I liked it a lot. There were plenty of good fights. Oh, there was some of that love stuff, too, the kind you don't want to see when you're nine, but just when I'd start thinking there was too much kissing and silly talk, whoop! Errol Flynn would be whipping hell out of someone.

But watching that movie got me kind of mixed up, so when we were riding the streetcar home, I asked Aunt Lorinda about it. "I thought Joe Louis is the champion," is what I said. Every kid knew about Joe—and every colored child and grownup, too, loved our Brown Bomber.

"He is, sugar."

"Then that was just a story. I mean, it's something someone made up. There isn't really a Gentleman Jim."

"See, Sugar," Aunt Lorinda said, "Gentleman Jim, he used to be the champion a long, long time ago. He was a real man and the movie tells you about some of the things he really did. Oh, I don't guess it's all true, but there's lots in it that is pure gospel."

It was right then I knew what I was going to do someday. I was going to make a movie.

I was nine years old. I'll be forty-one next October. You know how it is. Like just about all of us, I've forgotten about most of the kid dreams I used to have.

But I'll be damned if I don't someday make my movie!

Of course, I don't know a thing about the mechanics of movie making. But when I have my bundle, you can bet I'll hire the best cameraman and the best sound man you can find. Then all they're going to have to do is exactly what I tell them—because I've been through my movie a couple million times in my head and I know just the way everything has to look and sound.

Now I've got to tell you I haven't figured out a name for my movie yet. And I'm not quite sure how I can let the people in the audience know that everything that happens takes place in 1938 down in Mississippi. I've seen

movies that put white lettered signs right over the picture
to tell you things like that, but I think that looks wrong—
and there can't be any one single thing looking wrong in
my movie.

My movie starts like this:

There's a dusty road leading up to a small wooden
house. There are these big trees behind the house and
more trees on both sides. It's the kind of house poor farm
people used to live in, but it's not all run-down. It's
pained a fresh white and the porch doesn't sag in the
middle. It's just a nice little house.

Then there's this black boy that walks out of the house.
He's got no shoes and he's not wearing a shirt and his
overalls are held up by just one strap. He's saying something to himself, you know, the ways kids do when they're
trying to sound like grownups. He says, "Sure a fine day."
Then he goes to the edge of the porch and sits down.

Now this is going to be really hard to show in a movie.
That's why I've got to get the best cameraman there is.
See, the sun is shining real bright, and the boy feels it
on the back of his neck. The movie has to make the
audience feel just exactly what it is that the boy is feeling,
right there, where there's that little knob on the back of
his neck. I guess that camera is going to have to be right
inside that boy so we know just how it is when his skin
drinks up all that sunshine.

Okay, the door opens again. A tall man comes out.
He's got on a white shirt and there are suspenders holding
up his pants. The boy turns and looks at him.

Did I say the man and the boy have to look a lot alike?
They do, they surely do.

The man steps on over to the boy and the boy has to

lean his head way back to see him because the man is so tall he's near like a giant.

"I'm goin' to the store, Son," the man says. "You go with me?" The man and the boy walk down the road. The man looks like he always takes great big steps but now he has to walk slow because the boy is with him and you can tell the man doesn't mind. After a while, the man takes hold of the boy's hand. Then the man starts singing:

I'm gonna leave, gonna go off to France.
I'm gonna leave, gonna go away to France.
Gonna go to France—jus' to give the ladies a chance!

The boy laughs. It's only when the man and the boy are off on their own that the man sings songs like that, and even then the boy has to promise he won't say a thing about it to Mama.

The man sings that song and then another one and they keep walking until they get to the crossroads. There's a store there with a sign in front that says: "Cooper's Groceries, Sundries, and Supplies."

That's where the man and boy go, but, before they get there, the boy asks, "Daddy, can I have a Hershey?"

The man says, "Every time I take you to Cooper's you 'spect a Hershey."

The boy says, "Ain't been to Cooper's but four times."

Then the man says, "We ain't come here to buy candy, son." He looks a little sad, like he wants to buy the boy a treat, but these are hard times and there's no money for candy.

Then they're in the store. There's a big fat white man

in an apron behind the counter and he's drinking a Coca-Cola. That's Mr. Cooper. He owns the store. There's two more white men over by the window near the rack that has the magazines, and they're looking at the Police Gazette and The Shadow Mystery Magazine. The man on the left is skinny and he's got an Adam's apple about twice as big as a real apple. His eyes are always moving back and forth, back and forth. The other man, well, he doesn't look like much of anything.

" 'Lo, Claude," is what the skinny one says. His big Adam's apple goes bouncing.

The man still holds the boy's hand and he says, "Afternoon, Mister Winthrop." Then he looks over at the other white man, who doesn't take his eyes off The Shadow, and he says, "Afternoon, Mister Deland."

The man and the boy go to the counter. Mr. Cooper sets his soda bottle down next to a box full of plug tobacco. He says, " 'Lo, Claude. What can I do for you?"

"I come about my bill, suh," is what the man says.

"Oh yeah, yeah," Mr. Cooper says. "I told your Essie about that." He messes with some papers that are stabbed on a spike alongside the cash register. "Here it is. Nine dollars and thirty cents. Want to pay all that now or you give me just some of it and settle up as you can? Course I don't like to let these things go on too long."

"No, suh, Mister Cooper, suh," the man says.

Mr. Cooper acts like no one's said anything at all to him. "Bein' you a good customer, Claude, and you always . . ."

"No, suh, Mister Cooper," the man says. He's not talking loud, but he's talking in a way that gets heard.

"What's that, Claude?" Mr. Cooper says.

"No disrespect, Mister Cooper, but the bill's wrong. I don't owe but six dollars and eighty-seven cents."

Mr. Cooper says, "What's that you sayin'?"

"These are hard times, suh, and I can't afford to be payin' what I'm not owing."

"Claude," Mr. Cooper says, "you sayin' I'm out to cheat you? You better watch that kind of talk."

Now we take a look at the white men by the magazine rack. They're still holding the magazines, but they're watching what's going on.

Then we look at Mr. Cooper. He's got both hands on the counter and he's leaning way forward and every time he opens up his mouth to say something, we feel like he's going to swallow up the whole theater full of people watching this movie.

"Goddamn it, boy! I figured out your bill. I never cheated nobody, no white man or nigra, in my entire life."

"Ain't sayin' cheat, Mister Cooper," the man says. "I jus' think you mistaken in your figurin'. I can't do nothin' with a pencil and paper, but I'm good with numbers in my head. You made a mistake . . . Mister Cooper, suh."

Mr. Cooper shakes his head. His face is red. He looks like he's run twenty miles using only one leg. "Goddamn it!" he yells—and then he really starts hollering. "Well just goddamn it and double goddamn it all to hell! You just get your black ass outta here!"

Now the little black boy looks like he doesn't know what's going on. He's never heard anyone talk that way to his daddy. Mr. Cooper keeps on hollering. "You don't owe me nothing no more! You surely do not! And I don't need your trade and I sure don't want you taking up space that ought to belong to customers who know I'm a fair man." He aims a big, fat finger at the boy.

"Get on out and haul your little nigra with you."

The white men are a still over there by the magazines. Mr. Cooper looks at them. Then he smiles like he's going to tell a secret joke just for the three of them. He says, "That is, if he is your little nigra."

Now here is where the man doing the sound for my movie will have to do a very careful job. I want the whole store to fill up to bursting with the laughter of those white men. I want the two magazine men laughing, and Mr. Cooper laughing, and it gets louder and louder and louder, and then, all of a sudden, there's no sound at all. *Nothing*.

And everything happens slow from now on, and we see it all just the way the little black boy is seeing it, as his daddy's black fingers go around the neck of that Coca-Cola bottle on the counter, and he picks up the bottle and swings it back and then that bottle is going *Crash!* right across Mr. Cooper's big, fat, laughing white face.

Green chunks of the Coca-Cola bottle hang in the air. Blood that looks like a red hand stretching out its fingers is all over Mr. Cooper's face and one drop makes a big, thick splat on the counter.

Now it's outside and the boy and the man are walking away from the store. There's yelling and screaming behind them, but they keep on walking down the road like there's never been any trouble at all.

And they walk on home.

That's it.

I guess there can be some music or something there, but that is the end of my movie.

No, we don't have men coming round with guns. We don't have a black man grabbing his chest and falling off the porch and lying there kicking on the ground with the blood making a puddle on his clean white shirt and shooting out of his mouth like a fountain.

We don't have a black woman waving her arms and screaming, "Sweet Jesus, sweet Jesus, help him!"

No.

There's no little black boy looking down like he doesn't know what's happening as he watches his daddy die on the Mississippi dirt.

No.

That's not in my movie, not that part.

It doesn't happen this time.

No.

Not this time.

Party Time

MAMA HAD TOLD HIM IT would soon be party time. That made him excited but also a little afraid. Oh, he liked party time, he liked making people happy, and he always had fun, but it was kind of scary going upstairs.

Still, he knew it would be all right because Mama would be with him. Everything was all right with Mama and he always tried to be Mama's good boy.

Once, though, a long time ago, he had been bad. Mama must not have put his chain on right, so he'd slipped it off his leg and gone up the stairs all by himself and opened the door. Oh! Did Mama ever whip him for that. Now he knew better. He'd never, never go up without Mama.

And he liked it down in the basement, liked it a lot. There was a little bed to sleep on. There was a yellow light that never went off. He had blocks to play with. It was nice in the basement.

Best of all, Mama visited him often. She kept him company and taught him to be good.

He heard the funny sound that the door at the top of the stairs made and he knew Mama was coming down. He wondered if it was party time. He wondered if he'd get to eat the happy food.

But then he thought it might not be party time. He saw Mama's legs, Mama's skirt. Maybe he had done something bad and Mama was going to whip him. He ran to the corner. The chain pulled hard at his ankle. He tried to go away, to squeeze right into the wall.

"No, Mama! I am not bad! I love my mama. Don't whip me!"

Oh, he was being silly. Mama had food for him. She wasn't going to whip him.

"You're a good boy. Mama loves you, too, my sweet, good boy."

The food was cold. It wasn't the kind of food he liked best, but Mama said he always had to eat everything she brought him because if not he was a bad boy.

It was hot food he liked most. He called it the happy food.

That's the way it felt inside him.

"Is it party time yet, Mama?"

"Not yet, sweet boy. Don't you worry, it will be soon. You like Mama to take you upstairs for parties, don't you?"

"Yes, Mama! I like to see all the people. I like to make them happy."

Best of all, he liked the happy food. It was so good, so hot.

He was sleepy after Mama left, but he wanted to play with his blocks before he lay down on his bed. The blocks were fun. He liked to build things with them and make up funny games.

He sat on the floor. He pushed the chain out of the way. He put one block on top of another block, then a block on top of that one. He built the blocks up real high, then made them fall. That was funny and he laughed.

Then he played party time with the blocks. He put one block over here and another over there and the big, big block was Mama.

He tried to remember some of the things people said at party time so he could make the blocks talk that way. Then he placed a block in the middle of all the other blocks. That was Mama's good boy.

It was himself.

Before he could end the party time game, he got very sleepy. His belly was full, even if it was only cold food.

He went to bed. He dreamed a party time dream of happy faces and the good food and Mama saying, "Good boy, my sweet boy."

Then Mama was shaking him. He heard funny sounds coming from upstairs. Mama slipped the chain off his leg.

"Come my good boy."

"It's party time?"

"Yes."

Mama took his hand. He was frightened a little, the way he always was just before party time.

"It's all right, my sweet boy."

Mama led him up the stairs. She opened the door.

"This is party time. Everyone is so happy."

He was not scared anymore. There was a lot of light and so many laughing people in the party room.

"Here's the good, sweet boy, everybody!"

Then he saw it on the floor. Oh, he hoped it was for him!

"That's yours, good boy, all for you."

He was so happy! It had four legs and a black nose. When he walked closer to it, it made a funny sound that was something like the way he sounded when Mama whipped him.

His belly made a noise and his mouth was all wet inside. It tried to get away from him, but he grabbed it and he squeezed it real hard. He heard things going snap inside it.

Mama was laughing and laughing and so was everyone else. He was making them all so happy.

"You know what it is, don't you, my sweet boy?"

He knew.

It was the happy food.

Love, Hate, and the Beautiful Junkyard Sea

IT WASN'T UNTIL THE THIRD grade I learned I could love.
It was in third grade I met Caralynn Pitts.

Before that, seems to me all I did was hate. I had reason. As everyone in Harlinville knew and let me know,
I was trash. The Deweys were so low-down you couldn't
get lower if you dug straight to China and kept going.
My daddy was skinny, slit-eyed, and silent except in his
drunken, grunt-shouting, crazy fits that set him to beating
my mother or me. Maybe it was the dark and dust of the
coal mine—he worked Old Ben Number Three—that got
inside him, poisoned him to turn him so mean. My
mother might have tried to be a good momma, I don't
know, but by the time I was able to think anything about
it, she must have just given up. In a day she never said
more than ten words to me. At night, she cried a lot.

Trash, no-account trash, bad as any and worse than most you find in southern Illinois, that's what I was, and if you're trash, you start out hating yourself and hating your folks and hating the God Who made you trash and plans to keep you that way, but soon you get so hate filled, you have to let it out or bust and so you go to hating other people. I hated kids who came to school in nice clothes, with a different shirt everyday, the kids who had Bugs Bunny lunch-boxes with two sandwiches on bread so white it made me think of hospitals, the kids who lost teeth and got quarters from a tooth fairy, the kids whose daddies never got drunk and always took them on vacations to Starved Rock State Park or way faraway, like Disneyland or the Grand Canyon. I hated all the mommas up at the laundromat every Monday morning, washing the clothes so clean for their families. I hated Mr. Mueller, at the Texaco, who always told me, "Take a hike, Bradford Dewey," when I wanted to watch cars go up on the grease rack, and I hated Mr. Eikenberry, the postmaster. Mr. Eikenberry had that breeze-tingly smell of Old Spice on him. My daddy smelled like whiskey and wickedness.

If you hate somebody, you want to hurt them, and I thought of hateful, hurting things happening to all the people I hated. There wasn't a one in Harlinville I didn't set my mind on a wish picture for, a hate-hurt picture that left them busted up and bleeding and dead. I imagined a monster big as an Oldsmobile grabbing up Rodney Carlisle—his daddy owned the hardware store on the square—and ripping off his arms and legs, a snake as long as the Mississippi River swallowing Claire Bobbit, Patty Marsel, Edith Hebb, and all the girls who used to tease me, and an invisible vampire ripping the throats out of all the teachers at McKinley School.

You might think, then, that I really did try to hurt people, I mean, use my hands, punch them in the nose or hit them on the head with a ball bat or something like that, but that's not so. Never in my whole life have I done that kind of hurt to anyone. What I did was to find another way to get people. I started lying. You tell someone the truth, it means you trust them. It's like you got something you like them enough to share with them. Doesn't have to be an important piece of truth, either, it can be a little nothing: "I went to the show last night and that was one fine picture they had," or "It's really a pretty day," or "My cat had kittens," or anything at all. You tell someone the truth, it's the same as liking them.

So when you lie to a person, it's because you got no use for them, you hate their guts—and what makes it so fine is you're doing it without ever having to flat-out say what you feel.

So I lied, lied my head off. I told little lies, like my Uncle Everett sent me five dollars because I was his favorite nephew and I did so have a wonderful birthday gift for Rodney Carlisle but I wasn't giving it to him because he didn't ask me to his party, and I told monster whoppers, some of them crazy, like I was just adopted by the Deweys but my real parents were Hollywood movie stars, or I had to kill this three hundred pound wolf with just my bare hands when it attacked me out at the junkyard.

I didn't really fool anyone with my lies, you know. That wasn't what I was trying to do. All in all, I'd say Miss Krydell, the third grade teacher, was right when she used to say, "Bradford, you are a hateful little liar."

Moon on the Water

But all that changed when Caralynn Pitts came and showed me the beautiful junkyard sea.

*   *   *

You've probably had to do it yourself, stand in front of the class and tell who you are and all because you're the new kid, and you're supposed to be making friends right off. It was the first week in May, already too hot and too damp, an oily spring like you get in southern Illinois. The new girl up by Miss Krydell's desk was Caralynn Pitts. She had this peepy voice about one squeak lower than Minnie Mouse. Her eyes and hair were both the same shade of black and she was wearing this blue and dark green plaid dress.

Caralynn Pitts didn't say much except her name and that she lived on Elmscourt Lane, but in a town the size of Harlinville, everyone knew most everything about her a week before she'd even moved in. Her daddy was a doctor and he was going to work at the county hospital and her momma was dead.

Well, Caralynn Pitts wasn't anything to me, not yet. I went back to drilling a hole in my desktop with my yellow pencil.

A week later I talked to Caralynn Pitts for the first time.

It was ten o'clock, the big Regulator clock up near the flag ticking off the long, hot seconds, and that was "arithmetic period," so, like always, Miss Krydell asked who didn't do the homework, and then she started right in on me: "Bradford Dewey, do you have the fractions?"

"No, ma'am."

Mort Castle

"Please stand, Bradford, and stop mumbling. Didn't you do the homework?"

I actually had tried to but, when I was working at the kitchen table, my daddy came up and popped me alongside the head for no reason except he felt like it, so I lit out of the house.

I wasn't going to tell Miss Krydell any such thing. "Ma'am, I did so do the homework. I don't have it is all."

"Why is that?" said Miss Krydell.

I felt this good one, a big, twisty lie, working its way out of me. "I was on the way to school and I had my fractions and next thing I knew, the scurlets come up all around me and that's how I lost my homework."

"The scurlets," said Miss Krydell. "Please tell us about the scurlets."

There was a laugh from the first row, and someone echoing it a row over, but Miss Krydell swept her eyes over the classroom and it got dead quiet real quick.

I said, "The scurlets aren't all that big. No bigger than puppies, but they're plenty mean. There's a lot of them around every time it gets to be spring."

"Oh, is that so?" Miss Krydell said.

"Yes, ma'am. It was running away from the scurlets so they wouldn't get me that I dropped my homework and I couldn't go on back for it, could I? See, the scurlets have pointy tails with a stinger on them and if they sting you, you swell up and turn blue and you die. And when you're dead, the scurlets eat you up . . ." I was really running with it now. "They start on your face and they bite out your eyes the first thing . . ."

"That will be enough, Bradford."

". . . I guess for a scurlet, your eye is kind of like a grape.

It goes 'pop' when they bite down on it. . . ."

"Enough, Bradford."

I stop right there. Miss Krydell says, "You are a liar, Bradford, and I am sick and tired of your lies. You'll stay after school and write 'I promise to tell the truth,' five hundred times."

I sat down, thinking how much I hated Miss Krydell and how bad my hand was going to feel when I finished writing all that.

The day went on, and, it was strange, but every time I happened to look around the room, there was Caralynn Pitts looking at me with those black eyes that were big as the wolf's in "Little Red Riding Hood." I didn't quite know what to make of that.

After school, I wrote and wrote and wrote, each "I promise to tell the truth" sloppier than the one before it. With my hand feeling like someone had taken a sledgehammer to it, Miss Krydell finally let me go. I cut back of the school through the playground to take the long way home. I heard this shh-click like someone running on the gravel, and then, she was calling my name—somehow I knew it was her right off—so I stopped and turned around.

She ran up to me and before I could say anything, she said, "You can see things, can't you?"

Not knowing what to make of that, I said, "Huh?"

"See things," she says.

I figured Caralynn Pitts had hung around school just to tease me like Claire Bobbit, Patty Marsel, Edith Hebb did, and so I answered in kind of a nasty way, "Sure can." I pointed over at the monkey bars. "You go hang by your knees and I can see your underpants. What do you think about that?"

Caralynn said, "You can see the things other people don't, can't you, Bradford? Like the scurlets." Then she started whispering, "Bradford, I can see things, all kinds of things, too. I can see tiny people living under sunflowers and I can see giants jumping from cloud to cloud and I can see bugs that fly in moonlight and spell out your name on their wings and once I saw a stone in the sunshine trying to it turn itself into apple jelly!"

I said, "What are you talking about?"

"Both of us, we can see things, so that means we ought to be friends."

I said, "No sense to what you're talking, Caralynn. I can't see anything much, nothing like what you're saying, and if you can, then you sound crazy."

Caralynn said, "I can't tell my daddy about what I see because he says it's only pretend and I'm too old to pretend that way. I used to tell Momma, before she died. She said I had imagination and sometimes, when there was nothing worth seeing in the whole world, all you had was your imagination. When Momma was so sick, she was dying, I guess, it seems like it rained every day. I used to sit with her, and we'd look out the window and every day, Bradford, every day I could see a rainbow. It had twelve colors, that rainbow, colors like you don't ever see in a plain old rainbow. I used to tell Momma how the sun made the colors change from second to second. Momma said that was our rainbow. That was the rainbow over the graveyard the day we buried Momma. It wasn't even raining, but I looked up and there it was, and where it bent and disappeared on the other side of the world, I saw Momma and she was waving to me."

"I don't know," I said. "I don't know anything about that or rainbows."

"Bradford," Caralynn said, "there's something I want to show you. Something beautiful. Can I?"

"I guess," I said.

I'm not a bit sorry about saying that, and haven't been since the words slid off my lips, but in these years gone by, I sure have asked myself why I didn't tell Caralynn to just get lost.

Maybe the reason is, I was small and my whole life was small but packed inside was this big hate—and hate is an ugly thing—and so I guess I was tired of all that ugly and ready to be shown something . . . beautiful.

Not that I believed Caralynn Pitts had a thing to show me, but I did go with her, all the way past the edge of town, through Neidmeyer's Meadow, and then along the railroad tracks until we came to the curve, and there, by this rusted steel building that I guess the railroad must have once had a use for but didn't anymore, was the old junkyard.

It wasn't the kind of junkyard where'd you go to sell your falling-apart car. It was an acre or so where everybody dumped the trash that wouldn't burn and was too big for the garbage men to haul off. It was all useless, twisted garbage, a three legged wringer washer with the wires sticking out the bottom, and a refrigerator with the basket coil on top, and an old trunk without a lid like maybe a sailor once had, and a steam radiator, and a bathtub, and hundreds of pipes, and a couple of shells of cars, and thousands of tin cans. Everywhere you looked were hills and mountains of steel and glass and plastic, all kinds of trash that came from you didn't know what stuff. Flies swarmed in bunches like black cyclones, and over it all, hanging so stink-heavy you could see it, was the terrible smell.

That was what Caralynn Pitts had to show me.

Not more than a spit away, a rat peeked from under a torn square of pink linoleum, its nasty whiskers quivering. I chucked a stone at it. I told Caralynn Pitts maybe she thought she was funny but I didn't think she was funny— and I started to run off.

I didn't get a step before she had my elbow. "Bradford, can't you see it?"

"It's the junkyard. That's all it is."

"It's the sea, Bradford, it's the beautiful junkyard sea. You have to look at it the right way. You have to want to see it, to see how beautiful it is. Please look, Bradford."

So I did. And Caralynn Pitts started talking to me in this peeping voice that seemed to crawl from my ear right into my brain. "Look at the water. Can't you see how blue and green it is? See the waves..."

... the water goes beyond nowhere, the waves gentle as a night breeze, the rippling tiny hills rolling in to wash against the diamond dotted golden sands where we stand ...

"... and a sea gull ..."

... its wings are made of air, its eyes magic black ...

"... and way out there ..."

... there, at the horizon ... a whale ...

there

... whales, the song of the whales, placid rumbles un-earthly and eternal ...

154

"Bradford," Caralynn said. "Can you see it, the beautiful junkyard sea?"

"No," I said, and that was the truth, but in the moment before I said it, I almost saw it. It was like someone had painted a picture of the junkyard on an old bedsheet and the wind catching that sheet as it hung on a line was making everything ripple and change before my eyes.

It was because I almost saw it—and because, I know now, there was a fierce want in me to see it—I came back to the junkyard day after day with Caralynn Pitts.

On a Wednesday, in the afternoon, a week after school let out, it happened.

I saw the beautiful junkyard sea.

The forever waters, sun light slanting, cutting through foam and fathom upon fathom, then diminishing, vanishing into the ever night depths. The sea gulls, winged arrows cutting random arcs over the rippling waves. A dolphin bursts from the sea, bejeweled droplets and glory, another dolphin, another and another, an explosion of dolphins . . .

Far off, a beckoning atoll, a palm-treed island. Far off, a coral reef, living land. Far off, the promise of magic, the assurance that a lie is only a dream and that dreams are true.

Good thing you don't have to learn or practice love, that it just happens.

In the fine sea spray
in the clean mist of air and salt water
I kissed Caralynn Pitts on the lips.
I told her I loved her.
I loved her and I loved the beautiful junkyard sea.

* * *

Every day that summer, Caralynn and I visited the beautiful junkyard sea. It was always there, always new, always wonderful.

Then late in August, Caralynn Pitts told me she was moving. Her daddy was joining the staff of a hospital in Seattle. I said I would always love her. She said she would always love me.

"But what about the beautiful junkyard sea?" I asked her.

"It will always be ours," she said. "It will always be here for us."

She promised to write to give me her address once they were settled in Seattle. We would keep on loving each other and when we grew up, we'd get married and be together forever.

The next week, she moved. Months and then years went by and there was no letter.

But I had the beautiful junkyard sea. And this is the truth: I never stopped loving Caralynn Pitts or believing she would return to me, return to the beautiful junkyard sea.

* * *

She did.

I was 22 years old. When I was 12, my daddy got drunk and drove the car into a tree and killed himself. What with his miner's benefits, and no money going out on whiskey, Mama and I got by. I'd scraped through high school, pretty bad grades, but I learned in shop class that I had a way with engines. Pop the hood and hand me a wrench, and chances were good to better yet that I could fix any problem there was, and so I was working at Mueller's Texaco.

On a sunny day in late April, Caralynn Pitts drove her white LTD up to the regular pump and asked me to fill it up, check the oil, battery, and transmission fluid.

Stooped over, I just kind of stood there by the open car window, jaw hanging like a moron. There was a question in Caralynn Pitts's big eyes for a second—and then she knew.

"It is Bradford, right?"

"Yes," I said.

"You've changed so much."

"I guess you have too," I said. That was probably the right thing to say, but to tell the truth, she hadn't done that much changing. It was like she was still the kid she had been, only bigger. "You came back, Caralynn," I said.

She gave me another funny look, and then she laughed. "I guess I have. I work out of Chicago—I'm in advertising—and I was on my way to St. Louis and, well, I needed gas, so I didn't even think anything about it . . . just pulled off I-57 and here I am."

"You came back to our beautiful junkyard sea," I said.

"Huh?" Caralynn Pitts said. She laughed again. "Oh, I get it. I remember. The beautiful junkyard sea, that was some game we had. I guess both of us had pretty wild imaginations."

"It was no game, Caralynn," I said. "It isn't."

"Well, I don't know . . ." She tapped her fingers on the steering wheel and looked through the windshield.

"Could you fill it up, please? And do you have a rest-room?"

I told her, "Inside." I filled the tank. Everything checked out under the hood. When she came back a min-ute later, I said, "Maybe we could talk a minute or two, Caralynn? It's been a long time and all and we used to be good friends, special friends."

She took a quick look at her wristwatch. Then, when her eyes touched mine, I saw something like what used to be there so many years ago. "We were, weren't we?" she said. "Maybe a quick cup of coffee or something. Is there someplace we could go?"

"Sure," I said, "I know the place. Just let me tell Mueller I'll be gone awhile."

I drove her LTD. She told me she had gone to college, Washington State, majoring in business. She told me she and a guy—I forget his name—were getting serious about one another, thinking about getting engaged. She told me she hoped to be moving up in advertising, become an account executive in another year or so. When we got out past the town limits, she said, "Bradford, where are you taking us?"

"You know," I said.

"Bradford . . . I don't know what's going on. What are you doing? You're acting, well, you're acting strange." I heard it in her voice. She was frightened.

"There's something I want to show you," I told her, and I drove to the junkyard.

She didn't want to get out of the car. She was scared. She said, "Bradford, don't . . . don't hurt me."

"I could never hurt you, Caralynn," I said.

I took her arm. I could feel how stiff she was holding herself, like her spine was steel.

"Here it is, Caralynn," I said. "Here we are."

We stood on the sun-washed shore of the beautiful junkyard sea.

She jerked like she wanted to pull away from me but I held her arm even tighter. "I don't know what you want, Bradford. What am I supposed to say? What am I supposed to do?"

"What do you see, Caralynn?" I asked.

"I . . . I don't see . . . anything, Bradford."

"Don't say that, Caralynn. I love you. Don't make me hate you."

"Bradford, I . . . I can't see what isn't there. This is a junkyard. That's all it is, just an ugly, stinking junkyard! Please . . ."

They never found Caralynn Pitts. I left her car there and walked back to town. The police did have questions, of course, since I was the last person to see her, but like I said, I know how to lie, and so I made up a few little lies and one or two big ones that made them happy.

I haven't gone back to the beautiful junkyard sea. Maybe I never will.

But I can't forget, won't ever forget, and don't want to forget how Caralynn looked

when the waters turned black and churning and the lightning shattered the sky and the sea gulls shrieked and the fins of sharks circled and circled and the first tentacle whipped out of the foam and hooked her leg, and another shot out, circled her waist, and then one more, across her face, choking off her screams, as she was dragged toward that thing rising in the angry water, that great, gray-green, puffy bag that was its

159

head, yellow eyes shining hungrily, the corn colored, curved beak clattering, as it dragged her deeper, deeper, and then she disappeared and there was blood on the water and that was all until,

at last

the sun shone
and all was quiet in
the beautiful
junkyard

sea

FDR: A Love Story

FDR WAS OUR FRIEND. WE needed a friend, The Depression was a sticking gray film over the land.

Almost immediately, because he understood magic, he gave us initials on decals and shoulder patches.

WPA

CCC

NRA

And *more*

And *Eleanor!*

FDR gave us Eleanor to be our very own aunt. A ridiculous smile exactly like the first laugh of the first baby that broke into a thousand pieces and became fairies in Never-Neverland. And that sweet-silly hat that promptly collapsed on her crazy curls as soon as it touched her head.

She always had a pecan pie fresh-popped in the oven for us. She always greeted us, "Hi, hi . . ."

(And how many times did she go into the deepest South, where the Depression lay like a blue tick hound in a shed, baring its teeth to defend its right to be there as though its family had been paying property taxes for five generations, and there she discovered a mumbling black convicted murderer on the chaingang, then one week later, he was free, pardoned, strumming guitar and singing "Jim Crack Corn" at a White House dinner? No one is lost. No one is eternally damned.)

No, FDR could not leave his wheelchair. Had he been able he would have come, knocked on our each and every door, knocked on the hood of the Model-T Ford where we lived, knocked on the paper and tin side of our Hooverville, knocked on the concrete of the conduit in which we squatted, held out that big strong hand to us, said, "Don't worry it will be all right."

There was another way.

We had radio.

We had Atwater-Kent. We had Philco. Sears-Roebuck sold a seven tube model for less than thirty dollars and offered credit.

So, throw us out of a thousand cold water flats, and Mother will scream, "You can't! We have children, for God's sake," and Father, humbled, impotent, jobless, will make a bad joke, "Take down the wallpaper, we're moving," but we've got our radios.

No, we have no fireside.

FDR did.

He shared.

"My friends . . ."

the warm voice the good
the good voice is upon the land
the good
that is the only and right word
the good voice is upon us he is with us our good friend good
is with us he is with us

"My friends . . ."

yes tell us now in this our hour of national sunset when
we are alone with our each and only greatest fear now be
with us

"My friends . . ."

(Sure, Walt Disney's Three Little Pigs whip the Big, Bad Wolf, and in our hearts we understand symbols, but that is only a movie, and life is real.)

and we are afraid

and we are afraid

The Depression continues

So does FDR.

So do we all.

Until a war, a day that will live in infamy, and we win, but FDR is dead. Inside that massive skull, there has been an explosion.

We line the streets.

All of us, his friends.

And we weep him into history.

Moon on the Water

JAZZMEN MAKE IT TEN OR twenty years after they die.
Fats Navarro, Yardbird, Coltrane . . . Sure, there were
people who dug them while they were here to lay it down,
but it's *now*, years after the final bar, and gangbusters,
right?

So I'm thinking it's soon going to be Breeze's time. The
past year, there've been a couple reissues of sides we cut
years ago, decent sales and good reviews in Downbeat and
even—hip to this?—Rolling Stone.

And Breeze's trip is the stuff that makes for a cult following. He was a junky, you see. Good box office there—
check with Lady Day and Bird and Chet Baker.

And they did fish Breeze out of Lake Michigan one
cold autumn day in '59, found him with his fingers on
the keys of his sax.

Moon on the Water

*   *   *

Any city's a rough-old, tough-old dues paying time for a jazzman, but Chicago was better than New York for Breeze and me. That's why we blew Apple Major, where cool and post bop and hard bop pretty much ruled, and where, pre-Coltrane revelations, if you were into something new, and you were ofay besides, it was guaranteed nowheresville.

And Chicago was a better scene, too, if you were in "the life." If you kept your cool, the heat did not jump all over you when you went on the prowl in search of white powder.

And Chicago had the lake. First time he saw it, Breeze said, "Yes." I knew what he meant. Looking one way, all you'd see was city. Then you could turn your back on it, forget it, and there was endless water, frozen in two a.m. moonlight, making you understand loneliness and eternity. And maybe you had the kind of thought that's like smoke, curling and disappearing, thinking about magic and just how small we all are and maybe you even dreamed the kid-dream of dream monsters that swim and slither just under the surface of water and just out of sight.

Yeah, for the good solid citizens of Chicago, the city that works is also the city that sleeps and when the square johns were doing Morpheus, there were many times when you could find Breeze and me by the lake. Breeze would have his horn. Most everywhere he went—then—the sax was with him. Sometimes when it was really right, the heroin rushing through you and turning your vision incandescent, you could see the radiance, the notes shining on the water, perfect and pure for an instant before they shattered and changed into foam.

So, for us Chicago did indeed make it. We had a two room dump just off Wells Street. We scored scag, did not get strung out, did not get burned, did not get beefed and we swung enough gigs to pay the freight.

It was Chicago that we found Micah and really started to get it together. Micah was standup bass. He was shadow-skinny and yes, he had the hands, long, long fingers and fast. Micah was younger than we were, a dude who'd dropped out of college to do the jazz thing, but there was a monkey on Micah's back, too, so we got music-tight, junky-tight and it was like it was all supposed to happen.

And we were working on and getting to and sometimes touching, really touching—close to the sound.

Uh-huh, the sound. What was it we wanted? What we were after?

What we did not want: tired-out, straight ahead swing. Not spit-it-out all flash and fingers be-bop. Not thud and boom and stretch it so they think you're saying something when you're only blowing smoke.

A moment for metaphysics, okay? A moment to direct your eyes on what those Impressionist painters, Renoir and Monet and Degas and Caiillebotte and Cassatt and Manet, the masters of the moment, were doing with rivers and sunrises and railroad stations.

We wanted morning light coming through the clouds the second before the sun goes orange-pink. We wanted not a dream but the way you feel when you almost remember the dream. We wanted it be a little bit like you think maybe God is.

And looking back and thinking back and sometimes, oh, way down there, really going back, I wonder if we didn't want the moon on the water?

Maybe that. Maybe.

Breeze played alto. I was guitar. Micah, on the bottom, was the heartbeat. We didn't have drums, didn't need them with Micah. Here's the root, here's the core, here's the center, that was Micah on bass. No reason to make a clash and clatter.

Of course, Mulligan, the Jeru, with his quartet gigging our in Citrusland, did not have drums, either, but he was going his horn-rimmed academic glasses way and we were into something entirely else.

There were times when we laid it down, the calm and the ease and the gentle. There were times when we found the song inside you that you didn't even know was there.

There were good times.

* * *

And then she came out of the lake.

* * *

It was summer, around three in the morning. There were "No Trespassing—Keep Out" signs, but there was also a six-foot section of chainlink fence that was down. We'd left Micah at a restaurant, soothing his junky craving for sweet with Danish and coffee with lots of sugar. It was just Breeze and me and his horn.

It wasn't a beach for people. Rocks, great lumping boulders, and smaller ones, smooth here and jagged there, making walking something entirely else, an unearthly experience best appreciated when seriously high. Ahead of us, the beach curved. A long, falling-down pier stabbed into the moon gleaming water like a giant, arthritic finger pointing your way to nowhere.

We drifted, the two of us and the muggy quiet, our steps taking us close to the waterline. We stood on the rocks. Spray splashed our shoes. Breeze squeezed the mouthpiece between his lips. He shut his eyes, doing some key-flipping to clear the horn. Then he let a few notes slide out of the bell, full of breath, just on the verge of breaking. There was no set time to what he laid down. It was just this shaky, brute insistence to continue, like an old man marching heavy-footed to the end.

Then he went to this riffing thing, kind of a squeak-jump-around, like the feeling you get when your arm's tied up, you've got the bubbling hit, your bubbling hit, in the dropper, and you know in just one eye-blink you'll be spiking that vein for the big rush.

That was when I saw something in the water and that was when Breeze's tune changed. Way out there, way beyond the pier, someone was swimming.

Breeze's horn was going slow, notes rounded with a tired moan edge, like a bad morning when you've got to reach for the white port to kill the pain. Sure, I knew Breeze's stuff—knew where he was coming from and how he got there—but he was putting down a sound I had never heard before. It went way back to the beginnings, to swirling fog of wishes and visions. His sax was luring and welcoming. It was the curved Viking horn bringing the far-traveled dragonship into the bay, to safe harbor and warm greeting and balance.

What was out there was a lady, a lady in the lake. She came swimming toward shore in rhythm to Breeze's music. Behind her was an ever-vanishing trail in the water. From second to second, the connection from where she was to where she had been was disappearing.

When she reached the shallows, she stood up, came walking out. She moved sure-footed on clicking pebbles, like a dance.

Breeze lowered the horn, let it swing on the cord.

She did not look frightened or surprised. All she looked—here's a word so tired it sags—was beautiful.

The moon was a halo behind her head. Her long lake-gleaming hair hung tangled like tree snakes on jungle branches. She had magic-cruel eyes and her mouth was the soft passion of a bitch-goddess.

And I remember thinking she should have been naked. Oh, she wasn't, had on bra and panties made translucent with wetness, but she should have been.

She came up to us and, in the moment before she spoke, I felt it. You get tight with a dude, hang with him, do good times and bad, there are flashes when you know you're touching just what the other cat feels. That was how it was with Breeze and me.

She was working on Breeze, doing a real number.

How? Cannot say. The old bluesmen sing about the hoo-doo. The square heads write songs for square heads about enchanted evenings and crowded rooms. But, when it all comes down, who the hell can really say?

"Hey, what are you guys doing here?"

The spell—and that's no real word for what it was—was gone. I heard the over-control in her voice that hipped me to her being pretty well juiced and there was a heavy slash of booze on her breath, too.

"We're jazzmen," Breeze said, like that explained everything. In a way, maybe it did.

"Jazzmen . . . You know what I am?"

"A chick," I shrugged, always cool, even though, well, you never did feel cool around her.

"That's all right," she said. "I'm a chick who got in the car and went cruising. I was looking for something, God knows what. I don't, not anymore, if I ever did. But you know, it seemed to make sense that I'd find it in the lake, so I went swimming. There were a couple of times when I nearly reached the place where the moon was right on the water, but then it moved. It always moves just when you're there."

"That's the way it goes," I said, thinking about drunk talk and crazy ladies, neither of which is supposed to make sense but both do if you think about it when you're not really working at thinking.

Her eyes did three beats on me, then triple that on Breeze; she was deciding something. "Jazzmen," she said. "I want you to come with me."

Maybe this is just "years later" wisdom talking, but I think I was a little afraid. But hell, cool means you go the way it goes and you flow the way it flows.

She'd left her clothing under the pier. Without any attempt to dry off, she slipped into a beige dress, and then we followed her to her car, parked not too far away. She had a dark blue Lincoln.

We went to an apartment building on the Gold Coast. The doorman lamped Breeze and me with a look that said it wasn't his business what kind of whatevers rich people hung with but that didn't mean he had to dig us.

She lived so way up there in the ozone that she could have gone next door to borrow a cup of flour from God. Massive furniture that made you feel like you'd disappeared when you sat down. Windows providing a view of the city that half-convinced you everything was all right down below. And the bar at the end of the living room was a juice head's dream of heaven.

The three of us, two jazzmen and a crazy lady, sat sipping wine, and on the hi-fi set—she had a solid classical collection—was Respighi's *Pines of Rome*. And then the mood, whatever it was, was broken by the click-click of the closing grooves of the record. The crazy lady smiled and said, "Which one of you is going to bed with me? Or is it going to be both?"

I shook my head. Sorry, lady, but even before H kills your ability, it knocks out your interest. But Breeze nodded and he went off down the hall with her, leaving his sax on the sofa.

I drank more wine. I put Vivaldi's *Four Seasons* on the turntable. I listened to that fine baroque sound from that time when music and the world were tight and structured and I heard something else. Breeze and the crazy lady were definitely getting it on, the old push-rub-tickle.

Weird, huh, because, like I said, dope is guaranteed to un-do your ability to do. All I could figure was that the chick had really gotten to Breeze and that no chemical negativity could out-do what she had done to him.

Think enchantment or conjure or sex magic or as Screamin' Jay has it, "put a spell on you."

The solid truth? The *emmis*? In the end, it doesn't much matter.

*   *   *

Who was she?

Some of this I picked up pretty quick and other stuff I only fell onto later.

Name: Lanna Borland. Heiress of a family that made many, many coins shilling their chocolate bars to America's super-sweet tooth.

Occupation: Full time fun-seeker, liver of the good life, from Port-au-Prince to the Riviera. Three divorces. Notch the bedpost to kindling with all the affairs. A bullfighter in Madrid, a member of the Dutch royal family, a sometime starving charcoal artist in New Orleans, a Hollywood alleged actor who never did figure out if he dug women, men, or both.

Goals in life: Something new. Something different. Kicks.

Philosophy of life: Get what you want.

Call it the classic poor little rich girl riff: You get everything, you get it all, and none of it really does it to you, nothing ever quite manages to knock you out, to wig you, zonk you, and knock you over and so, maybe after a while, nothing means anything and you just keep on looking for something.

This time around, figures me, Lanna Borland's something was a jazzman.

And, man, she had him. Righteously. Breeze was solid gone on the crazy lady. Dead solid gone. She just started being there, being there all the time. She was a bringdown and a hangup to the music. Breeze and Micah and I trying to work up new charts, she was there. While we were blowing onstage at the Fickle Finger, she was there at a stage side table, those eyes lamping and vamping, doing a back beat on Breeze and his style. And when Micah and I tried to put it back together, to get it right and tight and true like it had been—sometimes—just the three of us grooving to the sounds inside we used to share, uh-uh, it wasn't three of us—it was four.

No. Not four. Split that. It was two and two. Micah and I. Breeze and Lanna.

She had Mr. B, one hundred and two percent, had him so that she was it—and there was nothing else.

There are women like that. And sometimes I'd get into this off-the-wall mind shpritz about her, how she came out of the lake, and how, oh yeah, every little kid knows it before you teach him otherwise, way, way out in the water, way deep in the water, that's where the real monsters live.

Lanna drained Breeze. She zombified him. And she slipped this dream into his head and blood to take the place of everything that was meant to be there. "Lanna's Song." He was going to write a tune for her. His mind was exploding with it, that's what he said, but that song didn't happen for a long time, for sure not then.

Breeze tried, tried like hell. And sometimes he thought he had it, asked me to do a minor slide-and-drift thing behind him. Then he'd shut his eyes and lay down a few notes. But those notes were never part of a song. They were always unconnected and alone.

Fact: The music went to hell. We fell into routines, repeating ourselves, re-tracing paths we had already worn out. When jazz is making it, it's as real an exploration as what Christopher Colombus pulled off; it's a voyage to a new world. But when you are not making it, uh-uh, you've got a nowhere trip on the city bus.

It was wrong. It was wrong for Breeze and Micah and me.

And naturally, Micah and I wanted Lanna Borland G-O-N-E gone. We did not hate her or anything like that. When you're cool, you do not hate.

Gone was just the way it had to be for her and for her to be gone was cool, okay?

*   *   *

Take it to the starting days of a cold autumn. It was a Saturday afternoon, the kind of dragging-slow time when you don't feel alive because most of you isn't. We were at the pad Breeze and I still shared but where he was spending less and less time.

We were there.

Micah and I.

Breeze and Lanna.

She was next to Breeze on the Salvation Army reject sofa. She wasn't wearing makeup and she had on jeans and a black turtleneck. Maybe she thought she was a beatnik. "Look," Micah was saying, "we've got to get it set, and get it down, and soon." He was moving jerky all around the room, staccato steps and twitching. He wasn't long for needing to fix.

"Okay, man," Breeze said. "Stay cool, okay?"

"Cool is cool and fool is fool," Micah said. A junky will say something like that and another junky will take it for profound.

The A and R man at BACA Records had been riding us

for a while, pressing to get us into the studio to lay down some new sides. This time around, looked like there'd be real distribution, thanks to a push we got from a critic at Metronome.

But Breeze was making bad kibosh on recording. We had to be ready. We wouldn't be ready, so sayeth the Breeze, until we had "Lanna's Song."

"Go slow, go slow," Breeze said. He stayed cool, but Lanna came on mucho cooler. She was turned toward him, knees up on the couch, and she was eye-balling him like the Amazing Kreskin.

"Go slow," Micah said. "Indubitably."

"Hey," Breeze said softly, "you're like some strung out. Why don't you unlax yourself?"

It was a good idea. Micah looked as though he were ready for the crawly-shakes. He was in need of a calm-down, slow-down trip to the no-nerves jangling beyond.

Micah nodded and said, "Yeah."

He turned to me. "I'm carrying but I'll need your works."

Call me Boy Scout with a merit badge in "Heroin": I was prepared. He started to follow me into the bedroom, but Lanna said, "I want to watch." There was something pretty wild working in her face. It was more than curiosity. Maybe it was hope.

Sure, she had known all along that the three of us were in the life. That's not a number you can hide from someone who's always there. But she'd never seen any of us fix.

You see, it was different then. The needle and you, that was a private thing, your time of prayer with your private god.

Breeze shrugged and said, "So she sees. So?"

So she saw. And so she dug what she was seeing, you could tell.

Micah was one smooth and careful user. He did the cooking slow, the tip of the flame caressing the bowl of the spoon. Dr. Kildare couldn't have been more precise drawing up the junk through the thin, sterilized needle.

Micah had me tie up his arm with my belt. He worked his fist to pump up the vein. I kept glancing at Lanna. The princess watching Rumpelstiltskin spin straw into gold.

"There we go. Nice one," Micah said when a clean and fat vein popped up, ready. He dabbed the inside of his elbow with an alcohol wet cotton swab. He raised the needle. He hit perfect the first time, and the fiery good news was on the way.

He didn't even have the needle out when it hit him.

"Christ," Micah said. "Beau-ti-ful." And you could see the transfiguration.

"Yeah," I said. I was getting a sympathetic rush off him. He began bobbing his head, drifting with music only he could hear.

"That's what I want," Lanna said.

"Uh-uh," Breeze said.

Micah came out of his bipping-trance scene. "What you want, baby?" he said. "Huh? You tell Papa Micah what you want."

She pointed at his arm where a drop of blood was a ruby on the blue river of the vein. "I want you to fix me up."

Nothing had to happen. I mean, there's no script in the skies that shapes your life. Lanna Borland did not have to suddenly come up with a new want, did she?

Or maybe she did. Maybe she had to because of the same reason she went swimming way out in the lake, trying to reach the place where the moon lay on the water. Maybe she thought the needle had that promise— and could deliver.

Breeze got up and walked to the window. He stood with his back to us. "How about it, Breeze?" Micah said. "She's your chick."

On the couch, Lanna was rolling up her sleeve. Breeze said nothing.

"Come on," she said.

"Right," Micah said. "Initiation time." Then he said to me, "The works, if you please."

All the time we were getting the fix ready, there wasn't a word from Breeze, not even a glance from him. We tied her up and watched the vein rise, bulging and ready.

"Give it to me," she said.

"You got it," Micah said. He swabbed her arm and my eyes met his.

The thing is, I think I knew. I think I could have stopped him. Maybe.

But the other thing, the bigger thing, is that I didn't want to.

And so he popped her. And then he said, "There you go. Now, kinda walk around and feel it."

She stood up and *Zoop!* Oh, yeah, she felt it. Her face went white. Her eyes rolled back. She dropped to her knees. She made one short sound that was not a word, and she flopped down hard on her face, and she was dead.

Breeze had turned around by then. His mouth hanging

open, he just mechanically shook his head from side to side.

Nobody did anything for a minute, and then it was time for somebody to do something, so I did. I got Breeze seated on the sofa. It was like moving a dude with a brand new lobotomy. I told him to stay put, not to move muscle one.

The way he was, I was sure he wouldn't.

And then Micah and I straightened up. I had to fix before I could get thinking the way I had to think, but we took care of it.

*   *   *

Life is not like TV's *The Line-Up* with the cops solving everything just before the last commercial. At least, it wasn't back then, okay? This was when *The National Enquirer* was a fake and nobody bothered investigating what the right folk didn't want investigated.

Lanna Borland was found a week later in a forest preserve near one of the city's northwestern suburbs. It was not front page, primetime news, not in those days. Back then, if you had money, you could buy "hush," and so, when a chocolate bar heiress makes an OD exit, there are things happening behind the scenes to guarantee, ultracool, no muss, no fuss, no scandal—and what we have here is "death by misadventure."

Micah split for the coast.

And Breeze and I stayed together. That is, we kept the pad. But the way Breeze was, I could have been the oily character in the turban taking care of the mummy in one of those antique Universal flicks.

178

Like you might figure, music was out.

Until one night, a few weeks later.

The temperature had dropped, not yet winter, of course, but a promise of certain winter. It was down in the 20s and there was that knife slice of wind that is exclusively Chicago's own.

Breeze left our place at midnight. His horn was with him. I was with him. I don't know if he wanted me, but there I was.

We went to that rocky beach that belonged to the summer. With the wind doing its work on the lake, the water looked as jagged and tearing as the rocks we stood on. I kept my hands in my pockets, wished my jacket were warmer. I wondered if I'd ever be warm again. I was high. I had the feeling I knew everything that was going to happen, everything that had to happen.

"She is out there, you know," Breeze said. His voice and the wind were one.

I started to say something. I didn't.

The moon was full. Far out there, where the world ended, the moon lay on the water. It was a place where you could maybe find monsters down deep in the lake, or maybe the exact spot on the earth where dreams died, or maybe the one point where you'd expect a crazy lady to be.

Then Breeze had the mouthpiece between his lips and he was playing. And he played warm as your own breath when the blanket's up over your chin. Then he turned it cold, and his cold was the midnight cold when you're alone in the house and every tick-tick of a pipe and the slow drip of a leaky faucet remind you of that aloneness.

And finally, he played a curling mist that was every dream that never will be.

179

He was playing a song. And I knew it was "Lanna's Song." He was still playing, variations on an end theme, as he walked stiff-legged into the waves.

That was how it had to be. So I let it be. And it seems I heard "Lanna's Song," the echoes of it, even when there was no reason to hear it anymore.

There are times I know I hear it still.

The Call

HOW DO YOU ANSWER THEIR questions?

How do you answer the question?

Just a smile, a "hello and how's it going" kind of guy down the block. 14 years a husband, ten years a father. He had a mortgage like the rest of us, okay? His kids seemed like sweet kids, pretty much, nice but not all that outgoing. For that matter, he wasn't that outgoing, not him or the wife.

Pretty wife. Remember back to the old kiddy shows on TV, the live ones when you could turn on the set and they'd have somebody playing kid games and showing cartoons and all? Beth Morgan had that sort of "live TV kiddy show host" smile. Not perfect, just pretty. But you saw her, you figured you'd probably like her.

Back to the question—

Well, Marv was pretty much a guy just like the rest of us, okay? You know what I mean.

What else can you tell the police or the reporters?

Marv Morgan. Mr. Enigma and a hell of a lot worse than that. But, okay, the reporters and the cops will go away after a while, and most likely, even the documentary TV videotapers will be gone and that is that. El Fin. All he wrote.

Yeah.

Written in . . .

So what you do is tell the kids they'd damned well better always let you know where they are and how long they're going to be there.

It probably is time to get dead bolts for all the doors. Hey, this old world is not what it used to be. Fact of life, and it sucks, but that doesn't make it any the less a fact.

And, you know, okay, you're a bullshit liberal but might not be a bad idea to have a gun in the house and you and the wife take some lessons in firearms usage: "How to Kill the Ass of Anybody Fucking with You . . ."

Might not be bad to—

—quit hammering your very own personal head with the question:

What in the name of God and/or the Devil makes a guy do something so . . .

—because you don't have a clue, Mister. Not doodley, not Jack, not nothin'.

You don't know about the telephone call that began it, that started it all . . .

*   *   *

He left the dinner table at the ringing and walked down the hall. He went to the small stand at the foot of the staircase and picked up the telephone.

"Hello," he said.

"Marvin."

He felt it then, the trill of the heart, the sudden onrush of vertigo and joy. He was confused and happy.

"Yes," Marv Morgan said.

"Do you remember what was done?"

"Yes," he said, and his lips moved as though he were praying. "It is now the time, Marv. It is now our time."

"Yes," he said. "Yes, yes, yes!" Then he put down the phone. He took in a breath, held it for a count of five, released it. He went back to the dining room and stood a moment in the doorway.

He looked at the two girls.

His children.

Beth Morgan.

His wife.

"Something wrong, dear?" she asked. His wife. "You look . . ."

He realized he was smiling, the kind of smile you have when you leave the dentist's office, nitrous oxide still bubbling in your brain and Novocain freezing your mouth. His daughters—his—chewed and swallowed and ignored him.

"No," he said, "everything is fine."

Then he sat down at the head of the table. His table, the head of the table. He looked at his wife, he looked, in turn, at each of the girls.

He laughed and didn't give a damn how it sounded.

Then he began to eat ravenously.

*　　*　　*

There has to be a reason. Has to be, has to . . . People just don't . . . Well, shit, yes, they do. Obviously they do. We've got the goddamned proof.

Okay, then, so we can't find a reason in the present, can't even find him, then it's time to go bopping into the past.

Talk to his high school teachers. His grade school teachers.

Talk to his relatives. His parents. A good boy. A shy boy, sort of. Liked to be alone with his thoughts. Hey, you could probably say all of us were like that, even those who pretended not to be.

Well, there was the "thing" with the dog when Marv was ten, but that didn't seem all that much. He said the dog ran off. Said it slipped the leash. Said he couldn't find it.

It was a pretty nice dog. Golden retriever, mostly. Had a happy face. Marv didn't cry or anything. He wasn't much of a crying kid, all in all.

But the dog never got found.

Marv Morgan. A kid like all the other kids. Average grades. Bicycle for Christmas. Helped with the household chores if you stayed on his back. Didn't really find anything all that funny in jokes, but he wasn't any kind of . . .

You know, if you try right this minute to picture his face in your mind, there's going to be sort of a blankness there. He just wasn't the kind of kid or, later, grown-up, that you would notice.

Oh yeah. He went to summer camp when he was 12. Camp Totem Pole. (Try that for stupid-plus names!) It was sponsored by an affiliation of suburban churches. Didn't cost too much.

Something did happen there.

Maybe . . .

*   *   *

He had just finished stowing his gear under the steel bunk's frame when cabin three's counselor walked in. He had seen counselors for other cabins. They looked like overaged campers themselves.

The man who stood at the door of the wood and wire mesh was different. His black hair was long, almost to his ears, his eyes were deep-set and dark.

"Hi, guys," he said. "I'm Peter. Peter Revson."

"Hi, Pete!" squalled the fat boy sprawled like a skin full of suet on the bed next to Mike's.

The counselor looked at the fat boy with a look that said nothing. "I'm your Camp Totem Pole counselor." He smiled for all of them then. "I'm supposed to teach you things."

The fat boy clapped his hands "Way to go!" His voice was a yip, like that of an injured dog. That was what Marvin thought. "Pete is neat! Pete is neat!"

Peter Revson pointed. "You."

It became quiet. He had that kind of voice. Outside, boys marched to their cabin by a counselor who was leading them in an offkey but spirited "Onward, Christian Soldiers."

"Me?" Fat boy was blinking.

185

Peter Revson nodded. "You," he said. "Stand up."

Bed springs squeaked. Fat boy's shorts were stretched tight over his watermelon gut and hung down to his baggy, elephant-skin knees. His Camp Totem Pole T-shirt stopped over an inch above his navel.

"What's your name?"

"Albert." Blubber lips shaped the syllables. "Albert Quanstrom."

"All right," Peter said. "Sit back down now, Quanstrom."

Peter's dark eyes went over the other boys one at a time.

He looked at Marvin. He smiled.

And Marvin Morgan smiled back.

Peter said, "Okay," and he left.

* * *

Who was there who really knew him, was really like tight with him? Not the neighbors, but somebody, though, someone along the way. Best friend or something. Has to be, right? Like when he was a kid. Uh-uh. You wouldn't call him unfriendly, but he wasn't best friends with anyone in particular, and that's a matter of record, assuming anyone ever thought there was a reason to keep a record on a bland-o, ho-hum, so what and who cares nonentity like Marvin Morgan.

Best friends? A real Kemo Sabe? Blood brother. Secret handshake and spit?

Nah, no one like that—

—that we know about . . .

No one . . .

*   *   *

It was Sunday afternoon. He'd slipped away from the hymn singing in the "long house." (Indian words. Respect for Native American culture. "We are all God's children." Sure. Smoke-um peace pipe and then slaughter your red asses.) He lay on his bunk, arms behind his neck. Overhead, a spider wove a web in the corner where two beams joined.

Maybe if he watched long enough, he would see a fly get trapped. He'd like that. It would give him a funny feeling in the base of his spine and his belly and brain.

The screen door creaked. He heard steps. Then Peter Revson stood over him. "You're supposed to be singing right this very instant. Don't you like to sing praise to Him from Whom all blessings flow, verily, verily?"

"It's okay. I just didn't feel like it."

"What do you like to do better, Marv?"

"I like to think."

Peter sat down on the side of the cot.

"Oh, I understand, Marv. You think about our world and all the people in it, that's what you think about. There's something else you like to think about, too."

"*What?*"

"How you're going to keep on fooling them, pretending you're just the same as they are."

Marv sat up. "I don't understand what you mean."

Peter Revson nodded in the direction of the long house. "You can hear them all the way over here. Make a lot of noise. It doesn't mean anything, though. They don't mean anything."

"Peter," Marv said, "well, hey! I don't get it. What are you saying?"

"Thing is, they think they have it all. 'The meek shall inherit the Earth.' They really believe they've got it already."

"Yeah," Marvin Morgan said. "That's like something I heard in Sunday school, I guess."

Peter put a hand on Marv's shoulder. His voice was soft, like a woman's. He spoke gently. "Our day is coming. Wheels turn. That is what wheels do. 'To everything there a season.' Maybe you got that in Sunday school, too."

"Maybe," Marvin said. "I don't remember. What are you getting at, Peter?"

Peter Revson tapped himself on the chest with his thumb. "I'm not one of them and I know it. I've always known it. They have names for those who are like us, when they occasionally recognize our existence. They don't want to consider Nietzsche. They don't want to consider the 'Myth of the Superman.' They just try to pretend we don't exist." Peter's thumb rapped again on his chest. "But I exist." He touched Marv's forehead, his index finger like the tip of a gun barrel. "You exist."

"I don't . . ."

"Don't fuck around, okay?" Peter Revson said. "You fuck around, you play the stupe from beyond Stupeland, it makes me want to knock your fucking head in. You know who we are, you do. You've always known."

"We're different," Marv said.

"That is right. We are different. And soon there will be a lot of us. You can feel it happening. When our time comes, we will be together and we will be strong. It will be our turn then. It will be our world."

"Peter, are you sure I . . ."

"Yes, I'm sure. I'm as sure about you as I am about me. That is my gift. I look and I know."

Then he rested his hand on Marv's shoulder. "You knew, too, didn't you? Knew me when you first saw me."

"Yes," Marv said, "I hoped . . ."

He started to cry.

*   *   *

So let's search the past. Go over it with a microscope. Logic. Deduction. Let's hope that hindsight has a value. The shrinkers want to know about nail-biting and bed-wetting, try to seek unresolved Oedipal conflict, Ego locked in battle with Id.

Then we get the "spiritual philosophers," hard to distinguish from the phony miracle prayer cloth assholes on the Christer programs, and they talk about the breakdown of family values, the turning away from belief, the . . . You know. No way to figure. Not really. Violence is now part of the 100 percent homemade, all-American pie. Don't think so? Try taking a walk at night on a city street. You'll have your throat cut because you scratched your nose and it looked like a "gang sign" to some degenerate asshole.

Catch the news a week or so ago? That kid who took daddy's assault rifle (AK-47 compatible!) and dusted four of his classmates. Not like he didn't have a reason. Hell, they gave him some shit about his Air Jordans. No sir, you can't dis a guy's athletic shoes and get away with it.

But you know it used to be better when we were kids. It was a less dangerous and an easier time. Remember, sitting around a campfire or something, late at night, dreaming about how terrific and just different it would be when you grew up?

Remember?

* * *

The fire crackled and pinpoints of red and orange flew wildly into the night sky. They were in a small clearing, on the other side of the lake. They had hiked all day. They were many miles from Camp Totem Pole.

Albert Quanstrom's pudgy hand slapped at the back of his neck. "Got him," he squealed. It was a moment of triumph for the fat boy. He rolled the mosquito's gooey remains between his thumb and index finger.

Peter Revson laughed. "All right, you killed him! Way to go. Now is it fun to kill a fucking mosquito or is it fun to kill a fucking mosquito?"

Albert's doughy face was puzzled in the firelight. "Hey, you're not supposed to talk like that!"

Peter Revson smiled. So did Marv. "Like fucking what? How the fuck am I supposed to fucking talk?"

"Well, you know . . ." Albert said. He blinked stupidly.

"Oh, I think I get it!" Peter said. "You mean because I'm a counselor at a fucking church camp I shouldn't say fuck. It's not a fucking Christian thing to do, huh?"

Marv laughed quietly.

"I mean," Peter said, "most good Christians wouldn't say fuck if they had a mouthful."

190

Albert scratched the side of his neck. "This is weird. How about . . ."

"Weird? What's weird, you fat fuck?" Peter Revson said. "Marv, do you think this is weird?"

"Definitely not weird," Marv said.

"Definitely not," Peter said. He opened the flap of his pack. Slowly took out the knife. The five-inch blade gleamed with the reflected fire. It looked beautiful, Marv thought, and he could smell the steel of it. His heart beat fast. "You see," Peter said, as he rose, the knife at waist level, "what's going to happen, Albert, is that we are going to kill you. Trust me, there's not one fucking thing weird about that." Albert's eyes filled his entire face. He snapped a horrified look at Marv.

"Marv, hey! Tell him to quit kidding around."

"Peter," Marv said, "quit kidding around." Marv smiled.

"I'm not kidding."

"He's not kidding," Marv said to Albert. "I'd say that one of the things Peter is not doing is kidding." Marv shrugged. "That's my opinion, anyway."

Peter moved toward Albert. Albert shuffled back on his hands and heels.

"What it is," Peter said quietly, "is I want Marv to see just how it is. Nothing to it, really. And it feels so . . . it feels so fine!"

"No!" Albert rolled, pushed himself up, tried to run.

But Marv was in front of him, grinning. He kicked him right in the balls.

Albert *whuffed* and made moist gagging sounds, doubling over. And then Peter was behind the fat boy, locking his left arm around Albert's neck. Now there was a snuffling sound along with the gagging and snot and drool and tears were wetting the boy's big-eyed face.

Marv moved closer. He wanted to see everything. He wanted to feel it. Albert's arms were waving spastically. Peter pressed him down, brought him to his knees, squatting behind him. He moved his left arm to cup a hand under Albert's blubbery chin. He pulled back the boy's head. He brought up the knife.

"Yes," Marv whispered. "Yes. Yes . . ."

The fire-shining blade lay across Albert Quanstrom's neck. Peter pressed the knife down hard and drew it across the boy's throat.

Albert's mouth opened wide. He looked surprised. A thin dark line appeared magically on his throat. It quickly thickened and bubbled and then gushed. Dark spray hit Marv's face and sizzled in the fire.

"See, Marv," Peter said, "nothing to it."

Peter and Marv talked late into the night. They spoke of a day, the day, that would come. It would be a while yet, but it would not be forever. There were others like Peter, right now, finding others like Marv.

And they were all of them born to kill.

Until their time—our time—until then, Marv would have to go on pretending, acting as though he were one of the others. His whole life had to keep on being a fake, but he must never stop believing in the promise of their bloody day, their killing time, their victory.

Peter would not forget him.

They were brothers. Blood brothers who found each other here at Camp Totem Pole. Marv realized it was a joke so he laughed.

Later, they hid Albert Quanstrom's body, disposed of the knife. Peter Revson was good at cleaning up. Nothing to worry about; he told Marv he had done this sort of thing 30, maybe 35 times. Kids, men, women, each one was different and each one was "exquisite." Yes, that was the only and right word.

"Yes," Marv said. He understood.

The next morning, they returned double-time to Camp Totem Pole. Albert Quanstrom had just wandered off. They spent the whole night searching, but couldn't find him.

Their story was believed.

"Of course," Peter said later, "this is what they want to believe, you see. If we told them, well, we took that puddle of puke out in the brush and cut his fucking throat, they would have a bitch-kitty of a time believing that."

Rangers, campers, and counselors, along with the town police, looked long and hard. The woods were dense. Dragging the lake revealed nothing.

It was a shame. Why, you could see how awful that poor young man, Peter Revson, felt. "It's all my fault," that's what he said again and again.

And Marvin Morgan, well, he must have been really good friends with poor Albert Quanstrom. The kid just lay on his bunk sobbing, and you could hardly get him to eat anything.

So the disappearance of Albert Quanstrom was a dark blot on the otherwise golden summer of the children, all the fine youngsters, at Camp Totem Pole.

* * *

Really, what's there to say? Just one of those things that happens and there is no way you, Sigmund Freud, or Dick Tracy can figure it.

What happens is just that your ordinary dude goes *el bonkers grande mucho-mucho*, and does something incomprehensible and horrible.

What you try to do, then, is just forget it, or forget about it as much as you can. Hell, with time, everything passes and all that bumper-sticker philosophy BS. And as you're working at forgetting it, you of course do think about it, right? Maybe you are watering the lawn or sitting in the tub wishing the kids had not used up all the hot water, and then you ask yourself, *Jesus H. Christ on a Harley, just what could have been going through that whack-adoo's mind before he did that?* You get a little shook, then, hoping, hoping to God you have never had thoughts like that—whatever they were—in your very own skull . . .

*   *   *

Marvin Morgan checked his Timex. It was two-thirty in the morning. He studied the small room he used as his office. It was nearly organized. There was a place for everything and everything was in its place.

Morgan smiled. This was not his room. It belonged to the pretender.

The pretender who had died with Peter Revson's telephone call. The pretender who, that night, had hugged the two children he fathered, had tickled them, laughed with them for a half hour at the Tasmanian Devil cartoon special on the Nickelodeon station. The pretender who had made love, slowly and gently, with Beth Morgan, who now lay asleep and unaware of his pretending.

No pretending.

Not anymore.

Not for him.

Not for any of them.

Marvin Morgan clicked off the light as he left the room. He walked down the hall, past the girls' bedroom. He listened to the special breathing sound made only by sleeping children. A few more steps took him to the master bedroom at the head of the stairs. Beth was a blanket-covered mound on her side.

He went downstairs, in the kitchen, he opened the drawer nearest the sink. The knife he chose was a good one, a Sabatier.

Then he went back up the stairs.

*　　*　　*

So, to sum it up, to give it definition and pretend that understanding comes with it, let's say Mr. Marvin Morgan (wherever he might be!) went ultimate psycho, okay? Let's say the elevator went all the way to the top and kept right on going.

Let's say . . .

Nothing that you don't pick up on every day.

Ten month old baby gets pitched into the incinerator. Says Momma dearest, "I just couldn't take her crying anymore, y'know? She was trying to drive me crazy, she really was, an' what she done was drive me crazy . . ."

A screwball senior citizen gets tired of pissing and moaning about the lumps in the mashed potatoes and so he takes a pump 12-gauge and goes at it on the whole first floor of the retirement center.

Junior high kid in Texas gets paddled three good whacks on the butt, for smoking, so he puts three .38s in the principal's head: that's an equation that makes sense to him.

Wife says she wants the carpet cleaned and next thing you know, hubby is giving her a pseudo-Sassoon haircut with a Black and Decker chainsaw.

Our world, ladies and gentlemen. A world in which we do have these awful insanities. These hideous, but isolated instances of homicidal dementia.

But it sure as hell is a damned good thing these lunatics are too warp-o to ever get together with one another.

Damn, they could really raise hell then, couldn't they?

Hansel, Gretel, and the Witch: Notes to the Artist

Dear Aline,

Your letter flatters me, even as your preliminary sketches honor me. (Just "silly scribbles" you call them, you modest young woman. And I can call you that, child, in that I am a far-too-boastful old woman!) I am certain our collaboration will be a marvelous success! After our discussions last summer, I cannot believe there is the slightest disparity in our most deeply held convictions regarding literature for young people. Moreover, though miles by the thousands are between us, I feel it is important that in our undertaking we demonstrate in our own way that people who know and hold to the True and the Good are the same in many nations, is it not so?

I pause now to positively blush as I read the para-

graph I have just written, so stodgy and pompous I am. Deliberately I began this note without a conventional heading, so that it might be no more formal than the many good "chats" we had last year when I visited your country. But, my dear Aline, it is possible that formality, even a rigidity of manner, is our national curse! Perhaps it is because your nation is so young, a child among nations, really, that you can, like children, candidly express your enthusiasm without undue social restraint.

I will soon send by postal air the opening of the book. I am excited over our working strategy, for with my submitting to you sections in sequence for your illustration as I write them, I will thus have your art to inspire me as together we grow a book for the beloved young people of a nation.

As I have heard in your country, "Let us put the show on the road."

* * *

Our beginning is as old as stars and sweet things, or maybe even older. I am certain you know it.

Once upon a time, a woodcutter and his family lived in a simple hut just beyond the town and just this side of the ever so deep woods. The woodcutter was a good man. He loved his country and he loved his God and he loved his wife and he loved his two children.

It would not surprise me any more than a potato pancake if you knew the names of the children.

The boy was named Hansel.

And the girl was named Gretel.

Ah ha! Is that what you say? You know this story, then? Fine, you may ah ha now, and even ah ho or ha ha ha if you wish, but sadly, dear children, though you think you know the story of these two precious ones, our Hansel and our Gretel, I must tell you that you do not.

Oh, no!

You do not, that is, know all of the story.

But you should.

And there are some parts of the story that are ever so much more sad than you could even imagine.

But that means, of course, as surely as sun shining down, that the ending of our story is destined to be gloriously, magnificently, and wonderfully happy.

To know the true story of Hansel and Gretel is to know and to understand how Good must always—always, always, always—triumph over Evil.

Then let us ask a question:

You know, of course, that the mother of Hansel and Gretel died.

But do you know how it was that she came to die?

You see, three days before God embraced her in His loving arms, she journeyed to the town to do her marketing. Times then were hard, and so she had to shop ever so very carefully, buying only what she absolutely needed. She admired a dainty thimble for her little Gretel but could not afford it. She regretfully regarded a shiny metal whistle on a chain for her little Hansel, but could not buy it. She felt unhappy because she could not give her children special gifts. Yet at the market, even during these so hard times, there were to be seen a very few people clothed in the finest, most gaudily expensive garments. They spent lavishly on this and on that, and on that and on this, and on two of anything else beside. Sometimes they talked among themselves in a strange language that sounded like a wicked song, a song like a frog might sing if it wanted to sound like a vulture.

Hansel and Gretel's mother became ill at ease when she noticed these rich ones gazing at her, gazing in a furtive way that was not meant to be noticed, their dark faces all pinched at the eyes and the heavy, purple lips too wet.

Hurriedly, she concluded her shopping, thinking how glad she would be to be gone from town and back again— safe—in her own home. And oh, if only she had returned to her loving home straightaway.

But she was hungry and she was thirsty. She could afford no food, but water was free at the well, and she drank deeply . . .

*　　*　　*

Dear Aline,

If I have any quibble (quibble, this is the word?) with your memorable renderings—and this quibble is hardly even of such a nature as to be termed a "true quibble"—it is in the way you give us the "little man who looked as much like a troll as a man, who sneaked and slipped around at night like a great rat, who sputtered in the daylight and muttered in the night's dark . . ." This character is a vassal of the Witch, of course, yet he delights in doing evil for its own sake. He was born to it. So at midnight, when he is poisoning the well, you have a perfect opportunity to make his grotesque visage still more bizarre and vermin-like

*　*　*

. . . clever, and when cleverness is bent upon wickedness (let all good people be vigilant and resolute!). The poison was a terribly cunning concoction of a nature most peculiar.

Upon a sturdy or robust person, it might have no effect, or cause only the slightest of stomachaches or headaches. But upon those of a delicate constitution, or upon those who were very young or very old, or upon those who had been weakened by the unnatural physical rigors and mental strain caused by poverty, this hideous poison had a far more grave and morbid result.

Thus did our poor Hansel and Gretel come to be bereft of their good and loving mother.

Thus did an overwhelming grief seize the poor woodcutter. Now, he worked harder than ever, setting his mighty ax to ringing on trees deeper and always deeper into the endless deep that was the deep woods. He worked until he could no longer raise his long-handled ax, until he could no longer raise his arms, until he could no longer raise his head. Only then, too weary to work and too weary to weep, would the sorrowful man return to his home.

But one day . . .

*　*　*

I wish even a hundredth part of your artistic gift were mine, my dear Aline, so that I might share with you in a drawing, no matter how crude, the missing quality I feel needed here, but the truth is, I appreciate your talent not just for its own sake but because I can do nothing with pencils, chalks, watercolors, or oils. Even as a very young child, I was berated by my teachers who would say that if I drew a simple stick figure, it would be too round.

So, let me remind you of a woman we greatly laughed about when you were so kind as to take me to the game of baseball at the Wrigley Field. Surely you will recall her, sitting behind us in the stands, with her loud and overly exuberant family.

She could have been thought quite pretty in a haughty way, but you had the right of it to say she doubtless had to wax her mustache at least three times a week! And when she spoke in that voice that could curdle milk or etch glass, there was no question of what she was

*   *   *

. . . a short distance from the hut.

"Father loves her," Hansel said.

"Very much," Gretel replied.

"She does not love him," Hansel said.

"No," thoughtfully replied the good Gretel. "It is as though she says the words of love, but they are not true. It is as though she wears a mask of love, but it fools him. It does not fool me."

"Nor am I fooled, dear sister," said Hansel with a sigh, "but I cannot speak to Father about this. I have tried and he will not listen. He gets a sad and unbelieving look on his face and asks me why I hate so much a woman who loves us so much."

Gretel nodded, saying, "She pinches me. She scratches me. I have marks. She slaps me. I do not cry." Then with firm, if sorrowful, resolve, she added, "I will never cry before her."

"She wishes to do us great harm, I have no doubt," Hansel said. "Last night, she thought I was sleeping, but, though my eyes were closed, I lay awake in my bed as she stood over me . . . She was whispering in the way a serpent might whisper. She said, 'My mistress will be pleased with you, my little Hansel. Ever so pleased with you!' I do not know what she means, Gretel, but I fear her."

"As do I," Gretel said. "Brother dear, what can we do?"

"We can pray to the good God above, that He will notice our plight and come to our aid."

And there, my dear, children, trusting in the Lord . . . our Hansel and Gretel knelt and folded their hands, and a narrow sunbeam from the holy sun of heaven fell upon them and it seemed to silently speak a golden promise . . .

* * *

Perfection itself! So cunning the trap! This is the house of the Witch! In their innocence, feeling betrayed and abandoned, there is no wonder that this gilded palace of wickedness beckons them and they heed its call

* * *

. . . for as great as were her magical evils, no less formidable were her talents as an actress. "I am Judith," said the Witch from the doorway, a claw-like hand gesturing to entice Hansel and Gretel closer. "I am alone and I am

203

lonely because of my ugliness. Grown-up people are cruel, but children have hearts pure and good. It is to your hearts, pretty ones, that I appeal as I entreat you to come into my home, to be happy and end my loneliness . . .

* * *

. . . hoped by now to see Judith the Witch; I am so certain she will be a memorable horror indeed, far more terrifying than Mr. Disney's witch in the cartoon movie you took me to see, Snow White and the Seven Dwarfs. If, however—er, you are having difficulty "designing" her (Is that the proper term? What an artist might say?), let me suggest that you give her a prominent, beak-like nose. It would be good, too, I think (and I know I am not an artist, so if this is foolish, forgive me) to make Judith's eyebrows wild and fiercely black, like the rough fur of a predatory animal and

* * *

. . . the unknown letters, if indeed they were letters, twisted and evil, almost as though they were diabolically squirming upon the ancient pages.

This book, little Gretel thought, was the source of Judith's power! If only she might learn the secret language of the old book, she could free Hansel from the cage and they would flee this dreadful house and the horrible witch!

"You little fool!" Judith's shout made Gretel spin about. The Witch had sneaked up on her, and now stood, cackling insanely and joyfully, waggling a bony, long-nailed finger at her. "My magic is in the book, that is what you think!" Judith's voice made a bubbling and breaking sound, like a cauldron on a fire. "But what of all my other magic? Look there!"

Judith the Witch pointed to the entrance of the house, where, on the door-post, was a foreign-looking charm adorned with a wavering, three-fingered design like the mark of a crowfoot in the dirt.

"Look there!" Judith the Witch pointed to an upside down crucifix over the mantelpiece, and Gretel seemed to see Our Dear Lord writhing in anguish, and seemed to see Him dripping blood from his hands and feet and side, and seemed to see Him dripping blood and tears from His endlessly patient eyes, and seemed to hear Him say, "And still they kill Me, and still these perfidious people murder me!"

"Look there!" Judith the Witch pointed to the far corner of the room where Hansel, his eyes big, a filthy cloth in his mouth, and heavy ropes wrapped all about him, lay in the cage. "Oh, yes, pretty little girl, your brother's blood will be upon my doorposts and upon my lips. And then when he is emptied like a pig peasant's wineskin, into the oven I will pop him, and cook him for a feast that I will prepare for the Elders . . .

*   *   *

. . . waited and waited, checking the post faithfully. I attempted to telephone you yesterday, but, as you can understand with world events being what they are, it was impossible to have the connection made.

I do hope you are not ill, my dear Aline. I so look

forward to your presentation of Judith's demise, as Gretel hurls her into the oven, and she is consumed by flame to become smoke and ash and vanish forever from the face of the Earth

* * *

. . . a warrior. He was a great man, and so it goes without saying (although, the chatterbox that I am, I say it to you, my dear children) that he was also a good man, for only a good man can achieve greatness.

It was not mere happenstance nor anything as foolishly unreliable as luck that guided his steps through the deep woods. Our Good and Eternal God had heard the prayers of Hansel and Gretel, had heard the prayers of millions, and so

. . . shocked and sad, I truly thought we had commenced a long lasting and artistically gratifying collaboration.

It is not impossible I misunderstood your comments during the time we shared while I visited your country. Still, I thought your remarks about "those people," particularly your comments about their, let us say, over-representation, in the fine and performing arts, the medical establishment, and, most importantly, the world of finance, to indicate that you were not in disagreement with the views the majority of us are free to openly express in my country.

Life is strange, as well we both know, and I can only hope that, despite the vehemence of what you call your "final note" to me, there will come a time when we are

again creating together, when we are again friends.

Though you request I destroy your art, this I cannot bring myself to do. I will instead return it so that you may do as you choose.

It is my plan to seek out an artist in my own country, one who understands (your word) my goals and aims as I continue to write for the dear children, dedicating my work to the youth of today, tomorrow, and a thousand years of tomorrows.

Other Advantages

I WALK INTO THE STORE about one o'clock in the afternoon, and Mr. Rotello, the owner, is at the checkout, putting a quart of milk in a sack for an old lady who comes in every day.

"Hello, Manuel." Mr. Rotello gives me a big smile, like he's glad to see me, you know, and he smiles at the old lady, too. Mr. Rotello, he smiles a lot and he most of the time looks happy. He's got that kind of face, you know what I mean? Like nothing ever bothers him.

The old lady, though, she's not smiling when she walks past me and out the door, moving slow like there's no reason to hurry home because there's probably nobody there waiting for her anyway. There's plenty of people in the world like that, I guess, but it seems like most of them live around here.

I go into the back room, limping a little, my bad left leg hurting from the long walk to the store. I take the apron down from the nail in the wall by the door that leads back out into the alley. I'm whistling as I tie on the apron. I'm feeling pretty good. See, I only have this job about a week, but it's nice, you know? Mr. Rotello is a friendly guy and he pays me okay and if my mother asks me to bring something home, Mr. Rotello lets me take it for cost.

Tell you, it wasn't so easy for me to get a job, either, with the short leg and the way I sound when I talk English. I mean, the truth is I sound a lot like that cartoon guy you used to see on the TV commercials, the "Frito Bandito." But, okay, no problem for Mr. Rotello, he tells me. He says it's good to have a guy working for him that speaks Spanish because we have plenty of Puerto Rican and Chicano customers. My short leg isn't any big deal, either, is what Mr. Rotello says, because it doesn't matter when you're pushing buttons on a cash register or setting cans of Ajax on a shelf. Really, if the store wasn't in such a bad neighborhood, I'd think I had the best job there could be—for me, anyway.

With my apron on, I go up front. The boss is sitting on a stool behind the register. He's smoking a cigarette and he's real careful to put the ashes in an ashtray. A lot of guys that owned their own store wouldn't be careful like that, you know? They'd just throw ashes all over the place and grind out the butt on the floor because they're not the ones that sweep up. But the boss, uh-uh, Mr. Rotello, he's not like that.

"Well, boss," I say, "what do you want me to do first?"

Mr. Rotello scratches his head where there's not much

hair anymore and says, "Oh, the usual, I guess. It doesn't look like rain so it might be a good day to do the windows. I think we're running low on cereals, so bring in a couple cases from the back and get them on the shelves."

I turn to get the cornflakes for aisle three, but Mr. Rotello calls me back. "You see the movie on channel eight last night?"

Sometimes I get the feeling that the boss hired me so he'd have someone around to talk to. Probably it got boring for him being alone in a grocery all day.

"No," I tell him. "I don't watch a lot on the television. See, my mother she gets on me. She thinks you watch too much, it makes you lazy and stupid and all."

Then I realize what I said to Mr. Rotello, and how it sounds pretty snotty even if I didn't mean it like that, but the boss just says, "Your mother's probably right, Manuel," and he laughs and goes on, "but this was a good film. Lots of action. John Wayne . . ."

It does sound like a good film. Mr. Rotello gets kind of worked up talking about it, telling me how John Wayne shot the bad guy off the porch and he got the one behind the water trough and how he turned just in time to blast this guy sneaking up on him.

Anyway, we talk a little more and then Mr. Rotello tells me he's going out for a while and that I should keep my eye on things.

That makes me pretty proud, you know, the way he trusts me to watch the whole store and take care of everything.

So, the next couple of hours, I get the windows washed, inside and outside. I roll in a carton of cornflakes and get the boxes on the shelf, real straight and right so they don't all come down if someone buys a box. A couple of customers come in but nobody buys too much. People around here don't have a lot of money to spend.

Sometimes I wonder how Mr. Rotello makes enough money for himself and to pay me a salary both. I bet it's not easy.

After a while, I take a rest, sitting on the stool back of the counter. I'm really pleased with myself. The store looks good, no dust on the cans, no dirt on the floor. That's the way stores ought to look. Now some of the places around here . . . There's this "credit jeweler's" across the street with a load of shining, glittery junk in the window that you can spend the rest of your life paying for. There's the corner liquor store that sells muscatel and quarts of beer for twice what they should be to people who are too broken down to go to places farther away where they could get fair prices. Tell you the truth, plenty of the stores here are in business just to suck the blood out of folks who don't have anything much but their blood to pay.

Anyway, I'm just sitting, not doing anything really, and my eye lands on the gun. It's hanging on a peg on the underside of the countertop, and seeing that ugly piece of steel makes me a little bit nervous, you know what I mean? Oh, I saw that gun first day I came to work for Mr. Rotello, but still, every time I look at it, it doesn't make me feel too good. It's a .38, I think, like the detectives on the TV cop shows have, and sometimes I think what a lousy thing it is that a really good guy like the boss, who runs a good, clean store and doesn't bleed people with big, fat prices has to keep a gun for protection.

Mort Castle

Uh-uh, it's not a perfect world, but like my mother is always saying, it's the only one we've got.

So, I'm thinking about the world, and that can get you down, you know, but before I get too hung up on thinking, The Professor comes in. The Professor's about a hundred years old. He's shaking more than usual, but he still tries to give me a smile before he goes down aisle four. He stands there a long time, hugging his brown overcoat around his poor old shaking body, and looks over everything very careful-like before he makes up his mind about what he wants.

Today it's a bottle of soy sauce that he brings up to checkout.

The Professor's mouth is working like crazy, like this time, today, he knows exactly what it is that he wants to say. It must be real important, too, the way he's trying to get it said, but he just can't do it. He mumbles something that doesn't come close to being words. Finally, looking really disappointed, he pays for the soy sauce with pennies, nickels, and dimes.

"That's okay, man," I tell him, to let him know that if he ever manages to say it, I'll be willing to hear it, and I put his soy sauce in a sack. The Professor leaves, and I'm trying to figure out why people call him the Professor and just what it is that he does with the stuff he buys. Everyday he comes in and everyday it's something different: one time crackers, another time stuffed olives. I guess The Professor is a crazy, but there's a lot of crazies in the world and most of them never do anything bad or hurt anyone.

The boss is back around three or so and he's in a real good mood, singing to himself. He tells me I did a fine job on the windows and then he goes in the back to hang

212

up his coat. When he comes back to the counter, he asks me if there were a lot of customers while he was out.

"No, boss," I say.

"What?" he says, slapping his forehead and rolling his eyes. "You mean Mrs. Van der Rich didn't drop by to pick up her order of imported bamboo shoots? What about the squabs I special ordered for the Rockefellers?"

I tell the boss I don't know anything about those people and then I get the joke and we're both laughing. You laugh with a guy, it's a good feeling, you know, the kind of feeling that makes you think you can say anything at all and it will be all right. So I decide to ask Mr. Rotello a question that's been bugging me since maybe the second or third day I started work. I'm pretty sure the boss won't take it wrong.

"How come you have a grocery store, boss?"

Mr. Rotello stops laughing and his face gets real serious, like maybe he's remembering something from a way long time ago. Then he wets his lips with tongue and looks at me like he's going to tell me a real big secret.

"I guess everybody has a dream, Manuel," he says. "Do you think mine was to someday have my own grocery store?"

I don't answer his question, and it's bugging me that I didn't wind up really asking him what I wanted to in the first place. A lot of times, see, I'm thinking in Spanish and when I say it in English it's nothing like what I really meant to say.

"When I was a kid," the boss says, "I always thought I'd grow up and do something exciting. I mean, when I was eight, I wanted to be a cowboy. Cowboys were a big thing then, Manuel. Like Tom Mix or Buck Jones or Bob

Steele. Then, a couple years later, I figured I'd be a cop. I'm not talking about the kind of cop who spends his life writing parking tickets, you know. A real gangbuster, a G-man, Dick Tracy or something."

I nod my head to show Mr. Rotello I'm following him, even though he's not answering my real question, the one that didn't get asked. I tell him, "My grandfather used to tell me how he wanted to go to Mexico City to be a matador. He was a farmer instead until he came to this country to pick oranges and grapes."

"Oranges and grapes," the boss says. "Yeah, me too. I work with the oranges and the grapes. And cornflakes, and pancake syrup, and cans of ravioli. You know how it goes. I got myself married right after high school. Then there were the kids, one right after another for the first five years there. A man's got to earn a living. You've got to be practical. Then all you are is practical, you're practical all the time, and don't do much dreaming anymore."

He stops talking and even though his eyes are still on me I can tell he's looking somewhere else, somewhere way faraway. Neither one of us says anything for a while and I get this feeling I can't explain but don't much like. To get rid of that feeling, and because I still want to know about the boss and this store and all, I ask, "But why do you have a store in a crummy neighborhood like this?"

Sure enough, my strange feeling goes away when Mr. Rotello laughs, and there's this happy wrinkle by his eye, and he looks like maybe there's still a Dick Tracy or a cowboy he keeps inside of him.

But the boss doesn't talk about dreams or anything like that.

"See, Manuel, I bought this store at a good price. It

was what I could afford without getting up to my butt in debt. I don't have competition from the big supermarkets down here and I don't have to spend a fortune in advertising. Besides, this is only a half-hour drive from my house."

It's funny, but what the boss says doesn't seem to make a whole lot of sense to me. Okay, I can see a guy like the credit jeweler on the other side of the street running his business here because it gives him a chance to bleed people until there's nothing left but the crappy fake Rolex they bought that quit working five years ago and a monthly payment book with a thousand tickets left to go.

But Mr. Rotello, uh-uh, he's not like that, not that kind of guy.

So I say, "But Mr. Rotello, what I'm talking about is this crummy neighborhood and you know what I mean crummy, okay?" See, there are plenty of sad, lonely, broken-down people in this part of the city, but there are mean ones, too. Okay, the wineheads that cover themselves up with newspaper and sleep in doorways, they're too beat down to hurt anybody, but there are others, you know, like all the junkies that walk around looking like they just came out of the grave or the street punks that hang out on the corner just hoping for bad trouble. I mean some of the mean guys around here will cut your throat for a quarter. The junkies, well, they're crazy, and it doesn't matter how many cop cars cruise the streets. A junky goes crazy wild in the head when he needs his dope and he'll shoot you or slice you or hit you in the head if he thinks you've got any money or anything he can hock for money. It doesn't matter to a junky, you know, and then, there you are, just dead in the street or the alley somewhere.

"I mean, Mr. Rotello, in some stores I bet you don't have to keep a gun under the counter. You don't have to worry about a stick-up every five minutes, right?"

Mr. Rotello gets a look on his face, like maybe he has a secret or something but it's going to stay just between him and himself.

"I guess you're right, Manuel," he says. "This is a tough neighborhood, but I don't mind running my business. There are other advantages . . ."

But Mr. Rotello doesn't get a chance to tell about those "other advantages" because here comes Mr. Wood, a real old man, and he's yelling at the top of his lungs like it's us that's deaf and not him, and he wants me to show him where the catfood is. Of course, it's where it always is, but I limp down aisle three with Mr. Wood following, yelling about his new cat, real happy now that he's got twenty of them. Mr. Wood and I carry twelve cans of Hap-E-Cat up front and Mr. Rotello bags them all up.

The day goes on. People come and go, buy a little something, maybe say a few words to me and the boss. Somehow, though, as the day goes on, Mr. Rotello and I don't get to talking serious anymore.

Anyway, it's about a quarter to nine, near closing, and we're both standing behind the counter, and I'm about to ask the boss if he can give me a ride home the way he usually does, when we get trouble.

Two guys walk through the door. They're young, but they have an old bad look, like poison's in their guts and running in their blood. One guy is short and he's got real thin blond hair that looks like a sick halo. The other one is a tall guy. His hair is slicked back and greasy. They both are wearing long coats that have to be seven sizes too big, the kind of clothes you buy at the Goodwill for a dollar.

These guys walk down past the canned soda and they're standing there together talking in real quiet voices.

You know how the television cops are always saying, "I had a feeling of danger?" That's what it was for me, I guess, like I'd swallowed a brick or something, and, all over, I was cold like I'd been inside a walk-in freezer for a month.

"Mr. Rotello," I say, edging closer to him, "I don't like the way . . ."

"It's all right, Manuel," the boss says softly. "Nothing to worry about."

So I just stand there next to him, scared, thinking the boss is wrong. These guys are going to be something very bad. I can see it. The short, blond guy, he's a junky for sure. You can see the barbed wire under the skin on his face. The junkies lose their bones and get wire instead when they have to have their needle.

But Mr. Rotello isn't shook at all that I can tell. The two guys walk all around the store, and then the tall one goes over by the door and the blond guy is in front of the boss and me at the counter. He puts his hand in the pocket of that too big coat and comes out with a gun and he waves it at us.

You know, my mother's always saying I ought to go to church every Sunday, and right then I'm thinking she's right and I'm making all kinds of promises to God and hoping I don't have to stand before Him real soon.

I sneak a quick look at Mr. Rotello and then I feel just

217

a little better because the boss is so calm I don't half believe it. It's almost like this is all a movie he's seen a couple of times already and he knows that everything works out okay.

The blond guy aims the gun right at me and says, "You, put your hands on the counter and keep them right there where I can see them." He's got a squeaky voice, crazy-like, and it sounds like he's not all the way sure what he's doing but he's going to go ahead and do it anyhow.

Tell you, maybe guys on television are always looking into gun barrels and it doesn't shake them and they still talk tough and snotty and everything, but me, I slap my hands flat on the counter.

Then Mr. Rotello, sounding like he's just saying "Hello" or something, tells the guy, "There's not much in the register, friend. Why don't you and your buddy forget it and get out of here and save us all a lot of trouble?"

The gun gets pointed right at Mr. Rotello's head. "Shut up!" the guy says, and I hope that the boss does shut up. "Open the register and keep your big mouth closed."

Mr. Rotello hits the button. The drawer flies open and the register's "No Sale" flag goes up. The boss picks up the bills—there's not more than forty bucks, I guess—and hands them over.

The blond guy stuffs the money in his pocket with his left hand and says, "The change, too."

Mr. Rotello sniffs like he's going to laugh. I'm praying that he doesn't. The shooting could start any second. Then Mr. Rotello hands the guy the coins, too, and the blond guy starts backing to his pal at the door. The tall one opens the door and slips out and the blond guy starts to leave, too, when I feel—I mean, I don't really see—Mr. Rotello move.

He bends down, real quick, and takes the gun off the peg under the counter.

"Hey!" Mr. Rotello yells. The blond guy isn't outside yet. He turns and his eyes are real big. He starts swinging the gun back toward us, but there's this explosion and a flash of fire from Mr. Rotello's pistol, and the blond guy jumps straight up into the air like one of those dumb Saturday morning cartoon characters on television. He hasn't even hit the floor yet and Mr. Rotello is pushing past me and around the counter and out the door and then I get the idea: The boss is after the other guy!

I'm kind of ashamed of myself for acting like a big chicken and all so, when I can get my legs to stop shaking, I go running out, too. Maybe the boss will need my help or something. I have to step around the guy by the door, though, and what I see makes me a little bit sick. He's kind of in a heap, like dirty laundry, and some of his head is all punched in, and the floor that used to be so clean is real bloody.

With the short leg, I can't run too fast, but outside, up ahead, there's Mr. Rotello moving like he's after Olympic gold. He stops at the corner, under a streetlight, and he looks from side to side, and then he goes running to the left. When I get to the corner, I see the boss turn into the dead end alley that runs behind the store. I follow as quick as I can, and when I'm at the entrance to the alley, there's Mr. Rotello, standing still. His left hand is on his hip. He's turned sideways. His right arm is straight out. He's aiming.

The tall guy is racing down the alley past the garbage

cans and piles of trash and tossed away old furniture. The way he's moving, it's like he doesn't even see the brick wall ahead of him and he's planning to go right through it.

The boss shuts his left eye. Something real funny comes onto his face, then, and for a second, it's like nothing is real. Mr. Rotello's not real, the guy running away isn't real, there was no holdup, nothing. It's almost like I'm watching a movie or reading a comic strip, and everyone is—flatter—and less real than everything really is.

Then the gun makes a big bang in the boss's hand and his arm jerks up and everything is really real again.

The stickup guy looks like someone invisible hits him with a flying tackle and knocks the legs right off him. He spins right, slams into a garbage can, and bounces off onto a pile of trash.

He's starting to get up when Mr. Rotello shoots again and then that's it. The guy isn't moving or anything. He's just sprawled there on the trash.

Back in the store, we don't have long to wait. The sirens are screaming real soon and I'm sitting at the counter and there's a whole bunch of cops coming in. I look at the gun on the peg under the counter, and there's this sick feeling in my stomach like you can get when you're afraid something is wrong and you're even more afraid that you know just what it is.

Two guys in white get the blond guy off the floor, cover him up on a stretcher and haul him away. A couple of policemen are asking me questions, and I guess I'm answering because I can hear my voice, but what I'm really doing is watching what's going on in front of the counter. There's a big cop with a long face slapping Mr. Rotello on the shoulder and saying, "Man, you are something else. How many does that make?"

"Five, I guess," the boss says, "in the past eleven months."

"Damn," the big cop says, "Rotello, your killed and wounded record's better than any officer's in the precinct."

I guess I'm acting strange because the policeman who's talking to me keeps asking me to repeat answers to questions that I thought I'd already answered. But, you know, I'm just not feeling good, no good at all. I'm remembering the way Mr. Rotello looked back there in the alley, and I think I'm understanding maybe why his face looked the way it did, and I have this idea why he has the store in this crummy neighborhood.

So I'm sick to my stomach, and maybe sad or something, too, but whatever it is I'm feeling, it's all squeezed up real tight in my throat, and I'm thinking I have to quit this job because I don't want to work here anymore.

Big Brother Mulbray and the Little Golden Book

WITHOUT SPEAKING, MULBRAY SITS IN the passenger seat of the Volkswagen as his younger sister, Wendy, drives away from the town and onto one of the many gravel farm roads. Soon now, Mulbray knows he will have to talk, that the reason Wendy said, "Hey, want to take a ride?" is because she wants to talk to him alone, without their parents being anywhere around.

But for now, Mulbray finds it good to breathe in the gritty dust that encircles the car and to pretend he is no one. Not the divorced, couldn't make it work, failure Mulbray, not the Fatherly Flub-a-Dub, not the nowhere piano man in a nowhere cocktail lounge, not anyone, no, not anyone at all.

"Well, let's go down here," Wendy says.

All right, he's willing to go anywhere. He doesn't even

have the responsibility of driving to worry about—and that's the way he likes it. He needs time to float, to do nothing and be no one.

Wendy turns the wheel and the VW slides onto a narrower still dirt road, hits a dip that slams Mulbray's head into the roof, then a bump that jerks him back down. "Sorry," Wendy says. "I should have warned you."

A little ways down the road, Wendy pulls into the drive of a Depression era deserted farmhouse. She says, "You smoke, don't you?"

"Yeah, sure," Mulbray says.

He understands that the distance between them is very great—ten years and who knows how many incidents—and that so great a space can only be bridged by ritual.

"In the glove compartment," Wendy says. "I didn't know if you smoked or not."

"Yeah, sure," he says. He takes out the baggy filled with dried bits of brown and green, package of rolling papers peeking from the top of the plastic. "When I first went to Chicago, I used to go out to the South Side and jam with some of the black dudes down there. Around Sixty-third and Vincennes. Real dump. Just walk in and pow! Smoke was real thick in there. Two deep breaths got you off."

Mulbray talks and tries to roll a joint, but it does not go well, too many stems and seeds, and each time he thinks he has it, a jiggle of his hand separates the whole into little unconnected dots in the valley of creased paper. "Yeah," he says—jiggle-jiggle, stems here, seeds there, goddamn—"used to toke with those dudes. You know, between sets"—jiggle-jiggle, goddamn—"Dude on drums had real good hands. Fast. I learned a lot from those black dudes."

Sure did, thinks Mulbray, fingernail directing marijuana where it belongs, *That bastard on the beat-to-hell bass used to blow me right off the stage. How did he get that bass to boom louder than a goddamn piano, huh? Fucking coons. Between their smiles and their dope they convinced you that you were a white McCoy Tyner or maybe even the white race's edition of Teddy Wilson. Oh, you were hip, you were outta sight, you were with it, running those single line John Lewis right hand improvs while those dudes grunted "Go, man," and "You got it." All the time you were laying it down, showing off your chops, they were laughing their asses off behind their black masks of cool. One night you came for a gig, and, before the set, the bass player took a lit joint from his mouth, handed it to you, and said, "Here, man, take a hit. Then fuck off." The joke was over.*

"Here," Wendy says. "Let me roll that."

She rolls a perfect bomber of a joint in 18 seconds flat. Mulbray says, "You know, it's been a while. When I was gigging with those black dudes I used to roll 'em one-handed, like a cowboy."

He realizes he is talking too damned much: "The Adventures Of Mulbray And The Black Jazzmen." Jesus Christ.

Wendy puts the finished joint on the narrow ledge of the dash and immediately begins work on another.

The Volkswagen's windows are up so none of the smoke can escape. The interior of the car smells like all of Italy set ablaze, a warm earth and oregano odor mingled with Mulbray's sweat. Two joints are gone, a third begun, and Mulbray is not only relaxed but buzzing with awareness of the whorls of his fingertips, his toenails catching the threads of his stockings, his nose and his knees. Each sensation is a second's focal point.

"Good stuff, huh?" Wendy says. She passes him the joint.

"Dynamite." A fine tingling emanates from the nape of his neck, branching into two humming wires that terminate directly behind his earlobes. Certainly they will be able to talk soon, Mulbray decides, now that his buzzing wires are in place.

And so, it begins, with Wendy saying, "How are you?"

"Fine," he says, "Just fine."

"No, I mean really. I mean, the divorce and all."

"It wasn't that bad," Mulbray says. In fact, he thinks, it was oh so civilized: his lawyer, her lawyer, several meetings in offices, a few words before a judge, "I don't" and "I don't" and then they weren't, and that was that, visitation rights, and no complications, no marriage. Goddamn, what a hell of a country we live in.

"No," says Mulbray, "it really wasn't too bad."

"That's good."

Yeah, thinks Mulbray.

"See," Wendy says, "one of the reasons I wanted to talk to you, well, I mean, see, there's this guy I'm kind of going with, more or less and, well, it's not serious yet, but it's looking like it could get serious.

"So, anyway, how are you supposed to know if you love somebody?"

"I don't know," says Mulbray.

"You were married and you were in love, right?"

"Yes."

"So?"

225

"So."

"A lot of times, see, I get these real silly fears, things that I know don't make any sense or anything because I know we are both really in love, I guess. But all the time I know we're in love, thinking that things aren't the way they should be, like maybe there's something wrong. Maybe nothing will work out like it's supposed to. You see what I mean?"

"Yes," says Mulbray.

"So, I guess my question is, how can you tell if you're really in love?"

Mulbray sighs. Damn it, he has lived a long time; he is obligated to have knowledge of such things, to have had experience with the things that matter. And so he says, "There's no scale or chart," and then he halts, realizing he will sound like the baritone lead in a grade-Z musical comedy.

He must choose his words carefully, for what he says now will affect, may even shape, his sister's entire life. He reviews his knowledge of love, but cliches keep interfering: "Love and marriage go together like a horse and carriage; falling in love with love; it's wonderful, it's marvelous; some enchanted evening you may meet a stranger; love is something deep inside that cannot be denied; love makes the world go round. Everything goes around and around and around . . ."

So does Mulbray's marijuana-melted mind.

"Huh?" says Wendy.

All right, he has it now. He will tell her a story, a story that perfectly illustrates all that love is, can be, and should be.

He will tell Wendy a true story.

* * *

"Look, Wendy, when I was seven—you were only two then, so you probably won't remember any of this—I saw a sailboat in the window of Wellman's toy store. You know, the one on the square. It had a fire engine-red hull, and two stiff white sails. It was right there between the Fort Apache set and a big can of Tinker-Toys, there was a Daisy rifle that shot corks, too, I remember, and I think there was a big cardboard picture of that Filipino kid, Johnny, the Duncan yo-yo kid. He used to go around to all the school playgrounds and show the kids how to do the fancy yo-yo tricks, stuff a lot trickier than spank-the-baby or walk-the-dog. Stuff like you can't believe. I saw him one time. The string broke and the yo-yo hit Alice Meyer in the face."

It is definitely time to pause. Dope has energized Mulbray's mind and his thoughts are moving at three times the speed of light. He has the feeling he has already passed by what he wants to say.

He has to slow down. If he is to wishes to say something worth saying about this mysterious topic of love, he had damned well better focus his attention. The trick is to close his eyes and keep the sailboat in sight.

"Okay," he continues, "So the boat was right there in the window. It must have been there a long time because the part that wasn't shaded by the big can of Tinker-Toys was all faded by the sun.

"I wanted that boat.

"I guess part of the reason I wanted it was because of this 'Little Golden Book.' See, I had this 'Little Golden

Book.' It was called *The Sailboat That Ran Away*.

"There's this kid who takes his sailboat to the park lagoon. The sailboat runs away to have an adventure. Well—the sailboat doesn't have a good time. It gets attacked by fish and frogs and a giant snapping turtle. Its keel gets caught in the weeds. It nearly wrecks itself on a submerged rock.

"Then a big storm comes up. Lightning is shooting all over the place and a big old jagged bolt nearly hits the sailboat's mast. The sailboat starts crying. It sings a sad little song.

*In Johnny's toybox is where I should be
It's too scary to go sailing on the big, bad sea.*

"So the boat heads back to the shore and there's the kid waiting for it, and it gets put in the toybox and it never runs away again and that's the end."

"I must have had fifty 'Little Golden Books,' but that one was my favorite. I can remember everything in it. I got a paper cut from the last page. There's a circle of blood in the middle of a kid's forehead on that picture where he's lifting the boat out of the water."

Mulbray wonders if it is possible his mother has kept that Little Golden Book. No, no it cannot be. Not that she has thrown it out, things just disappear from a person's life and that's all, that's the way it is.

"So?" Wendy says.

"Yes," Mulbray says. His voice is strange to him, hardly his at all, more like that of one of the old 'Dead End

Kids' who used to star in Monogram Pictures. What was that one who always tried to sound tough?

"See," says Mulbray, "I guess I could kind of understand how the little sailboat felt. I think it was something like that."

"I don't understand," Wendy says.

"I'm getting to it," Mulbray says. He had better hurry on with his story if he is going to make his point. "Well, the boat cost four dollars.

"You know how long it takes a kid to get four dollars. I mean, how long it used to take. I mean back then? I had an allowance. I think it was like fifty cents a week. I started saving. I didn't buy anything. No comic books, no cupcakes after school. I didn't buy anything. I even sold my Duncan yo-yo, that one that the Filipino yo-yo guy used when the string broke and it hit Alice Meyer in the face. I got a dollar for it.

"You know Andrew Arthur, I guess. You know his family, anyway. They still live around here. So, I guess what happened was Andrew Arthur was walking on the square with his mother on the way to the dentist's to finish some root canal work, and he started to cry or something, because he was going to have to sit in the waiting room for an hour with nothing to do but look at Highlights For Children or a couple of ripped up 'Archie' comics, so, to keep him quiet, his mother went into Wellman's and bought him the boat."

"Look," Wendy says, "you don't have to . . ."

"No," Mulbray says, "that's all right. See, it was Andrew Arthur got the boat I was saving for. See?"

There, at last he is finished.

Andrew Arthur, what a prick.

"I'm sorry", says Wendy. "I just don't get what you're trying to say."

Mulbray sighs. "That's all right," he says, as the Golden Book closes and the sailboat sails away, forever, sails away.

Altenmoor,
Where the Dogs Dance

ONE DAY IN SPRING, WHEN the boy came home from school, he did not find Rusty in the backyard, on the screened-in porch, or anywhere downstairs in the house. He knew Rusty could not be up with Grandpa. Last winter, when the weather had gone so cold, Rusty's back legs had gone cold, too, so cold he could no longer climb stairs.

The boy's mother took him into the kitchen and tried to explain, though he hadn't asked her. "Rusty's gone, Marky."

He hated being called "Marky," but she was his mom, so what could he do? Dad called him "Mark," and sometimes "Son," and that was better but it still wasn't right.

Grandpa knew and always called him "Boy." He felt

like a "boy," not "Mark," or "Son," or (phoo!) "Marky!"
Once in a while he wondered if that would change when
he got older.

Mom said Rusty was very old. In a dog way, Rusty was
more than a hundred. She said Rusty had had a very good
life because everyone loved him a lot, and now Rusty's
life was over.

The way Mom talked made the boy think she was trying not to frighten him. Then she hugged him so hard
all his air rushed out and he thought Mom was trying not
to be frightened, too.

But the boy didn't understand, so he said, "I'll go see
Grandpa." Grandpa knew how to talk about things so the
boy understood because Grandpa was very smart. He was
so smart that long ago, when he could still see, Grandpa
even used to write books.

"He'll like that," Mom said. "Go see him."

Upstairs at the end of the hall, across from his own
room, the boy knocked on Grandpa's door. He waited
one-two-three, then heard Grandpa say, "Enter."
Grandpa always made him wait one-two-three, never one,
or one-two, or one-two-three-four.

Grandpa sat in a straight-backed chair by the window.
Grandpa didn't have a rocking chair and the boy knew
why because once Grandpa had told him. "Old people
are supposed to sit in rockers. Seldom in my life have I
done the 'supposed to's.' "

Through the window, the sun shone a square of light
at Grandpa's feet. The boy stood with his sneakers at
the edge of the square. If he stepped inside, it might
break, the yellow oozing out like the yolk of a poached
egg.

The boy said, "Grandpa, Mom says Rusty is gone."

"Your mother is truthful enough," Grandpa said, "though so sadly lacking in imagination it's often difficult for me to acknowledge her as my daughter."

"Oh," the boy said. Sometimes Grandpa talked funny, except he never did when he was talking about important things—like Altenmoor.

"Mom says Rusty was very old," the boy said.

"Indeed," Grandpa said.

"You're very old."

"Once more, indeed."

The boy remembered when Grandpa had been old— but not very old. Grandpa got very old when the cloudy looking white film covered his eyes. After that, Grandpa couldn't read anymore, not even the Altenmoor books Grandpa had written himself.

"I'll miss Rusty," the boy said. "You know, like how he used to sleep with his head between his paws. He had big paws."

"I will miss that too, Boy," Grandpa said. "The picture of Rusty asleep and the sound of his adenoidal snore are preserved and treasured in my memory."

Grandpa tipped his head. For a second the boy thought Grandpa wasn't blind at all because the boy could almost feel himself being seen. "Do say on, Boy," Grandpa said.

"Is Rusty dead?" the boy said.

Grandpa said, "There are some who would say and some who would believe it as well. And you? What do you say? What do you believe?"

The boy thought. Then he said, "No."

"No?"

"Rusty went to Altenmoor," the boy said and he hoped

he believed what he was saying. "He went once through the Rubber Tree Woods and he jig-jogged left past the Marmalade Mound. Then he followed the winding Happy-To-You River to Altenmoor."

"Continue, Boy." Grandpa leaned forward, elbows on his knees, hands folded under his chin. "Speak to me of Altenmoor. So long since I've written of the noble realm and longer still since I've gone a'journeying there."

"In Altenmoor, every morning is a Sunrise Surprise and the buttercups thunder like twelve tubas."

"Only louder," Grandpa said.

"Much louder! And the winds are all hot winds and happy winds and wild winds!"

"And the animals?"

"Oh," the boy said, remembering the animals. "The pigs whistle 'Dixie' in four part harmony and the cats play silver cymbals in three-quarter time."

"And the dogs?"

"The dogs dance!" the boy said. "The dogs do dance all the day!"

"You see," Grandpa said, "it was time for Rusty to be where the dogs dance. Yes. Rusty has gone to Altenmoor."

The boy smiled but the smile didn't feel all the way right because it pinched at the corners of his mouth, and so he had to ask. "Really?"

" 'Really?' The modern rephrasing of the ageless 'What is Truth?' The metaphysicians ponder as they will, all we truly know, we know only here." Grandpa patted himself on the chest.

The boy said, "There is a real Altenmoor?"

"Were there not, could I have written the seventeen

books that comprise the complete Altenmoor chronicles? If there were no Oz, could Mr. L. Frank Baum have related the adventures of Dorothy and Tin Woodsman and Scarecrow? What of Treasure Island and Never-Neverland, or savage Pellucidar and Wonderland? If they did not exist, how could people tell of them?"

Again Grandpa patted himself on the chest. "Books, Boy, are from the heart and of the heart. That makes them not merely true, but truer than true. Do you understand?"

"Some," the boy said. "Not everything."

"Some is more than most people," Grandpa said. "It will suffice."

The boy had something else to ask. "But how could Rusty get to Altenmoor, Grandpa? It's a long, long way and his legs were no good."

"Excellent point, Boy," Grandpa said, "and logic demands an answer."

Grandpa stretched out his arm and spread his fingers. In the sunlight the veins of his hand were ripply blue and strong. "I touched Rusty's head, you see. I patted that bony knob at the back of his skull and tickled between his ears. I touched him, and all the strength I could give, I gave to Rusty so he could make the trek to Altenmoor."

"And then he went?"

"He did," Grandpa said. "He went once through the Rubber Tree Woods and he jig-jogged left past the Marmalade Mound."

"Then he followed the winding Happy-To-You River to Altenmoor!" the boy and Grandpa said together.

"Yes," Grandpa nodded, "and now Rusty is dancing, he

is dancing where the dogs dance. I believe that."

"I do too," the boy said.

* * *

On a winter night so cold that the house could not keep out all the winter chill, the boy awoke. He thought at first that a dream had frightened him awake, but he realized he was not frightened.

Then he knew it was a thought that had pulled him from his sleep.

He got out of bed. Even through the carpet the floor was shivery, so he slid his feet along instead of lifting them. He did not need a light.

He stepped across the hall and quietly knocked on the door. It would have been wrong to wake Mom and Dad. They did not mind getting up if he had a stomachache or a bad dream, but his stomach felt fine and he was not dreaming.

The boy waited one-two-three.

Then he waited four and five and six and seven before he gently turned the knob and went in.

Winter moonlight seeped through the window. Grandpa was in bed, lying on his back, the blankets drawn halfway up his chest. His hands were outside the blankets, fingers of the right over those of the left.

"Grandpa?" The boy stood beside the bed, thinking one-two-three-four-five-six.

Then the boy thought about what he would miss about Grandpa, things he wanted to keep in his memory. There were a lot of things, and once he was sure he had them all, the boy touched the back of Grandpa's hand, then took hold of three of Grandpa's fingers and squeezed.

Grandpa's eyes opened. Beneath the milky glaze his eyes looked right at the boy, and this time the boy was almost certain Grandpa could see him.

"Yes? What is it, Boy?"

"Are you going to Altenmoor now?" the boy said.

Slowly Grandpa sat up. "Yes, I believe I am."

"Then I have to help you."

"Yes." Grandpa nodded. "Keep hold of my hand, Boy."

The boy did. It took a long time, but he could feel himself giving all the strength he could give to Grandpa. He knew it was happening because he started to feel as though he were going to sleep, the way he did in the back of the car after a long day at the beach.

Then Grandpa said, "Thank you," and took away his hand.

"Grandpa, will you go now?"

"Shortly." Grandpa said. "No longer than it takes a pig to whistle 'Dixie.' Now you must return to bed. There is still much of a winter's night to sleep away."

"Okay," the boy said. He went to the door, then stopped and looked back. "Grandpa, you know. The Rubber Tree Woods and the Marmalade Mound and the winding Happy-To-You River."

"Of course, Boy," Grandpa said. "Where else?"

The boy said, "Goodbye, Grandpa."

The next morning the boy was up early because his mother and father came to his room and woke him and told him he wouldn't be going to school. Dad stood by the door. He had the same look on his face he'd had when someone stole the car last year.

Mom held the boy close to her. She was crying. She said, "Grandpa is gone, Marky."

"Yes," the boy said. He wished he could explain but he knew she would never understand.

Dani's Story

William Raley, Editor
AFTER HOURS MAGAZINE
P.O. Box 538
Sunset Beach, California

Dear William,
Thanks for asking me for a story for the last issue
of AFTER HOURS.

Sure, I've got a horror story. I have lots of them.

Don't we all?

Best,

Mort Castle

"I'm scared," she says. "You don't think so, maybe, but I am. I'm scared a lot now, even when there's no reason."

I tell her she'll get over it with time. I say, "It's all right."

Scared.

I do not tell her, *I understand.*

I do not say, *I think maybe we all are.*

All the time.

*　　*　　*

Let's flashback. It's okay. The world is non-linear, right? One leads to two? No, sir, and once you realize Our Cosmic King has repealed the Law of Cause and Effect, you'll be less frequently disappointed.

So . . . Flashback:

The city is Chicago and the time is Spring and dusk and the weather is just about perfect. You can taste Summer on the breeze off Lake Michigan.

Let's walk with her. We can do that, after all. This is fiction. I make the rules.

People and street lights and patterned reflections in store windows and random silica glitter in the sidewalk and sounds that are distinctly and distinctively city sounds

A bus groans a turn onto Jackson and two Orientals laugh quietly behind her and she wonders if this is the first time she has ever heard Orientals laugh in real life and not in a movie or something. Overhead, the El train, metal on metal, comes to a stop.

You know, a night like this, you understand how it was the Impressionist painters came to see in the way they saw. It is only that instant of soft-focused precision that can capture this complete world within how many worlds, that can make you feel this

NOW

This

SUCHNESS of things.

And she is happy now. Her name is Dani. Well, her real name is Alison, spelled with only the one "I," but this is fiction, so I can call her Eustacia Visigoth Marmalade if I choose. Dani is ON! HER! OWN! in the city, because she is ALL GROWN UP!

(Well, okay, there is some financial help from the folks, until she gets it all together, okay, and she will pay them back, 'cause how else, right now, could she afford an apartment in the ultra-slick, toney-clique Lincoln Park area?)

(Hey, Dani works for a living, you know? Graphic design, a small but getting noticed ad agency where a certain amount of goof-around—not goose-around!—is encouraged, part of the creative process . . .)

Happy. Dani is happy because
it is Spring
now
in the city.

And let's get cornball, my friend, let's get sentimental and silly, because, hey, you are supposed to avoid diabetes-inducing sentiment in fiction, but goddamnit, life is loaded with sentimentality, ain't it, and this is, for real fellas and gals, friends and pals, the McCoy, the true gen, the *emmis*.

So, if this instant you peered right into Dani's brain, you would discover that right now she does indeed believe totally in Magic. Believes that everyone is entitled by birth to One Wish That Comes True. Believes That It is A Wonderful Life. Believes there is a Caring Celestial Eye on The Sparrow and You.

If Dani told you this, well, now that she is an adult, she'd probably feel stupid and say, "God, did I say that? That was dumb! I mean . . ."

She might blush.

I think you might fall in love with her then.

* * *

Of course I am free to share Dani's thoughts with you. Dani is a fictional character in a work of fiction . . .

According to Webster's Dictionary, Fiction is Bullshit. Phonius Baloneyus.

> *You just make it all up, right?*
> *It's all out of your head.*

> *Uh-uh. Out of my head.*
> *Yessirree, Bob. Not that much*
> *to it, frankly.*
> *Think it up and write it*
> *down and when you're done, you stop.*
> *And here is insight into the workings of*
> *a fiction writer's mind. I*
> *chose the name Dani because*
> *it's sort of close to Demi,*
> *and people used to tell our*
> *main character that*
> *she reminded them of Demi Moore,*

Moon on the Water

or, at least the way
Demi Moore looked in Ghost.

* * *

"Thing is," Dani says, "I never thought Demi Moore was such a much, okay? I mean, if I were lezzy, I would not want to go to bed with her."

Dani smiles, but it's the sort of smile that makes you feel wrong. She says, "I'm not pretty anymore."

Is she going to cry? Please, I hope not. I thought she was over that part of it, the tears that explode out of nowhere . . .

So, in that I am something of an obtuser, what I say is, "You are pretty. You will be even prettier. Today plastic surgery is no big deal, so you don't have to and you will never have to worry about yourself in the loveliness department, okay?"

"Okay," Dani says. Laughs. "Hell, you think any girl younger than you is Big Time Lovely."

My turn to laugh. Har-dee-har-horseshit.

Fact: I am forty eight, and, starting last year, it felt like every girl and every guy and everybody who matters in the round world was younger than yours truly, Mort the Moi.

Sometimes I think about it.

Aging.

I guess I think about it often, probably.

Sometimes, sometimes it makes me sad.

Sometimes.

Often.

Often it makes me deeply and profoundly sad.

243

*   *   *

No.

Dani says she is really sorry, really, but she does not like most of what I have written so far. She says no way could she have been so Pollyanna sweet, naive and assholic. I've made her just too nice.

"It's just bogus, you know."

Besides, why don't I just get on with it? Her story. Just charge into the beginning, chainsaw through the middle, and then, Tah-dah!

At last!

The End!

The End!

That will be IT!

That will take care of it. I know that is what she hopes in a vague and inexpressible way that manages to irritate the hell out of me.

So, hey, why doesn't she write it?

No, no thank you, Mort. I lived it. That takes care of my obligation, yes?

Dani thinks I have magic. Mort the Writer. Published and everything, published in languages I do not even speak.

Okay, maybe I reside at the Lower End of the U.S. Economic Ladder, but I am, to Dani, and a few others, Mort The Shaman

And I can do magic

Get HER story into print.

That will give purpose to the horror.

Purpose. Not catharsis.

Moon on the Water

Catharsis? Doesn't happen.
And I cannot will not
will not tell her
that it is just there
the horror
the horror
will always be
the horror
she has known
the horror
we know

*   *   *

Let's go to that Friday night in early autumn.
We are done screwing around.

It's going to happen.

*   *   *

September 5, 1994

Dear William,

Sorry it's taking longer to get you a story for AFTER
HOURS than I'd planned. Slow going and rough at this
end of the mail chute.

But as you know, sometimes things have to come at
you and come together in their own way.

245

Mort Castle

And Raley, some of this is your own damned fault! Check out the resonant and evocative title you slapped on your magazine.

After Hours. Hey, pal, what is it we hear "after hours"? Who is it?

There are voices, you know, and they talk to me—after hours. Truth is, I'm hearing them more and more often. I don't sleep well, not anymore, and so, two or three in the morning, I'm up reading, trying to write, trying not to feel sad, whatever. And it is then "The After Hours Voices" (sounds like the name for the Chorus on an old Jackie Gleason album!) are keeping me company. Oh, they don't scream. They are soft, insistent, and regretful. They are not unlike the haze around a mountain peak in an Oriental painting, and just as real.

The After Hours Voices talk to me . . . "Sing sorrow, sing sorrow . . ." That is an English folk song, "The Lass From The Low Country," and I feel that sort of feeling as I listen to voices call from memory and from the peculiar nowhere that is the desolate realm of hopes gone to hell.

Voices you can hear only after hours.

They whisper intimations of horror.

And so, begin again.

Moon on the Water

Best,

Mort Castle

* * *

Because it did happen and so now it has to

On her floor, the 16th . . .

Dani waits for the elevator. Waiting is not impatience. No foot-tapping. No running fingers along the strap of her purse.

Horror waits for her.

Not a monster.

Not a demon.

Not a ghost.

You do not need a ghost to be haunted.

Horror is WHAT IF? above all, and forget the bullshit metaphysics, horror is the impossible to control hurting we do to ourselves. If the toothache eases, hey, we just have to stab the old tongue in there to get it fired up and screeching again, don't we?

So—WHAT IF?

WHAT IF?

WHAT IF?

What if she had not decided to go out that night?

What if Cathy Lynn and Cathy Cole, AKA "The Two Cathys," AKA Cathy One (Lynn) and Cathy Two (Cole) had suggested they meet at the Hard Rock Cafe a half-hour later? A half-hour earlier? It didn't matter, really. Cathy Two's boyfriend was working the door. They could always get in.

What if the elevators had been out of order? "I work out twice a week, but forget the free stress test, pal."

What if she had had a cold? "God deh snibbles, an' just wanna read a boog an' stay warm inna beddd."

What if he had never been born?

He . . . What if Mr. Horror had been struck by lightning/run over by a Purolator truck/mangled beyond recognition by a punch press?

What if? What if? What if? What if? What if?

Let's push it over the top, to the utterly impossible, and ask, what if Dani had done what no kid in the history of the world has done, what if she had actually listened to her mother and father?

Her parents did not want her going so far away to the city.

Dani grew up in Monticello, just about the middle of Illinois, and what was so bad about it, anyway, answer me that, young lady?

Dad was the State Farm Insurance man with his office right there on McHemie Street—Like A Good Neighbor, State Farm Is There!—and Mom processed loan applications for United Savings and Loan of Monticello and Farmer City, and there was nothing wrong with the education Dani got in high school, was there (graduated seven, "lucky seven," in a class of 77), Dani had to admit that, what they couldn't understand, really not understand, was why she had to go study art at the Art Institute in Chicago, instead of, say, the U of I, or Illinois State University. You know, say what you want, a number of nationally known artists, like the sculptor Nick Africano, and the glass-blower, John Brekke (one of Mort's students when he was in high school!), they got all the art they needed right at ISU, not more than 50 miles away, okay, right there in Normal, Illinois.

Beginning of Dani's senior year:

"I do not want you in the city. No. I watch the news. I'm not paranoid and I'm not a hick, but I tell you, honey, I am afraid of the city."

"You're not afraid of a city, Dad. You are afraid of black people . . ."

"It's not that they're black . . ."

"Think about what you said, what you just said!"

"What I am thinking about is you! And you know me better than that, Dani. I'm no bigot."

"I know! I know. You always watch Bill Cosby. Why, some of your best friends would be Knee-Gah-rows, if there were any in Monticello."

Dad looks down, then, a hand to his brow so she cannot see his eyes. "I know you think this town is too little for you, okay? You're not going to be happy if the only major art exhibition you see is the new mural at the VFW Hall. There's a lot to you, a lot inside you, Dani."

"Dad . . ."

One of those long silences that so rarely happen in real life and that third-rate fictionists throw in when they are trying to contrive poignancy.

"I'm not arguing, okay? I am asking. Does it have to be Chicago?"

"Yes."

His voice is tight but there is nothing small or grudging in the words he finds hard to speak. "You have real talent, Dani, and me, well I do not pretend to understand talent. I am a plodder, and I realize it, and it's worked for me, so I'm not unhappy. But I know you cannot ignore talent and if that means Chicago, then that's what it means."

It meant Chicago.

Mort Castle

*   *   *

after hours voices

absent friends I

scott talks
to me over
telephone lines
comic edge and marlboro
rasp subdued now

says he's
just out
of a methadone clinic
says he's
all right
now

thinks
he is

says he's
just a goddamned
junky
is what
he is

laughs

Moon on the Water

a goddamned
junky

says he will go
to california
has to go
to california
now

a quest
sort of

something
like that
see the ocean
something about
healing waters and power
get it all
worked out

says he will
get settled
see the ocean
call me

that was 1975

directory assistance
cannot assist

Mort Castle

i
have not

heard
from him
since

after hours voices

absent friends II

It was the catcher in the rye, Holden Caulfield, who told us you can get to missing everybody, even the people you never knew.

I miss Groucho Marx. Josh White. Jack Benny. Blind Louie. Aunt Kate and Ozzie. Harry Truman. Thelonius Monk. Joe Louis. Franklin Delano Roosevelt. Gold Tooth Liboro. Delmore Schwartz. John Bubbles. Janis Joplin. John Coltrane. Uncle Nate. Martin Luther King. Miss Kitty. Jack Kennedy. Bobby Kennedy. Jackie Kennedy. Fats Waller.

You can get to feeling that everyone who was anyone is dead.

"Ain't it a gasser?"

     —The Late Lord Buckley

. . . the 27th of September, and I can't say
I've wrapped the story for your last ish.

But I am, however, hearing many muttering of The After
Hours Voices, and they ain't doing no meditative

Gregorian chants!

Know what, Will-yum, ain't impossible Mort has himself a kick ass mid-life crisis. But hey, I can handle it, and if you listen to any of the talk shows, you know you do get through it, put it all together into a viable philosophy without resorting to Shirley MacLaine religions or Everything You Need to Know You Learned in Reform School books.

And then, when you have GOT IT, Satori! Big Bingo!

Then you DIE!

Hit that one Sam Kinison style. The late Sam Kinison!

THEN YOU FUCKING DIE!

"*The only guarantee you get with life is your inability to survive it.*"

—H. L. Mencken

Now, isn't he one cheery motherfucker though?

*   *   *

"So, you want me to go ahead with it now, Dani?"

"Yes. You've fooled around long enough, haven't you? Story time, beginning, middle, end. It's you. You don't want to write it, do you?"

"I'll write it. I told you I would. Don't you worry about that." I will write it and what I want has nothing to do with it.

What I want has never
stopped a single tidal wave or a teenage suicide
or an IRA bomb or a two year old's AIDS death
What I want?
I am not God.
And judging by what I see, God isn't, either.

Mort Castle

Let's hold a sec with the
self-pity and the grandiosity, okay?

All right! We have another After Hours Voice.

I've been here before,
but you weren't listening.
You weren't willing to listen.

Okay, I am listening.
Tuned in. Going to
impart some wisdom or what?

Just the truth.

Vincent Van Gogh
looks through
mad eyes
of horror
and sees
sunflowers

Now, get back to Dani.
Her story needs telling.
And let's state the obvious, Mort.
It's not just for Dani
you're telling it

*   *   *

She is going to The Hard Rock Cafe where she will
meet her friends, Cathy One and Cathy Two. She is waiting for the elevator.

Moon on the Water

The orange-pink light over the bronze sliding doors. Down. The sound is *Bink!* It is exactly *Bink!* Later, she will hear that precision of sound in her head.

Dani steps into the elevator. She is the only passenger.

(That's right! You just caught it yesterday on the Geraldo-Oprah-Leeza-Sleeza-Sally-Jerry Jibber-Jabber Show! The guy—and it's ALWAYS a guy—who tells you ladies how NOT to be a VICTIM! NEVER get on an elevator alone! Never get on an elevator that has fewer than 1,232 people on it! Never get on an elevator if you can help it 'cause the fucking thing can faw down! If you absolutely MUST get on an elevator by yourself, have your WWII surplus bazooka in easy reach, strap a 55 gallon drum of MACE to your back, carry a starving weasel in your purse . . .)

Descending
BINK!

The Ninth Floor.
Stop.
Doors slide open.

He enters.

Horror

not just yet

I need to take a breath

okay

255

Mort Castle

here we go

> *What is it with you?*
> *Why does it always have to be horror?*

> *They used to ask my friend—my now absent*
> *friend—Bill Wantling,*
> *why he wrote so many poems about prison.*
> *Bill's final book was called* San Quentin's Stranger.
> *Bill did seven years in San Quentin*
> *and they used to ask him that.*
> *I write horror because*
> *that is what we've got.*

> *Please, no platitudinous re-bop*
> *about, "It's all in how you look at it,"*
> *and don't give me that*
> *"You decide if the glass is*
> *half-full or half-empty,"*
> *when the glass contains Jonestown*
> *Special Kool-Aid, and don't quote me*
> *that putz with ears, Wayne Dyer, or the*
> *putzette, Joyce Brothers,*
> *and don't give me any Reader's Digest*
> *inspirational tripe, "If life hands you a lemon . . ."*

> *". . . it was probably picked by*
> *a one-armed, hare-lipped, illegal*
> *alien who was the product of*
> *incest between his syphilitic sister*
> *and his hydrocephalic brother,*
> *and one day, Mr. Lemon Plucker will go*

Moon on the Water

wacky-wacky-WACK-oooooOOOOO!!!!
Fully transmogrified and
living up to his fullest
potential behind the meanest Mexican brown
and crack and animal tranq
and four gallons of
Liquid Plumber, and
he will climb on top of a building and
play rock 'n' roll Uzi on a
bunch of pre-schoolers on their field trip
to the zoo to see the newborn giraffe.

"The horror. The horror."
Good old Kurtz looked right
into the Heart of Darkness
and he had a take on it.

Yo, Mort, you like quotes. Here's one for you:

Upon this awkward ball
of mud
I see
All
All
is ecstasy

You know who wrote that?

Yes.

Bill Wantling.
Who wrote San Quentin's Stranger.

257

Mort Castle

Who was San Quentin's Stranger.
Who knew Caryl Chessman and Van Gogh's sunflowers.

*　　*　　*

All right. Dani. I guess we're both ready now.

Dani. In the elevator.

He has just stepped in.

Average height. Weight: 145-165—who can tell? Late 20s, early 30s, young 40s—who can tell? Dark blond hair. Maybe light red hair. Can't recall. Cannot summon or create a visual for the police.

Bland face. That's all. Dressed all right. Sports coat. Swirling tie, a touch too much on the polyester, too shiny, meaning he is not quite with it. Think of all the so-so/okay actors on the one or maybe two season television shows you "watch sometimes" instead of "really liked" or "really hated." You'll realize that you cannot recall any of their faces because they're just blah-ho-hum, they are people whose looks you can say are "average . . ."

But there is the smile. It's loose, teeth very TV commercial (Caps? Bonded?), and then, his breath, and she understands: he has been juicing. He is perhaps a jigger or so from utterly ossified. She sees it in his eyes that want to operate independently of one another. His voice, words too cleanly separated and enunciated. "You are very cute. I would like very much to go to bed with you. I would like to touch you and make love to you."

He is pathetic.

Barney Fife.

258

Frightening.

Lee Harvey Oswald.

She is confused and outraged.

His loose smile hangs here. It is all she sees.

She slaps him.

A slap in the face sounds like nothing else but a slap in the face. Smile twists like cartoony rubber. Solidity of cheekbone beneath oily skin.

God! She has not struck another human being in anger since second grade when Marsha Voerner called her a "pig poop."

Slapped him. Hates him. Hates herself.

God! Wants to kill him or to apologize wants

wants to get away because

now she sees

she is in trouble.

Hand to his face. Amazed. Sorrowful. "You hit me," he says. "You don't. You hurt me. You can't do that. You just don't hit people. That isn't right. You just don't."

And he moves and touches the magic button on the panel and the elevator stops and she is trapped.

She tries

Tries nothing.

Because she cannot scream. He has her throat with his left hand and he is strong. He has her slammed against the wall.

Rape her. Beat her. Kill her.

She must cooperate. Submit.

Whatever he says. Wants.

No!

Go along with him until you have a chance . . . Fight.

Pinned to the wall. Tries to kick him in the balls. Cannot. Cannot breathe.

Women of Power, All Ye Mighty Amazons, the fact is most men are stronger than most women. Men typically have a height and weight advantage. And even when there's a question, well, what kind of odds do you think we'd have for Roseanne Barr versus Roberto Duran?

He says, "You just stop right now." Orders.

Cannot breathe.

Is going to die.

Be killed.

And KILLED is worse than dying.

(And this is not the horror. This is bad, this is BAD, but this is NOT the horror!)

"You hit me in the face. I am going to hit you in the face. I'm going to hit you only once, but I am going to hit you hard. I want you to remember, don't you ever, ever, ever hit anyone. What is the matter with you? What is the matter with you, anyway?"

He draws back his right hand, a fist now. She is kind of zoned, like overmuch nitrous oxide at the dentist's, so, some things are all foggy, but she can concentrate intensely on others.

Like the sound of KRACKSHK and the crackling and squishing, an impossible, pulping, slow-motion sound, that fills her whole head when he punches her right on the nose.

This is no television punch on the nose. An honest to God punch on the nose is probably not as painful as having your appendix removed without anesthetic, but it's not exactly eating M & Ms, either.

Moon on the Water

Dani is gulping blood and snot and a little air, trying not to pass out, when he lets her loose.

She slides to the floor.

He starts the elevator.

Gets off at the next floor.

The elevator going down.

You know, Dani thinks. *Wow! That hurt!*

Stand up. Okay. A little shaky but some of that is just the elevator itself, right? Sure. Don't throw up. Try to be objective, and you know, the pain is really quite amazing. Really.

So, what we've got, I'd imagine, is assault and battery. A guy hit me.

Assault and battery. I hit a guy.

Got a punch in the nose. Bop in the beezus. Sock in the snoot. Snarfed your snufflupagus, girly, and smashed your schnozzola and slammed your Cyranose . . .

That is not horror, is it?

*　　*　　*

Gee, way back when, I thought you said something about your writing a horror story. Got any plans to get around to that during this incarnation? Come on, damn it! Just write it already!

Right. Nothing to it. After all, I write fiction. I just make up all this stuff. Why don't I do it already? Why don't I just do it already? Nothing to it, a little imagination and throw in a vampire and there you go!

Mort Castle

*   *   *

Uh, Suffering Artist,
lighten up a tad, okay?

Hey, there!
It's Mr. After Hours Voice,
not quite as well known
to us Baby Boomers as
Mr. Tooth Decay, but,
nonetheless, a real player
in my life.
What's to say?
Do we get . . . philosophical?

AFTER HOURS VOICE: *Soitainly!*
Nyuck, nyuck, nyuck! (A halfway decent impression
of the immortal Curley.)

MORT CASTLE: *(Struggling Writer Who*
Sometimes takes Himself
Too Seriously and has
a tendency toward
Self-Indulgence):
So, lay down your spiel,
yuh ole sidewinder,
and let me hear
the wisdom of the ages.

AFTER HOURS VOICE: *Uh, let's check on*
what you are listening to as

Moon on the Water

you work on this story
for William R. Sounds like the
Bill Evan's Trio. Sounds like currently dead
Bill Evans when he used
to be alive.
Sounds quite beautiful,
you know.

Sounds like Scotty LeFaro on bass.
Scotty was killed in a horror movie
of a car accident some
months after this recording.

And later, you will listen,
I'll bet, to Lady Day
and Chet Baker, and no one understood
sorrow like they did,
and they lived tragedies and
insanities, and they are gone now,
but what they left behind,
well, there is some of the horror
there, has to be,
goes with the territory,
but there is more, isn't there,
there is more, goddamnit.

They took it all in, and what
they created is this lastingness,
this music that is as close
as you're going to get
to the holy.

Mort Castle

> *Yes, pain has its place*
> *in the creation*
> *of this man-made sacrament.*

> *But so does EVERYTHING else!*

*   *   *

Dani, it is very late.
I will finish your story now.
Then we will rest.

*   *   *

Main floor.
Every broken noser out!
Dani has arrived.
Staggers. "Uh-hmmm . . ." A bubbling throat sound she
makes again and again, her *Bridge on the River Kwai* song
to keep her moving.
A step.
A step.
Has to keep moving. Must. "Uh-hmmm . . ." "Uh-
hmmm . . ." "Uh-hmmm . . ."
"Uh-hmmm . . ."
This is not the horror.
This is bad.
But this is not the horror.
The doorman is there. Just appears like he's following
a script. Hands on her shoulders. She flinches.
"All right," he says. "Okay." Broad, dark brown face.

Coat with epaulets. His good eyes narrowing. Concern. "All right."

Funny, you know. For a second, she thinks he is her father and everything is all right.

Click, and she's tracking right once more. The doorman is named Kelly Green. When she first heard it, she thought that was a funny name, especially for a black man; she wondered later if it was wrong to think that.

"Uh-hmmm . . ."

"Looks like something happened, didn't it? We get you fixed up real soon. First, let's just sit you on down . . ."

"Doan go . . ."

"No, no. It's all right. I'm here. Right here, okay? Just get my phone here and get you some help. Everything be fine. You see . . ."

She is sitting down. He has made a call. He is holding her hand. "Uh-hmmm . . ."

He is a nice man.

He says, "It's all right. Okay, now. It's all right. It's all right."

*   *   *

Dear William,
  It happens weird sometimes, you know? Here's what I thought was the ending of this story:

*   *   *

Okay, Horror Reader, you've been patient as hell, so now, at last (right?) this is—

Mort Castle

The Horror!

Dani is unable to identify her assailant for the police. She will always be afraid of him. If she lives 100 years, she will be waiting for him to explode out of her dreams and into her life.

Okay, no question the rhino repair surgeon will do a superb job, and not to sweat the financial, she has a fine medical package from the ad agency, so, really, you won't be able to tell she had a broken nose.

But the horror is that never again will Dani accept as a given that this old world is a good old world in which to be.

Think of: A butterfly torn apart simply because it was there for the tearing.

Think of: Your favorite uncle, the one who took you fishing and made jokes about the fish you caught, giving them Biblical names like Hezekiah, Jeremiah, and Nehemiah . . . How did it feel when you learned he was a suicide?

Think of: Yourself old and lonely and nobody calls.

Think this way, and you will feel something of the loss Dani has suffered. A unique dimension of her selfness is gone, can never be restored. Trust replaced by cynicism. She is smarter and she is bitter. The edge is there. She has that sharpened awareness that becomes city paranoia to enable her to survive.

It is no exaggeration to say Dani is gone. The Dani who was has been destroyed. She is lost to us and to herself.

And that is the horror, the horror conclusion of this horror story.

Moon on the Water

*   *   *

But William, that is not it, at all. The story
does not end that way. Dani won't let it.

*   *   *

"No," Dani says. "because it not true. It's not that way."
She tells me I have written the ending of my story.
Not her story.

"See, the ending of my story is Kelly Green. You know,
sometimes when it's real late, and I wake up frightened,
I can hear him. What he's saying is, 'It's all right, it's all
right.' And then after he says it for a while, I can get
back to sleep."

I ask, "So, then, how does your story end?"

"The way it should end. It ends with

*   *   *

sometimes I think us horror guys, William, can deal
with everything—except hope!

What happens, I guess, is we write a few
horror stories, then more of them, and
we get caught up in it, become darkness junkies,
and we put on these glasses that let
us see the horror, and by the time we
hit our 40s, we are wearing
horror bi-focals, good for seeing the

up-close horror and the distant horror,
and because we have picked up some
shakiness along the way, had our disasters
and disappointments, had too much that should
have gone right go dead wrong or just go away
forever because we have known too many losses,
after a while, all we see is the
horror of it all.

Horror. It gets so it's the only
thing. That is, it gets so we make it
the only thing.

And William, if I sound like
I'm either preaching or teaching, hell,
I'm entitled, it goes with my being an AARP
certified old fart, right?
So there!

So, you've got my story here. Not heavy
on plot this round, but there
is some fiction. Into each life
that comes my way, some fiction may fall!

That is, you have my story—Dani's story—once
we wrap it. We can wrap it with the
words that are a prayer, a prayer
of one person to another person, a prayer of
one person for another person, a prayer
without God getting in the way, a prayer to
speak mercy and touch you and know your
tears, a prayer to speak kindness

and ease and rest and know your pain,
a prayer of hope a prayer of hope
a prayer of hope

It's all right. It's all right.

The Old Man and the Dead

I

IN OUR TIME there was a man who wrote as well and truly as anyone ever did. He wrote about courage and endurance and sadness and war and bullfighting and boxing and men in love and men without women. He wrote about scars and wounds that never heal.

Often, he wrote about death. He had seen much death. He had killed. Often, he wrote well and truly about death. Sometimes. Not always.

Sometimes he could not.

Moon on the Water

II

May 1961
Mayo Clinic
Rochester, Minnesota

"Are you a Stein? Are you a Berg?" he asked.

"Are you an anti-Semite?" the psychiatrist asked.

"No." He thought. "Maybe. I don't know. I used to be, I think. It was in fashion. It was all right until that son of a bitch, Hitler."

"Why did you ask that?" the psychiatrist asked.

The old man took off his glasses. He was not really an old man, only 61, but often he thought of himself as an old man and truly, he looked like an old man, although his blood pressure was in control and his diabetes remained borderline. His face had scars. His eyes were sad. He looked like an old man who had been in wars.

He pinched his nose above the bridge. He wondered if he were doing it to look tired and worn. It was hard to know now when he was being himself and when he was being what the world expected him to be. That was how it was when all the world knew you and all the world knows you if you have been in *Life* and *Esquire*.

"It's something I don't think a Jew would understand. Maybe a Jew couldn't."

The old man laughed then but it had nothing funny to it. He sounded like he had been socked a good one. "*Nu?* Is that what a Jew would say? *Nu?* No, not a Jew. Not a communist. Nor an empiricist. I'll tell you who else. The existentialists. Those wise-guy sons of bitches. Oh, they get ink these days, don't they? Sit in the cafes and drink the good wine and the good dark coffee and smoke the bad cigarettes and think they've discovered it all. Nothingness. That is what they think they've discovered. How do you like it now, Gentlemen?

"They are wrong. Yes. They are wrong."

"How so?"

"There is something. It's not pretty. It's not nice. You have to be drunk to talk about it, drunk or shell-shocked, and then you usually can't talk about it. But there is something."

III

The poet Bill Wantling wrote of him: "He explored the *pues y nada* and the *pues y nada*."

So then so. What do you know of it Mr. Poet Wantling? What do you know of it?

F____ you all. I obscenity in the face of the collective wisdom. I obscenity in the face of the collective wisdoms. I obscenity in the mother's milk that suckled the collective wisdoms. I obscenity in the too-easy mythos of all the collective wisdoms and in the face of my young, ignorant, unknowing self that led me to proclaim my personal mantra of ignorance, the *pues y nada y pues y nada y pues y nada pues y nada* . . . In the face of Buddha. In the face of Mohammed. In the face of the God of Abraham, Isaac, and Jacob.

In the face of that poor skinny dreamer who died on the cross. Really, when it came down to it, he had some good moves in there. He didn't go out bad. He was tough. Give him that. Tough like Stan

Ketchel, but he had no counter-moves. Just this sweet, simple, sad ass faith. Sad ass because, what little he understood, no, from what I have seen, he had it bass-ackwards.

How do you like it now, Gentlemen? How do you like it now? Is it time for a prayer? Very well then, Gentlemen.

Let us pray.

Baa-baa-baa, listen to the lambs bleat,

Baa-baa-baa, listen to the lambs bleat.

Truly, world without end.

Truly.

Not

Amen.

I can not will not just cannot no cannot bless nor sanctify nor affirm the obscenity the horror.

Can you, Mr. Poet Bill Wantling? Can you, Gentlemen?

How do you like it now?

In Hell and in a time of hell, a man's got no bloody chance,

F____you as we have been f____ed. All of us. All of us.

There is your prayer.

Amen.

IV

"Ern—"

"No. Don't call me that. That's not who I want to be."

"That is your name."

"Goddamn it. F____you. F____you twice. I've won the big one. The goddamn Nobel. I'm the one. The heavy-

273

weight champ, no middleweight. I *can* be *who* I want to be. I've earned that."

"Who is it you want to be?"

"Mr. *Papa*. I'm damned good for that. Mr. Papa. That is how I call myself. That is how Mary calls me. They call me 'Mr. Papa' in Idaho and Cuba and *Paris Review*. The little girls whose tight dancer bottoms I pinch, the little girls I call 'daughter,' the lovely little girls, and A. E. and Carlos and Coop and Marlene, *Papa* or Mr. *Papa*, that's how they call me.

"Even Fidel. I'm Mr. Papa to Fidel. I call him *Señor Beisbol*. Do you know, he's got a hell of a slider, Fidel. How do you like it now, Mr. Doctor? Mr. Papa."

"Mr. *Papa*? No, I don't like it. I don't like the word games you play with me, nor do I think your 'Mr. Papa' role belongs in this office. You're here so we can *help* you."

"Help me? That is nice. That is just so goddamn pretty."

"We need the truth."

"That's all Pilate wanted. Not so much. And wasn't he one swell guy?"

"Who are you?" persisted the psychiatrist.

"Who's on first?"

"What?"

"*What's* on second! Who's on first. I like them, you know. Abbott and Costello. They could teach that sissy Capote a thing or two about word dance. Who's on first? How do you like it now, Gentlemen? Oh, yes, they could teach Mr. James Jones a little. Thinks he's Captain Steel Balls now. Thinks he's ready to go against the champ. Mailer, the loud mouth Hebe. Uris, even *Uris*, for God's sake, the original Hollywood piss-ant. Before they take me on, any of them, let them do a prelim with Abbott and Costello. Who's on first? That is good."

"What's not good is that you're avoiding. Simple question." The psychiatrist was silent, then he said, sternly, "Who are you?"

The old man said nothing. His mouth worked. He looked frail then. Finally he said, "Who am I truly?"

"Truly."

"*Verdad?*"

"*Sí. Verdad.*"

"Call me *Adam* . . ."

"*Adam?* Oh, Mr. *Papa*, Mr. *Nobel Prize*, that is just too pretty. How do *you* like it now, thrown right back at you? You see, I can talk your talk. Let us have a pretension contest. Call me 'Ishmael.' Now do we wait for God to call you his beloved son in whom he is well pleased?"

The old man sighed. He looked very sad, as though he wanted to kill himself. He had put himself on his honor to his personal physician and his wife that he would not kill himself, and honor was very important to him, but he looked like he wanted to kill himself.

The old man said, "No. Adam. Adam Nichols. That was the one who was truly me in the stories."

"I thought it was Nick Adams in . . ."

"*Those* were the stories I let them publish. There were other stories I wrote about me when I used to be Adam Nichols. Some of those stories no one would have published. Believe me. Maybe *Weird Tales*. Some magazine for boys who don't yet know about f——ing.

"Those stories, they were the real stories."

275

Mort Castle

V
A Dance With A Nun

Adam Nichols had the bed next to his friend Rinelli in the attic of the villa that had been taken over for a hospital and with the war so far off they usually could not even hear it it was not too bad. It was a small room, the only one for patients all the way up there, and so just the two of them had the room. When you opened the window, there was usually a pleasant breeze that cleared away the smell of dead flesh.

Adam would have been hurting plenty but every time the pain came they gave him morphine and so it wasn't so bad. He had been shot in the calf and the hip and near to the spine and the doctor had to do a lot of cutting. The doctor told him he would be fine. Maybe he wouldn't be able to telemark when he skied, but he would be all right, without even a limp.

The doctor told him about a concert violinist who'd lost his left hand. He told him about a gallery painter who'd been blinded in both eyes. He told him about an ordinary fellow who'd lost both testicles. The doctor said Adam had reason to count his blessings. He was trying to cheer Adam up. Hell, the doctor said, trying to show he was a regular guy who would swear, there were lots had it worse, plenty worse.

Rinelli had it worse. You didn't have to be a doctor to know that. A machine gun got Rinelli in the stomach and in the legs and in between. The machine gun really hem-stitched him. They changed his bandages every hour or so but there was always a thick wetness coming right through the blanket.

Adam Nichols thought Rinelli was going to die because

Rinelli said he didn't feel badly at all and they weren't giving him morphine or anything much else really. Another thing was Rinelli laughed and joked a great deal. Frequently, Rinelli said he was feeling "swell"; that was an American word Adam had taught him and Rinelli liked it a lot.

Rinelli joked plenty with Sister Katherine, one of the nurses. He teased hell out of her. She was an American nun and very young and very pretty with sweet blue eyes that made Adam think of the girls with Dutch bobs and round collars who wore silly hats who you saw in the Coca-Cola advertisements. When he first saw her, Rinelli said to Adam Nichols in Italian, "What a waste. What a shame. Isn't she a great girl? Just swell."

There was also a much older nun there called Sister Anne. She was a chief nurse and this was not her first war. Nobody joked with her even if he was going to die. What Rinelli said about her was that when she was a child she decided to be a bitch and because she wasn't British, the only thing left was for her to be a nun. Sister Anne had a profile as flat as the blade of a shovel. Adam told Rinelli he'd put his money on Sister Anne in a twenty-rounder with Jack Johnson. She had to have a harder coconut than any nigger.

Frequently, it was Sister Katherine who gave Adam his morphine shot. With her help, he had to roll onto his side so she could jab the hypodermic into his buttock. That was usually when Rinelli would start teasing.

"Sister Katherine," Rinelli might say, "when you are finished looking at Corporal Nichols's backside, would you be interested in seeing mine?"

"No, no thank you," Sister Katherine would say.

"It needs your attention, Sister. It is broken, I am

afraid. It is cracked right down the middle."

"Please, Sergeant Rinelli—"

"Then if you don't want to see my backside, could I perhaps interest you in my front side?"

Sister Katherine would blush very nicely then and do something so young and sweet with her mouth that it was all you could do not to just squeeze her. But then Rinelli would get to laughing and you'd see the bubbles in the puddle on the blanket over his belly, and that wasn't any too nice.

One afternoon, Rinelli casually asked Sister Katherine, "Am I going to live?" Adam Nichols knew Rinelli was not joking then.

Sister Katherine nodded. "Yes," she said. "You are going to get well and then you will go back home."

"No," Rinelli said, still sounding casual. "Pardon me, I really don't want to contradict, but no, I do not think so."

Adam Nichols did not think so, either, and he had been watching Sister Katherine's face so he thought she did not think so as well.

Sister Katherine said rather loudly, "Oh, yes, Sergeant Rinelli. I have talked with the doctors. Yes, I have. Soon you will begin to be better. It will be a gradual thing, you will see. Your strength will come back. Then you can be invalided home."

With his head turned, Adam Nichols saw Rinelli smile.

"Good," Rinelli said. "That is very fine. So, Sister Katherine, as soon as I am better and my strength comes back to me, but before I am sent home, I have a favor to ask of you."

"What is that, Sergeant Rinelli?"

"I want you to dance with me."

Sister Katherine looked youngest when she was trying to be deeply serious. "No, no," she said, emphatically. "No, it is not permitted. Nuns cannot dance."

"It will be a secret dance. I will not tell Sister Anne, have no fear. But I do so want to dance with you."

"Rest now, Sergeant Rinelli. Rest, Corporal Nichols. Soon everything will be fine."

"Oh, yes," Rinelli said, "soon everything will be just swell."

What Adam Nichols liked about morphine was that it was better than getting drunk because you could slip from what was real to what was not real and not know and not care one way or the other. Right now in his mind, he was up in Michigan. He was walking through the woods, following the trail. Ahead, it came into sight, the trout pool, and his eyes took it all in, and he was seeking the words so he could write this moment truly.

> *Beyond this trail*
> *a stream lies*
> *faintly marked by rising mist.*
>
> *Twisting and tumbling*
> *around barriers,*
> *it flows*
> *into a shimmering pool,*
>
> *black with beauty*
> *and*
> *full of fighting trout.*

Adam Nichols had not told many people about this writing thing, how he believed he would discover a way to make words present reality so it was not just reality but more real than reality. He wanted writing to jump into what he called the fifth dimension. But until he learned to do it, and for now, writing was a secret for him.

The war was over. Sometimes he tried to write about it but he usually could not. Too often when he would try to write about it, he would find himself writing about what other men had seen and done and not what he himself had seen and done and had to give it up as a bad job.

Adam Nichols put down his tackle and rod and sat down by the pool and lit a cigarette. It tasted good. There is a clean, clear and sharp smell when you light a cigarette outdoors. He was not surprised to find Rinelli sitting alongside him even though Rinelli was dead. Rinelli was smoking, too.

"Isn't this fine? Isn't this everything I said it would be?" Adam Nichols asked.

"It's grand, it sure is. It's just swell," Rinelli answered.

"Tonight, we'll drink some whiskey with really cold water. And we'll have one hell of a meal," Adam Nichols said. "Trout. I've got my old man's recipe." He drew reflectively on his cigarette. "My old man, he was the one who taught me to hunt and fish. He was the one taught me to cook outdoors."

"You haven't introduced me to your father," Rinelli said.

"Well, he's dead, you see. He was a doctor and he killed himself. He put his gun to his head and he killed himself."

"What do you figure, then? Figure he's in hell now?"

"I don't know. Tell you, Rinelli, I don't really think there's anything like that. Hell. Not really."

Rinelli looked sad and that's when Adam Nichols saw how

dead Rinelli's eyes were and remembered all over again that Rinelli was dead.

"Well, Adam, you know me, I don't like to argue, but I tell you, there is, too, a hell. And I sure as hell wish I were there right now."

Rinelli snapped the last half-inch of his cigarette into the trout pool. A small fish bubbled at it as the trout pool turned into blood.

A few days later Rinelli was pretty bad off. Sometimes he tried to joke with Adam but he didn't make any sense and sometimes he talked in Italian to people who weren't there. He looked gray, like a dirty sheet. When he fell asleep, there was a heavy, wet rattle in his throat and his mouth stayed open.

Adam Nichols wasn't feeling any too swell himself. It was funny, how when you were getting better, you hurt lots worse. Sister Katherine jabbed a lot of morphine into him. It helped, but he still hurt and he knew he wasn't always thinking straight.

There were times he thought he was probably crazy because of the pain and the morphine. That didn't bother him really. It was just that he couldn't trust anything he saw.

At dusk, Adam Nichols opened his eyes. He saw Sister Katherine by Rinelli's bed. She had her crucifix and she was praying hard and quiet with her lips moving prettily and her eyes almost closed.

"That's good," Rinelli said. "Thank you. That is real nice." His voice sounded strong and casual and vaguely bored.

Sister Katherine kept on praying.

"That's just swell," Rinelli said. He coughed and he died.

Sister Katherine pulled the sheets up over Rinelli's face. She went to Adam. "He's gone."

"Well, I guess so."

"We will not be able to move him for a while. We do not have enough people, and there's no room . . ." Sister Katherine looked like she had something unpleasant in her mouth. "There is no room in the room we're using for the morgue."

"That's okay," Adam Nichols said. "He can stay here. He's not bothering me."

"All right then," Sister Katherine said. "All right. Do you need another shot of morphine?"

"Yes," Adam said, "I think so. I think I do."

Sister Katherine gave him the injection, and later there was another, and then, he thought, perhaps another one or even two. He knew he had had a lot of morphine because what he saw later was really crazy and couldn't have actually happened.

It was dark and Sister Katherine came in with her little light. Rinelli sat up in bed then. That had to be the morphine, Adam Nichols told himself. Rinelli was dead as a post. But there he was, sitting up in bed, with dead eyes, and he was stretching out his arms and then it all happened quick just like in a dream but Rinelli was out of bed and he was hugging Sister Katherine like he was drunk and silly.

He's dancing with her, that's what he's doing, Adam Nichols thought, and he figured he was thinking that because of all the morphine. Sure, he said he was going to dance with Sister Katherine before he went home. "Hey,

Rinelli," Adam Nichols said. "Quit fooling around, why don't you?"

Sister Katherine was yelling pretty loud and then she wasn't yelling all that loud because it looked like Rinelli was kissing her, but then you saw that wasn't it. Rinelli was biting her nose real hard, not like kidding around, and she was bleeding pretty much and she twisted and pushed real hard on Rinelli.

Rinelli staggered back. With blood on his dead lips. With something white and red and pulpy getting chewed by his white teeth. With a thin bit of pink gristle by the corner of his mouth.

Sister Katherine was up against the wall. The middle of her face was a black and red gushing hole. Her eyes were real big and popping. She was yelling without making a sound. She kind of looked like a comic strip.

It was a bad dream and the morphine, Adam Nichols thought, a real bad dream, and he wished he'd wake up.

Then Sister Anne came running in. Then she ran out. Then she ran back in. Now she had a Colt .45. She knocked back the slide like she really meant business. Rinelli went for her. She held her arm straight out. The gun was just a few inches from Rinelli's forehead when Sister Anne let him have it. Rinelli's head blew up wetly in a lot of noise. A lot of the noise was shattering bone. It went all over the place.

That was all Adam Nichols could remember the next morning. It wasn't like something real you remember. It was a lot more like a dream. He told himself it had to be the morphine. He told himself that a number of times. The windows were open and the breeze was nice but the small room smelled of strong disinfectant. There was no one in the other bed.

When Sister Anne came in to bring his breakfast and give him morphine, Adam Nichols asked about Rinelli.

"Well, he's dead," Sister Anne said. "I thought you knew."

Adam Nichols asked about Sister Katherine.

"She's no longer here," the old nun said, tersely.

"I thought something happened last night. I thought I saw something awful."

"It's better you don't think about it," Sister Anne said. "It's war and everybody sees a lot of awful things. Just don't think about it."

VI

"Let's talk about your suicidal feelings."

"There are times I want to kill myself. How's that?"

"You know what I mean."

"Who's on first?"

"You pride yourself on being a brave man."

"I am. Buck Lanham called me the bravest man he's ever known."

"Hooray. I'll see you get a medal."

"Maybe I deserve a medal. I've pissed in the face of death." The old man winked then. That and what he had just said made him look ridiculous. It made him look ancient and crazy. "I have killed, after all."

"I know. You are a very famous killer. You have antlers and tusks and rhino horns. You've shot cape buffalo and geese and bears and wild goats. That makes you extremely brave. You deserve medals."

"Who are you to deride me?" The old man was furious. He looked threatening and silly. "Who are you to hold me in contempt? I have killed men!"

VII

The time is a drunken blur in his memory. It is the "rat race" summer and fall of 1944, and he is intensely alive. A "war correspondent," that is what he is supposed to be, but that is not all he can allow himself to be.

He has to go up against Death every time. With what he knows, oh, yes, he has to meet the flat gaze of Mr. Death, has to breathe Mr. Death's hyena breath, he has to.

That is part of it.

He calls himself a soldier. He wouldn't have it any other way. This is a war. He appoints himself an intelligence officer. He carries a weapon, a .32 caliber Colt revolver.

And don't the kids love him, though? God, he sure loves them. They are just so goddamned beautiful, the doomed ones and the fortunate, the reluctant warriors and those who've come to know they love it. They are beautiful men as only men can be beautiful.

You see, women, well, women are women, and it is the biological thing, the trap by which we are snared, the old peg and awl, the old belly-rub and sigh and there you have it, and so a real man does need a woman, must have a woman so he does not do heinous things, but it is in the company of men that men find themselves and each other.

These kid warriors, these glorious snot-noses like he

used to be, they know he is tough. He is the legit goods. He can outshoot them, rifle or pistol, even the Two Gun Pecos Pete from Arizona. Want to play cards, he'll stay up the night, drinking and joking. He puts on the gloves and boxes with them. He'll take one to give one and he always gives as good as he gets.

He has a wind-up phonograph and good records: Harry James and the Boswells and Hot Lips Paige. He has Fletcher Henderson and Basie and Ellington. The Andrews Sisters, they can swing it, and Russ Colombo. Sinatra, he'll be fine once they let him stop doing the sappy stuff. There are nights of music and drinking and in the following days there are the moments burned into his mind, the moments that become the stories. Old man?

Well, he can drink the kids blind-eyed and to hell and gone. He stays with them, drink for drink. The hell with most of the kiss-ass officers. They don't know how foolish they are. They don't know they are clichés. The enlisted men, John Q. Public, Mr. O. K. Joe American, Johnny Gone for a Soldier, it's the enlisted man who's going to save the world from that Nazi bastard. It's the enlisted men he honest to God loves.

The enlisted men call him "Papa."

How do you like it now, Gentlemen?

The kraut prisoner was no enlisted man. He was an officer. Stiff necked son of a bitch. *Deutschland uber alles.* Arrogant pup. *Ubermensch.*

No, the German will not reveal anything. He will answer none of their questions. They can all go to hell. That's what the German officer says. They can all get f___.

Papa shakes a fist in the kraut's face. Papa says, "You're

going to talk and tell us every damned thing we want to know or I'll kill you, you Nazi son of a bitch."

The German officer does not change expression. He looks bored. What he says is: "You are not going to kill me, old man. You do not have the courage. You are hindered by a decadent morality and ethical code. You come from a race of mongrelized degenerates and cowards. You abide by the foolishness of the Geneva Convention. I am an unarmed prisoner of war. You will do nothing to me."

Later, he would boastfully write about this incident to the soft-spoken, courtly gentlemen who published his books. He said to the German officer, "What a mistake you made, brother."

And then I shot that smug prick. I just shot him before anyone could tell me I shouldn't. I let him have three in the belly, just like that, real quick, from maybe a foot away.

Say what you want, maybe they were no supermen, but they weren't any panty-waists, either. Three in the belly, Pow-Pow-Pow, and he's still standing there, and damned if he isn't dead but doesn't know it, but he is pretty surprised and serves him right, too.

Then everyone else, all the Americans and a Brit or two are yelling and pissing around like they don't know whether to shit, go blind, or order breakfast, and here's this dead kraut swaying on his feet, and maybe I'm even thinking I'm in a kettle of bad soup, but the hell with it.

But have to do it right, you know, arrogant kraut-kopf or not. So I put the gun to his head and I let him have it, bang! and his brains come squirting right out his nose, gray and pink, and, you know, it looks pretty funny, so someone yells, "Gesundheit!", and that's it, brother. That's all she wrote and we've got us one guaranteed dead Nazi.

VIII

A rose is a rose is a rose
The dead are the dead are the dead except when they aren't and how do you like it
let's talk and
Who is on first
I know what I know and I am afraid and I am afraid

IX
HOMAGE TO SPAIN

1. An Old Man's Luck

The dusty old man sat on the river bank. He wore steel-rimmed spectacles. He had already traveled 12 kilometers and he was very tired. He thought it would be a while before he could go on.

That is what he told Adam Nichols.

Adam Nichols told him he had to cross the pontoon bridge. He really must and soon. When the shelling came, this would not be a good place to stay. The old man in the steel-rimmed spectacles thanked Adam Nichols for his concern. He was a very polite old man. The reason he had stayed behind was to take care of the animals in his village. He smiled because saying "his village" made him feel good. There were three goats, two cats, and six doves. When he had no other choice and really had to leave, he opened the door to the doves' cage and let them fly. He was not too worried about the cats, really, the old man told Adam Nichols; cats are always all right. Cats had luck. Goats were another thing. Goats were a little stupid and sweet and so they had not much luck.

It was just too bad about the goats, the old man said. It was a sad thing.

Adam agreed. But the old man had to move along. He really should.

The old man said thank you. He was grateful for the concern. But he did not think he could go on just yet. He was very tired and he was 76 years old.

He asked a question. Did Adam truly think the cats would be all right?

Yes, Adam said, we both know cats have luck.

Adam thought they had a lot more luck than sweet and stupid goats and 76 year old men who can go no farther than 12 kilometers when there is going to be shelling.

2. Hunters In The Morning Fog

Miguel woke him. They used to call him Miguelito but the older Miguel had been shot right through the heart, a very clean shot, and so now this one was Miguel. The sun had just come up and there was fog with cold puff-like clouds near to the ground. "Your rifle," Miguel said. "We are going hunting."

"Hey," Adam Nichols said, "what the hell?" He wanted coffee or to go back to sleep.

"Just come," Miguel said.

There were five of them, Pilar, who was as tough as any man, and Antonio, and Jordan, the American College professor, and Miguel, who used to be Miguelito, and

Adam Nichols. They went out to the field. Yesterday it was a battlefield. The day before that it had just been a green, flat field. Some of the dead lay here and there. Not all of the dead were still. Some were already up and some were now rising, though most lay properly still and dead. Those who were up mostly staggered about like drunks. Some had their arms out in front of them like Boris Karloff in the *Frankenstein* movie. They did not look frightening. They looked stupid. But they were frightening even if they did not look frightening because they were supposed to be dead.

"Say, what the hell?" Adam Nichols asked. His mouth was dry.

"It happens sometimes," Pilar said. "That is what I have heard. It appears to be so, though this is the first time I personally have seen it."

Pilar shrugged. "The dead do not always stay dead. They come back sometimes. What they do then is quite sickening. It is revolting and disgusting. When they come back, they are cannibals. They wish to eat living people. And if they bite you, they cause a sickness, and then you die, and then after that, you become like them and you wish to eat living people. We have to shoot them. A bullet in the head, that is what stops them. It's not so bad, you know. It's not like they are really alive."

"I don't go for this," Adam said.

"Don't talk so much," Pilar said. "I like you very much, *Americano*, but don't talk so much."

She put her rifle to her shoulder. It was an old '03 Springfield. It had plenty of stopping power. Pilar was a good shot. She fired and one of the living dead went down with the middle of his face punched in.

"Come on," Pilar said, commanding. "We stay together. We don't let any of these things get too close. That is what they are. Things. They aren't strong, but if there are too many, then it can be trouble."

"I don't think I like this," Adam Nichols said. "I don't think I like it at all."

"I am sorry, but what you like and what you dislike is not all that important, if you will forgive my saying so," Miguel said. "What does matter is that you are a good shot. You are one of our best shots. So, if you please, shoot some of these unfortunate dead people."

Antonio and Pilar and Jordan and Miguel and Adam Nichols shot the living dead as the hunting party walked through the puffy clouds of fog that lay on the field. Adam felt like his brain was the flywheel in a clock about to go out of control. He remembered shooting black squirrels when he was a boy. Sometimes you shot a black squirrel and it fell down and then when you went to pick it up it tried to bite you and you had to shoot it again or smash its head with a rock or the stock of your rifle. He tried to make himself think this was just like shooting black squirrels. He tried to make himself think it was even easier, really, because dead people moved a lot slower than black squirrels. It was hard to shoot a squirrel skittering up a tree. It was not so hard to shoot a dead man walking like a tired drunk toward you.

Then Adam saw the old man who had sat by the pontoon bridge the other day. The old man's steel-rimmed spectacles hung from one ear. They were unshattered. He looked quite silly, like something in a Chaplin film. Much of his chest had been torn open and bones stuck out at crazy angles. There were wettish tubular—like things

291

wrapped about the protruding bones of his chest.

He was coming at Adam Nichols like a trusting drunk who finds a friend and knows the friend will see him home.

"Get that one," said Jordan, the American College professor. "That one is yours."

Yes, Adam Nichols thought, the old man is mine. We have talked about goats and cats and doves.

Adam Nichols sighted. He took in a breath and held it. He waited.

The old man stumbled toward him.

Come, old man, Adam Nichols thought. Come with your chest burst apart and your terrible appetite. Come with the mindless brute insistence that makes you continue. Come to the bullet that will give you at least the lie of a dignified ending. Come unto me, old man. Come unto me.

"You let him draw too close," Miguel said. "Shoot him now."

Come, old man, Adam Nichols thought. Come, because I am your luck. Come because I am all the luck you are ever going to have.

Adam pulled the trigger. It was a fine shot. It took off the top of the old man's head. His glasses flew up and he flew back and lay on the fog-heavy ground.

"Good shot," Jordan said.

"No," Adam said, "just good luck."

3. In A Hole In The Mountain

It is not true that every man in Spain is named Paco, but it is true that if you call "Paco!" on the street of any city in Spain, you will have many more than one *"Que"* in response.

It was with a Paco that Adam Nichols found himself hiding from the fascist patrols. Paco's advanced age and formidable mustache made him look *Gitano*. Paco was a good fighter, and a good Spaniard, but not such a good communist. He said he was too old to have politics, but not too old to kill fascists.

Adam Nichols was now a communist because of some papers he had signed. Now he blew up things. For three months, he had been to a special school in Russia to learn demolitions. Adam Nichols was old enough now to know his talents. He was good at teaching young people to speak Spanish, and so for a while he had been a bored and boring high school teacher of Spanish in Oak Park, Illinois. Blowing up things and killing fascists was much more interesting, so he had gone to Spain.

There were other reasons, too. He seldom let himself ponder these.

The previous day, Adam Nichols had blown up a railroad trestle that certain military leaders had agreed was important, and, except for old Paco, the comrades who had made possible this act of demolition were all dead. The fascists were seeking the man who had destroyed the trestle. But Paco knew how to hide.

Where Paco and Adam were hiding was too small to be a cave. It was just a hole in a mountainside. It was hard to spot unless you knew just what you were looking for.

It was dark in the hole. Paco and Adam could not build a fire. But it was safe to talk if you talked in the same low embarrassed way you did in the confessional. Because they were so close, there were times when Adam could almost feel that Paco was breathing for him and that he was breathing for Paco. A moment came to Adam Nichols that made him think, *This is very much like being lovers*, but then he decided it was not so. He would never be as close with a lover as he was now with Paco.

After many hours of being with Paco in the close dark, Adam said, "Paco, there is something I wish to ask thee." Adam Nichols spoke in the most formal Spanish. It was what was needed.

Gravely, though he was not a serious man, Paco said, "Then ask, but remember, Comrade, I am an aged man, and do not mistake age for wisdom." Paco chuckled. He was pleased he had remembered to say "comrade." Sometimes he forgot. It was hard to be a good communist.

"I need to speak of what I have seen. Of abomination. Of horror. Of impossibility."

"Art thou speaking of war?"

"*Si.*"

"Then dost thou speak of courage, too?" Paco asked. "Of decency? Or self-sacrifice?"

"No, *Viejo*," Adam Nichols said. "Of these things, much has been said and much written. Courage, decency, self-sacrifice are to be found in peace or war. Stupidity, greed, arrogance are to be found in peace or war. But I wish to speak with thee of that which I have seen only during time of war. It is madness. It is what cannot be."

Paco said, "What wouldst thou ask of me?"

"Paco," Adam Nichols said, "do the dead walk?"

"Hast thou seen this?"

"*Verdad.* I have seen this. No. I think I have seen this. Years ago, a long time back, in that which was my first war, I thought I saw it. It was in that war, Paco *Viejo*, that I think I became a little crazy. And now I think I have seen in it in this war. There were others with me when we went to kill the dead. They would not talk of it, after. After, we all got drunk and made loud toasts which were vows of silence." Adam Nichols was silent for a time. Then he said again, "Do the dead walk?"

"Thou hast good eyes, Comrade Adam. Thou shootest well. Together we have been in battle. Thou dost not become crazy. What thou hast seen, thou hast seen truly."

Adam Nichols was quiet. He remembered when he was a young man and his heart was broken by a love gone wrong and the loss of well holding arms and a smile that was for no one else but him. He felt worse now, filled with sorrow and fear both, and with his realizing the world was such a serious place. He said, "It is a horrible thing when the dead walk."

"*Verdad.*"

"Dost thou understand what happens?"

"Perhaps."

"Then perhaps you can tell me."

"Perhaps." Paco sighed. His sigh seemed to move the darkness in waves. "Years ago, I knew a priest. He was not a fascist priest. He was a nice man. The money in his plate did not go to buy candlesticks. He built a motion picture theater for his village. He knew that you need to laugh on Saturdays more than you need stained-glass windows. The movies he showed were very good movies. Buster Keaton. Harold Lloyd. Joe Bonomo. John Gilbert. KoKo the Klown and Betty Boop cartoons. This priest did not give a damn for politics, he told me. He gave a damn about people. And that is the reason, I believe, that he stopped being a priest. He had some money. He had three women who loved him and were content to share him. I think he was all right, this priest.

"It was he who told me of the living dead."

"And canst thou tell me?"

"Well, yes, I believe I can. There is no reason not to. I have sworn no oaths."

"What is it, then? Why do the dead rise? Why do they seek the flesh of the living?"

"This man who had been a priest was not certain about Heaven, but he was most definite about Hell. Yes, Hell was the Truth. Hell was for the dead.

"But when we turn this Earth of ours into Hell, there is no need for the dead to go below.

"Why should they bother?

"And canst thou doubt that much of this ball of mud upon which we dwell is today hell, Comrade? With each new war and each new and better way of making war, there is more and more hell and so we have more and more inhabitants of hell with us.

"And of course, no surprise, they have their hungers. They are demons. At least that is what some might call them, though I myself seldom think to call them anything. And the food of demons is human flesh. It is a simple thing, really."

"Paco—"

"Si?"

"This is not rational."

"And art thou a rational man?"

"Yes. No."

"So?"

" 'The Living Dead,' maybe that's what somebody

would call them. Well, hell, don't you think that would make some newspaperman just ecstatic? It would be bigger than 'Lindy in Paris!' Bigger than—"

"And thou dost believe such a newspaper story could be printed? And perhaps the *Book of the Living Dead* could be written? And perhaps a motion picture of the Living Dead as well, with Buster Keaton, perhaps? Comrade Adam, such revelation would topple the world order.

"Perhaps someday the world will be ready for such awful knowledge, Comrade Adam.

"For now, it is more than enough that those of us who know of it must know of it, thank you very kindly.

"And with drink and with women and with war and with whatever gives us comfort, we must try not to think over much about what it is we know."

"Paco," Adam Nichols said in the dark, "I think I want to scream. I think I want to scream now."

"No, Comrade. Be quiet now. Breathe deep. Breathe with me and deep. Let me breathe for you. Be quiet."

"All right," Adam said after a time. "It is all right now."

A day later, Paco thought it would be safe to leave the hole in the side of the mountain. They were spotted by an armored car full of fascists. A bullet passed through Paco's lung. It was a mortal shot.

"Bad luck, Paco," Adam Nichols said. He put a bullet into the old man's brain and went on alone.

X

"You're really not helping me. You know that."

"Bad on me. I thought I was here for you to help me. My foolishness. Damn the luck."

"I've decided, then, we'll go the way we did before, with electro-convulsive therapy. We'll—"

I am for God's sake 61 years old and I am going to die because of occluded arteries or because of a cirrhotic liver or because of an aneurysm in brain or belly waiting to go pop, or because of some damn thing—and when I die I wish to be dead, to be dead and that is all.

"—a series of 12. We've often had good results—"

and, believe me, I am not asking for Jesus to make me a sunbeam, I am not asking for heaven in any way, shape, or form. Gentlemen, when I die I wish to be dead.

"—particularly with depression. There are several factors, of course—"

I'm looking for dead, that's D-E-A-D, and I don't want to be a goddamn carnival freak show act and man is just a little lower than the angels and pues y nada and you get older and you get confused and you become afraid.

"We'll begin tomorrow—"

no bloody chance because now the world is hell and if you doubt it, then you don't know the facts, Gentlemen. No bloody chance. We ended the war by dropping hell on Nagasaki and on Hiroshima, and we opened up Germany and discovered all those hells, and during the siege of Stalingrad, the living ate the dead, and ta-ta, Gentlemen, turn-about is fair play, and we're just starting to know the hells that good old Papa Joe put together no bloody chance and we're not blameless, oh, no, ask that poor nigger hanging burning from the tree, ask the Rosenbergs who got cooked up nice and brown, ask—Welcome to hell, and how do you like it now, Gentlemen?

When the world is hell, the dead walk.

XI

When they returned to Ketchum, Idaho on June 30, the old man was happy. Anyone who saw him will tell you. He was not supposed to drink because of his anti-depressant medication, but he did drink. It did not affect him badly. He sang several songs. One was "*La Quince Brigada,*" from the Spanish Civil War. He sang loudly and off-key; he made a joyful racket. He said one of the great regrets of his life was that he had never learned to play the banjo.

Later, he had his wife, Mary, put on a Burl Ives record on the Webcor phonograph. It was a 78, "The Riddle Song." He listened to it several times.

> How can there be a cherry
> that has no stone?
>
> How can there be a chicken
> that has no bone?
>
> How can there be a baby
> with no crying?

Mary asked if the record made him sad.

No, he said, he was not sad at all. The record was beautiful. If there are riddles, there are also answers to riddles.

So, so then, I have not done badly. Some good stories, some good books. I have written well and truly. I have sometimes failed, but I have tried. I have sometimes been a foolish man, and even a small-minded or mean-spirited one, but I have always been a man, and I will end as a man.

It was early and he was the only one up. The morning of Sunday, July 2, was beautiful. There were no clouds. There was sunshine.

He went to the front foyer. He liked the way the light struck the oak-paneled walls and the floor. It was like being in a museum or in a church. It was a well-lighted place and it felt clean and airy.

Carefully, he lowered the butt of the Boss shotgun to the floor. He leaned forward. The twin barrels were cold circles in the scarred tissue just above his eyebrows.

He tripped both triggers.

RED

JACK KETCHUM

Fans and critics alike hailed Jack Ketchum's previous novel, *The Lost*, for its power, its thrills and its gripping style, and recognized Ketchum as a master of suspense. Now Jack Ketchum is back to frighten us again with . . . *Red!*

It all starts with a simple act of brutality. Three boys shoot and kill an old man's dog. No reason, just plain meanness. But the dog was the best thing in the old man's world, and he isn't about to let the incident pass. He wants justice, and he'll make sure the kids pay for what they did. They picked the wrong old man to mess with. And as the fury and violence escalate, they're about to learn that . . . the hard way.

SECOND CHANCE

CHET WILLIAMSON

You are invited to a party. A reunion of old college friends who haven't seen each other since the late 1960s. It should be a blast, with great music and fond memories. But be forewarned, it won't all be good. Two of the friends at the party weren't invited. In fact, they died back in college. But once they show up, the nostalgia will turn to a dark reality as all the guests find themselves hurled back to the '60s. And when they return to the present, it's a different world than the one they left. History has changed and the long-dead friends are still alive—including one intent on destroying them all.

Dorchester Publishing Co., Inc.
P.O. Box 6640
Wayne, PA 19087-8640

Please add $2.50 for shipping and handling for the first book and $.75 for each additional book. NY and PA residents, add appropriate sales tax. No cash, stamps, or CODs. Canadian orders require $5.00 for shipping and handling and must be paid in U.S. dollars. Prices and availability subject to change. **Payment must accompany all orders.**

Name: _____

Address: _____

City: _____ State: _____ Zip: _____

E-mail: _____

I have enclosed $_____ in payment for the checked book(s).

For more information on these books, check out our website at www.dorchesterpub.com.
_____ *Please send me a free catalog.*